THE MYSTWICK SCHOOL OF MUSICRAFT

THE MYSTWICK SCHOOL OF MUSICRAFT

BY JESSICA KHOURY

ILLUSTRATED BY FEDERICA FRENNA

HOUGHTON MIFFLIN HARCOURT
BOSTON   NEW YORK

hmhbooks.com

The text was set in Garamond.

Library of Congress Cataloging-in-Publication Data
Names: Khoury, Jessica, 1990– author. | Frenna, Federica, 1990- illustrator.
Title: The Mystwick School of Musicraft / by Jessica Khoury ; illustrated by Federica Frenna.
Description: Boston ; New York : Houghton Mifflin Harcourt, [2020] | Summary: Twelve-year-old
Amelia gets the opportunity to attend a boarding school and learn how to use music to create magic,
hoping to become a Maestro like her deceased mother.
Identifiers: LCCN 2019001117 (print) | LCCN 2019002595 (ebook) |
ISBN 9781328625632 (hardcover) | ISBN 9780358164449 (e-book)
Subjects: | CYAC: Magic—Fiction. | Music—Fiction. | Boarding schools—Fiction. |
Schools—Fiction. | Fantasy.
Classification: LCC PZ7.K5285 (ebook) | LCC PZ7.K5285 Mys 2020 (print) | DDC
[Fic]—dc23
LC record available at https://lccn.loc.gov/2019001117

Manufactured in the United States of America
DOC 10 9 8 7 6 5 4 3 2 1
4500784917

For Madelaine,
who knew Amelia first

CHAPTER ONE

Prelude for a Chicken

I T'S HARDER TO CHARM A CHICKEN than you might think.

I guess it's because they have such tiny brains. Nothing against the chicken, of course—it's not like it *asked* to be stupid.

That's just the way it is.

Not that I'm in any sort of position to judge.

After all, I *am* lying flat on my back on a ground definitely covered in chicken poop, my upper half wedged under a shed and my flute clenched between my lips as I shimmy farther in. It's hard to charm a chicken in any position, but doing so while wedged under a shed is not exactly ideal. I'm pretty sure my music teacher would confiscate my instrument if she saw me like this.

But sometimes, life requires you to rescue a trapped chicken with a bit of magic, even if it means getting a little dirty.

Taking my flute out of my mouth—after thoroughly wiping my grubby palms on my jeans, of course—I try the regular, nonmagic route one more time:

"Here, chicken, chicken!"

The little rebel I'm after is crammed just above me, between the shed and the fence on the other side. She's attempting an ambitious escape, pecking at the metal fence wire.

Sighing, I turn my head just slightly and purse my lips over the flute's embouchure. It's an awkward angle, with my face half planted in dirt, and I wonder if this is *really* worth the five dollars Mrs. O'Grady offered me.

"Just a simple chicken charm, Amelia," she'd said this morning, standing on our front porch, her cheeks ruddy from working in her little vegetable garden. "It's that Rooter. She's got herself jammed again, I'm afraid."

Well, I *do* need the five dollars.

My fingers find the flute's keys, arranging themselves in preparation.

Before I start, I take a few deep breaths. It's no good playing when your heart's bouncing around your chest like a basketball in a washing machine. I might set Rooter and me and the whole chicken coop on fire.

As the First Rule of Musicraft states: *A spell can charm or do great harm. Before you play, clear the way.*

When I'm good and still inside, I purse my lips, then launch into the spell that usually works on Rooter: "The Ants Go Marching." A simple tune, good for calming someone's nerves and, if that someone's a chicken, luring them out from under a

2

shed. I could play it in my sleep, but it's not just about hitting the right notes. It's also about keeping tempo and staying focused, or I won't produce any magic at all. Go too fast or slow, and the spell will fall apart. Play it in the wrong key, and its effects could reverse, and I could end up scaring Rooter away rather than drawing her to me.

Anyone can pick up a flute and blow into it, but to turn music into magic, you have to play it *right*.

Mrs. O'Grady could have probably played the spell on her old harmonica and done the trick, if she weren't going tone-deaf. And I know she is because I once saw her try to summon an apple off a branch too high to reach.

The apple exploded instead.

So you can see why her attempting a charm on Rooter might end . . . *badly*.

A few notes in, the spell starts to work. The magic isn't strong —a few white wisps of light curl away from my flute and fade, shimmering, into the muddy ground. They reflect in Rooter's black eyes.

On the second repetition, the chicken's head perks in my direction and she stops her mindless pecking at the fence. Her head twitches this way and that, her feathers ruffle, and then she scoots my way. Curlicues of light swirl around her, the spell drawing her along and infusing her tiny chicken brain.

That's it, I think. *Come on, you old featherbutt.*

The magic swirls around like white feathers, and when it lands on my skin, I feel the slightest tingle. Sort of like snow-flakes, there and then gone.

I focus on Rooter, directing the flow of magic to her and not some other chicken in the yard. Playing while distracted is dangerous; the magic could get out of control fast without my willpower harnessing it and giving it a clear target. So I force myself to keep all my attention on the bird.

But Rooter stops dead, then begins to reverse, chicken rump wiggling this way and that as she shimmies back to the fence.

I've lost hold of her.

My stomach clenches with frustration.

I don't have much time till I have to catch the train to the city. Before then, I'll have to shower, pack lunch and my sheet music, and squeeze in a last-minute practice session.

"It's not like my *entire future* is on the line here, McNugget," I growl, catching my breath before trying again.

"What's that, dear?" Mrs. O'Grady calls.

I turn my head till I can see her feet—woolly socks in san-dals below the hem of her flowered nightgown. Mrs. O'Grady has reached the age where it's perfectly acceptable for her to wear a flowered nightgown no matter the place or occasion.

"Just making conversation," I say, adding under my breath, "with a *chicken*."

"Oh, that's nice," she replies. "Rooter's a good one for a chat. Understanding eyes."

I look at Rooter's eyes.

They wobble at me.

Wincing, I start playing again. It takes two repetitions of the melody before I can get Rooter's attention once more. This time I give it all I've got, keeping my gaze locked on the chicken's, until she starts moving forward again. Shimmying along, flute glued to my chin, I dare not go a smidgen faster or I'll risk messing up and breaking the spell.

Finally, I clear the shed, still playing, and Rooter's just a few chicken steps behind. The minute she's in the open, Mrs. O'Grady scoops her up and cuddles her, cooing and fussing. I finish the spell, then lie in the dirt and chicken poo a moment, catching my breath.

"Oh, Amelia, thank you, dear!" Mrs. O'Grady says. "Now, haven't you got somewhere to be?"

I blink up at her; the sun's in my eyes, and I shield it with a hand. "Gran told you about that?"

Mrs. O'Grady strokes Rooter's neck, and the bird coos happily. "You sound surprised."

I grunt, looking down at the ground. "She doesn't really like Musicraft much."

"No doubt that's because you remind her of your mother." Mrs. O'Grady sighs. "I remember her at your age, running around in the woods with that flute, charming the squirrels right out of the trees. Such a shame, what happened to her. I remember once my kitchen caught fire, and your mother—no bigger than you are now!—came running over and put it out with a spell. Saved the house!"

Swallowing, I squeeze my flute a little tighter. "Gran never told me that."

"Well, now, she does miss your mother an awful lot. Even after eight years, it's hard for your gran to speak of her." Mrs. O'Grady hands me a folded bill. "Here, now. You earned it."

"Thanks." I take the money. And blink. "Mrs. O.! This is too much!"

Maybe her eyesight is going as bad as Rooter's. She gave me a twenty, not a five.

"Hush!" she scolds, patting Rooter's head. "Now run home. Tell your grandmother I'll be around with more eggs tomorrow."

"Okay." Then my attention snags on her watch, and I jump like I've been electrocuted.

"It's nine o'clock already!?" I shriek. Holy mother of Beethoven—I have to go!

"Good luck, Amelia! You make us proud, now!" Mrs. O'Grady calls, as I dash away, leaping over the fence around the chicken yard.

It's only a minute's walk across Mrs. O'Grady's farm and through the weeds to Gran's house, but I cut it in half by going at a dead sprint, my flute clutched in my hand like a runner's baton. By the time I reach the front porch, I'm completely soaked in sweat. It's midsummer and the sun beats down like a spotlight. Even the pine trees behind the house look droopy, defeated by the heat.

"Gran!" I shout, running inside and letting the door slam behind me. "GRAN!"

She comes walking out of the kitchen, covered in flour, her hair still in rollers. "Now, now, no shouting inside, please."

"Gran!" I look her up and down, stomach dropping. "What are you *doing?* You should be ready to go. We're going to be late!"

"Late?" She frowns. "For what?"

"My *audition!*" I wave my flute, incredulous.

"Oh." She sighs and wipes her hands on her apron. "Is that today?"

"*Gran.*" I grab her keys and thrust them into her hand. "We have to go *now*. We're already going to miss the first train!" There's another that leaves soon after, but missing the first one means I'll *barely* make it to the audition in time.

She blinks at my clothes. "Don't you want to change first?"

She's stalling on purpose. That's probably even why she sent me to help Mrs. O'Grady, hoping I'd forget about my audition.

Gran is no fan of Musicraft. All my life, she's suggested other forms of "self-expression," giving me sports equipment for Christmas, making me try out for the school play, signing me up for horse-riding lessons and swim team and Girl Scouts. Anything that wasn't musical. But none of it stuck. None of it called to me the way magic does.

Always, I found my way back into Mrs. Parrish's after-school Musicraft classes, with the other kids in my little town who had musical talent. At first, we learned kiddie stuff—weak summoning spells on plastic recorders, or making our lunchboxes float with kazoos—but that wasn't enough for me. Mrs. Parrish somehow persuaded Gran to let her teach me on the weekends. And soon, it became my obsession. I practiced hours every day, woke up early to play before school, rode my bike to Mrs. Parrish's house whenever she'd open her door for me. I've probably spent more time with that flute pressed to my chin than I have sleeping or studying or anything else. By third grade, I could outplay all the other kids in elementary school. By fifth grade, I was getting invited to play with the high school marching band. I'll never forget the day Mrs. Parrish told Gran I might be the best musician she'd ever taught; Gran had huffed and sighed and looked at me like I was a crossword puzzle she was about to give up on, but I'd still glowed like a lightbulb with pride.

Amelia could be a true Maestro, Mrs. Parrish had said. *Only the second one to ever come from our town.*

Only the second one—after my mother.

But it'll all be for nothing if I miss this audition.

Leaving her to clean up, I race through the house and throw

9

a change of clothes into a bag, my heart pounding. Then I stuff in my sheet music and a bottle of grape juice. If I'm late for the audition, they won't even give me a chance to play. I'll be cut, just like that. I can't think of a stupider reason to ruin the single greatest opportunity I'll ever have.

"Let's go, let's go! We're going to miss the nine thirty train!" I yell, and I race through the house, leaping over the coffee table and sprinting outside. Gran ambles out, taking her time.

While she drives five miles under the speed limit, I clean my flute and go over my audition music in my mind, again and again, until the notes are engraved onto my brain. It's only three miles to the train station, and I'm starting to think riding my bike there would've been faster.

We drive by my school, which is quiet and empty during the summer, looking smaller without all the buses and kids. I see the trailer where my Musicraft class meets, and press my hand to the window in farewell.

If today goes as planned, I may never set foot in my old school again. It makes me sad to think about, but also queasy with nerves and excitement.

I can do this, I remind myself. *I HAVE to do this.*

I open my flute case and stare at the photo taped to the inside. It's the one thing that makes me feel calm before an audition or recital. It's been with me for as long as I've played the flute, always reminding me *why* I'm doing this.

This picture is one of the only ones I have of my mom. She was just eighteen in it, with curly dark hair and dimples. In the photo, beneath her graduation gown, she was wearing a sweater, and on the sweater was a crest: a wreath of ivy around a harp, and the word *Mystwick*.

I was four when she died.

My dad disappeared after it happened, and no one knows where he went. I guess he loved her so much that he didn't have enough love left for me. Of him, I have few memories at all, mostly of a deep laugh coming from someone who is always just out of sight. When I think of my parents, usually I just remember Mom, playing her flute—the same one I'm holding now—filling the air with crackling, glowing magic. But even of those vague memories, I'm not always sure which ones are real and which ones I made up.

"Gran," I say cautiously, "Mrs. O told me my mom once put out a kitchen fire for her. You never told me that."

Gran snorts. "That Clara is a gossip. Can't keep her mouth shut for anything."

"Were you there? Did you see it?"

But instead of answering, Gran just frowns at the road ahead. Her eyes pinch and her lips press flat, and like she always does when I ask about Mom, she closes up tighter than a scared turtle.

Well, I know one thing for sure: my mom is the reason I always hear music in the back of my mind. She is why I love

Musicraft, the art of spinning sound into spells. She is why I dream of it every night and long for it every day. It's a part of me because it was a part of *her*.

I need to find out how much of her lives in me.

And that means starting at the place she loved most: the Mystwick School of Musicraft.

CHAPTER TWO

The Itsy-Bitsy Fire

W<small>E HAVE TO WALK</small> four blocks from the train station to the hotel where the auditions are. I spent the whole two-hour trip watching the brass trio play the locomotion spell that powered the great metal train, and now I hum their spell as I walk beside Gran. The street is lined with tall brick buildings, the sidewalks flooded with people hurrying in all directions. Cars jam the road, horns blaring, taxi drivers leaning out of their windows to shout.

This is only the second time I've been to the city. The first time, I came with Mrs. Parrish and the other Musicraft students from school, to see a movie at the big cinema. That was one of the best nights of my life. They had a Maestro who played the film score on the piano while we watched it, and her spells had produced all kinds of effects—wind, rain, fireworks—so it had felt like we were *in* the movie. I'd been so starry-eyed afterward I'd barely noticed anything else after we left the cinema.

But now, I look around with my mouth hanging open, eyes as round as cymbals.

There is magic *everywhere.*

I've never seen so many types of instruments, or heard so many different spells being played at once: summoning and hovering spells, illusions and glamours. The air carries the smoky smell of magic, like the scent of a match right after you blow out the flame.

Through the open windows of a café, I hear a pianist playing a complicated concerto that delivers diners' plates and cups on glittering ribbons of magic. Across the street, on a fifth-floor balcony, a little girl plays "Au Clair de la Lune" on a plastic recorder, her magic coaxing a small potted lily to unfurl its petals. I recognize that spell—it's a common practice piece for young musicians, and I remember playing it over and over when I first began my training, until I was hearing it in my sleep. But the girl is having trouble focusing, because several balconies over, a man with a jug and a pair of castanets is playing a messy wind spell, perhaps trying to cool down his apartment. I wince at the din he produces; just because anyone *can* play a spell doesn't mean they should.

I watch them until Gran shouts at me to look where I'm going; I'd nearly tripped over a storm drain.

Newsstands bristle with papers, headlines screaming things like *Tokyo Philharmonic Staves Off Deadly Typhoon* and *Nigerian*

Maestro Composes New Cancer-Fighting Spell—But Is It Too Good to Be True? People on the corners hawk rolled spells in plastic tubes or hand out fliers advertising "Spectacular Performances by Musicraft's Best Illusionists! Witness Conjuration of Cosmic Proportion! One Night Only!" I take every flier they thrust at me, eyes wide, until Gran scowls and shoves them all into a recycling bin, muttering about charlatans.

I bounce impatiently alongside her, while the sounds of the city sweep over us. My ears can't help but pick up the melodies hidden in the noise.

Every place has its own music, if you listen hard enough. The woods have a quiet, whispery nocturne, all swishing leaves and wind, one of my favorite sounds. It makes me want to lie down and close my eyes and just breathe. But the city is a symphony, so many sounds all clashing and blending, rising and falling: honking cars, shouting people, and of course, the street musicians who perform magic for spare change. We pass a man who offers to smooth the wrinkles from Gran's face with a spell from his accordion.

"Honestly," huffs Gran, not even giving him a glance. But she looks at *me* with a scowl. "*This* is what you want to do with your life, Amelia?"

"These people are Novices," I point out. "When I've graduated from Mystwick, I'll be a Maestro, Gran. Like Mom. You *know* that."

She always pretends she doesn't know anything about Musicraft, like it's not important to remember the difference between Novices and Maestros. As if pretending none of it exists could convince me to stop playing.

Mrs. Parrish explained it to me years ago: While Novices are small-time spell workers, Maestros are more powerful, specially trained musicians. In groups called Symphonies, they travel the world, calming hurricanes and bringing rain to droughts and building bridges, all kinds of wonderful and beautiful things. Novices use their magic in small ways, like healing colds or propelling trolleys down the street, but Maestros?

Maestros change the world.

But to earn that special gold pin, you have to pass a series of very difficult Maestric Exams, which is almost impossible to do without the training found at the world's top Musicraft schools like Mystwick. And they only take the best of the best.

There are other schools, of course, like the Musicraft Academy in this very city, where Mrs. Parrish went, but not many people go there to become Maestros. Instead, they train to be Musicraft teachers or instrument makers, which are also important jobs . . . but I've always known that I wanted to be a Maestro, like my mom, like the people in the Symphonies on the television.

A trolley rolls past, wheels sparking with golden magic thanks to the saxophonist standing at the back, sweat shining on his face as he plays "Over the Rainbow." Across the street, I spot a five-piece brass ensemble in hardhats, aiding a construction crew with a hovering spell that lifts heavy beams and tools. Banners of golden magic unfurl from their instruments and slink through the air like slender dragons.

Back in our little town, there's only one professional musician besides our music teacher—Mr. Meadows. He's a guitarist who mostly does small spells in his little shop downtown —curing headaches, finding lost keys and pets, substituting when Mrs. Parrish can't teach our class. As a Novice, he can't do high-level magic, but he'll usually show me a few new tricks when I ask. Sometimes, he even pays me a little to help him, things like growth spells when they reseeded the baseball field or even, once, playing an elemental spell to hold off rain on the day of the big town-wide picnic. Gran knows *nothing* about that, or she'd probably have sold my flute on the spot, thinking I was trying magic too big for me. But there aren't many people back home who could play such spells, and certainly no other kids my age who could pull them off.

But here, it seems there's a musician on every corner. I've never seen so much magic at work all at once; the air is thick with it, glittering light and glowing ribbons of every color. I slow in front of a Spellstones store and peer through the window at the racks and racks of sheet music for sale, with spells covering everything from Novice healing magic and illusion work to restricted, dangerous spells that can only be bought and played by Maestros. I could spend *hours* in there, just leafing through all those papers. I've always dreamed of going into a Spellstones; they're the most famous chain of music stores in the world. They say you can find any sort of spell on their shelves — spells to recover lost memories or banish thunderstorms or slow the melting of the glaciers.

But then I see the tall building ahead, and I grab Gran's hand.

"There it is!" I shout. "The hotel where the auditions are!" I recognize it from the search I did on the library computer back when I first submitted my application. I glance at Gran's watch; my audition slot is in just twenty minutes. If we'd made the earlier train, I'd have had time to practice beforehand, but now I'll be glad if I just get a chance to change clothes first.

Gran shakes her head. "Go on, then. I'll catch up to you. But Amelia, be careful! Watch out for —"

"I'll be fine, Gran!" I don't need to be given permission twice.

I race ahead, pushing through the crowds on the sidewalk and clutching my flute case to my chest. I skid around the corner and then find myself standing right in front of it: the Hotel Rhapsody.

Tall and glass and modern, the building is fancy.

Seriously fancy.

I almost wait for Gran to catch up, but being even a minute late might cost me everything. So I put one foot in front of the other and walk past the two sparkling fountains to a huge revolving glass door.

The lobby echoes with voices and the splashing of an artificial waterfall that tumbles from the third floor. A valet walks and plays a guitar, and from it, yellow streamers of magic unfurl to carry a line of suitcases for a guest. I stare at him for a few minutes, wondering how he can juggle so many pieces at once. The silver music note pinned to his uniform designates him as a Novice, but the spell sounds pretty complicated, his fingers a blur as they pick the strings.

Off to one side is a table with a little sign on it: MYSTWICK SCHOOL OF MUSICRAFT AUDITIONS. A woman sits behind it, shuffling through a stack of papers.

I hurry over and set my flute on the floor, then cough to get the woman's attention.

She looks up, frowning. "Cutting it close, aren't we?"

I wince. "Sorry. There was this chicken and it was stuck and then we missed the first train — you know what, never mind."

She sets aside her papers. "Name?"

"Amelia Jones. Twelve years old. My birthday is April third—"

"Just the name will do, thank you." She hands me a paper with the number 242 on it, and as I give her my audition fee — mostly cash I earned charming chickens and doing odd jobs for neighbors — I think, *There are 241 other auditions today?*

"Um . . . how many spots are there?" I ask.

She blinks at the stack of mostly one-dollar bills, then sighs. "There are one hundred seats available in the freshman seventh-grade class, with four openings for flutists."

My heart drops.

Kids fly to the United States from all over the world just to audition. Who knows how many more are trying out all together? There are auditions being held all over the country this week, so probably thousands, all of them just as eager as I am to get into Mystwick.

"Young lady?" The woman at the desk eyes me. "Are you all right? You look pale."

"Uh . . . fine," I mumble. "How long till they call me?"

She consults a paper, then says, "You have about ten minutes, I imagine. You're lucky I let you in at all. Punctuality is key in a Mystwick musician."

I smile weakly. "Right. Sorry."

Looking out the front windows, I spy Gran waiting for a light to cross the street. Figuring I'd better use this time to clean up, I hurry past the waterfall and a restaurant where fancy people are eating fancy little meals. Glancing across the lobby, I see Ballroom A, where I'm supposed to wait for my audition to start. Looks like there are a bunch of kids there already, and I can hear them warming up. Discordant notes echo through the lobby, the woodsy drone of cellos beneath plinking piano and aggressive trumpets.

In the marble bathroom behind the restaurant—I wonder if the gold faucets are *actually* gold—I look into the mirror and groan.

On a good day, my hair is curly and bouncy, like copper coils. But on a bad day? *Frizz-a-palooza*. And yep, today is definitely a bad day.

Giving up on the hair, I put my bag on the counter and unzip it—and my stomach turns inside out.

In my rush, I didn't check the grape juice cap, and now it's poured all over my nice dress. And not just that, it's soaked my sheet music too.

I lean back with a groan.

"Okay," I mutter. I look in the mirror, take a deep breath, and plant two fists into the countertop. "No panicking. Pull it together, Amelia Jones. *Think*."

I quickly zip my bag shut, grab my flute case, and run out of the bathroom. There's an exit to the back of the hotel to my left.

I bust through the back door and into the parking lot behind the hotel. A dumpster sits to my right, and I duck behind it and spread out the contents of my bag: one soaking, grape-juice-stained dress and three pages of Handel's Sonata in E Minor. With everything laid out in front of me, I unsnap my case and take out my flute, sliding the pieces together until it's nearly the length of my arm.

I take a moment to exhale, lick my lips, and try to still myself.

Breathe in. Breathe out.

Find the tempo.

When I'm ready, I begin to play. Not Handel's Sonata, but a simpler tune everyone knows: "The Itsy-Bitsy Spider." It's an easy drying spell, for when you spill water on the floor or your laundry comes out damp.

As I play it now, bursts of blue magic float from the flute and settle on the soaked items like butterflies. The air around me starts to heat up a little, which means the spell is working.

But in my impatience and nervousness, I play a little too fast, and that, plus the heat of the summer, equals disaster.

Because the papers and the dress burst into *flames*.

With a yelp, I stumble backwards, nearly dropping my flute. The blaze leaps up, close to catching the garbage piled in the dumpster. Heat rushes over my skin.

I raise my flute, hands shaking, and try to think of a spell to conjure water. "Rain, Rain, Go Away"? No, that's another drying spell, the opposite of what I need. To reverse any spell, you have to transpose it to a parallel key, major to minor or vice versa. But that takes a lot of preparation, and I've never reversed this particular spell before.

My mind races, but it feels like every thought in my head caught on fire too. All I can do now is watch the flames leap higher and higher, just like the panic in my chest.

If I burn down the hotel, will they still let me into Mystwick?

Focus, Amelia!

Out of nowhere, I hear a swift flourish of violin music. I don't recognize the melody, but it's some sort of tarantella—fast and reckless, notes popping in the air. I look around in confusion—when a deluge of water dumps from the sky and douses the fire. It's like someone upended a bucket from one of the windows above. It splashes over my sneakers, washing a bit of the mud away.

In the resulting puddle lie the remains of my dress and papers—mostly ashes now.

Gasping, I look up to see a boy standing at the end of the dumpster, a violin tucked under his chin, his fingers flying over the strings, his bow slicing the air. He's wearing a black suit with shiny lapels, and I wonder faintly if he's here for a wedding or something. He looks very formal.

He plays for another minute, closing the spell, then lowers the violin. He has brown eyes and dark hair that flops in all different directions, and the biggest ears I've ever seen.

"Wow," I say. "You're *really* good."

He grins. "Drying spell gone wrong?" He has an accent, British I think.

I blink, then nod. "Itsy-Bitsy Spider."

He laughs, tucking his instrument into a case lying open at his feet. "I think your spider's a pyromaniac."

I let out a long sigh; my hands are still shaking a little. Without my sheet music, I'm going to have to play my audition spell from memory. *Great.* "Thanks for that. I could've burned down the hotel."

"I'm sure you'd have handled it," he replies with a shrug. "I just happened to be out here for a quick practice, and thought I'd pitch in."

Taking a second look at him, I ask, "You're auditioning?"

"You bet." He opens his jacket to reveal the number *241* on his chest. "I'm Jai. Jai Kapoor."

"Amelia Jones."

He frowns. "Amelia Jones . . . I feel like I know that name. Have you ever played in any of the big concert halls? London? Paris?"

"Yeah, a real famous one called My Treehouse," I laugh, thinking he's joking.

Then I realize he might actually be serious.

"Huh," he says. "Must have been someone else I was thinking of. So, Mystwick, huh?"

I kneel to pack my flute away. "Been dreaming of it my whole life. You?"

He shrugs. "Don't really have a choice. My parents went there, and my grandparents. We Kapoors are a tradition at Mystwick, they say."

It's strange talking to someone who's been dreaming of Mystwick too. Strange in a *good* way. Like meeting a person who's read all the same books as you. There were other music kids at my school, of course, but none of them cared about Mystwick the way I do.

"You're brave, going in for flute," Jai says. "That's the most competitive category, after piano. You'll have to outshine twice as many musicians."

I smile weakly. "*Brave*. Yeah, that's me. Just, you know, always trying to do things the hard way."

I should have guessed flute would be one of the more popular instruments.

They say you can tell a lot about a person by the instrument they choose. You can play any spell as long as your instrument is capable of carrying the melody, but certain instruments have their specialties—brass like tuba and trumpet are good at wards and hovering spells, for example, and flutes are particularly good at healing magic. Percussion is known for energizing spells, which is why you see drummers at sports matches a lot, and if it's elemental magic you need, the best choices are cellos or harps.

Mrs. Parrish had told me years ago, when I'd first told her I wanted to go to Mystwick, that choosing a less common instrument like the euphonium or organ would make it much easier to get in, with fewer musicians vying for those spots in the Mystwick roster.

But for me, choosing flute has always been based on one totally different and nonnegotiable reason: it was my mom's instrument. And if that means facing tougher odds, then I'm ready.

My insides may be slowly melting into trembling lumps of jelly, but I'm *ready*.

"Violin for you, huh?" I ask.

He nods, sighing a little. "It's not my favorite, but it's my strongest instrument. I wanted to go for guitar or saxophone, but my dad—"

"Jai!" shouts a stern voice from the hotel door, and we turn to see a tall, serious-looking man in a suit like Jai's standing there. He has a Maestro's gold pin on his lapel, polished to a shine. He has the same big ears as Jai, but a lot less laughter in his eyes. "You are supposed to be practicing."

"I was, Dad," Jai says. "But then—"

"But then you thought you'd waste time clowning around?" The man shakes his head, his eyes stormy. "Get inside and take your seat, and *focus!* It's time you got serious, son."

I lower my gaze, but see Jai grit his teeth. "Right," he says. "Coming."

We walk in together, Jai's dad several steps ahead, his shoulders stiff and his black hair perfectly combed.

"My dad says sax and guitar aren't *serious* instruments," Jai finishes in a whisper; then he makes a face.

In Ballroom A—which leads to a set of double doors labeled Ballroom B, where the auditions must be taking place—a bunch of kids are pacing around as they sing or hum the melodies of the spells they'll be performing for the audition; singing doesn't produce magic, so it's a safe and quick way to run through a spell. Mrs. Parrish calls it *solfège,* and sometimes we spend whole class periods just singing spells instead of playing them.

The kids look like strange, animated dolls, their eyes unfocused and their hands holding up invisible instruments. The sounds of all their voices and different melodies clash and harmonize. I can identify many of the spells they're practicing and realize most of them are way more difficult pieces than my sonata. But that doesn't bother me. It's better to nail a simpler spell than flub a fancy one.

Still, I eye a few flutists, trying to judge how good they are, though most of them scooch aside and stop their warm-ups as Mr. Kapoor pushes through.

"Your dad went to Mystwick too?" I whisper to Jai.

"Yeah. Now he's with the Austrian Philharmonic. My mum was supposed to bring me to the audition, but she got tied up with work back in London." At my blank expression, he adds, "She's the Minister of Musical Affairs for the UK, same as my grandad was before her."

Geez. Is there a nonmusical person in this kid's entire family?

"Dad had to miss a performance to come here," Jai adds. "Some big illusion show for the king of Denmark. So he's extra cranky."

"Oh," I say casually, as if missing performances for kings is a totally normal problem to have.

I can tell Jai is trying not to stare at me, but then he asks tentatively, "So . . . do you live on a farm or something?"

I glance down at my work boots, jeans, and T-shirt with a picture of Johannes Sebastian wearing sunglasses beneath the words I'LL BE BACH—all spattered with mud and chicken poop. At least they seem to have aired out a bit. That, or I've gotten used to the smell.

"Um . . . yes." It seems to be the easiest explanation.

Gran is standing outside the ballroom, looking around nervously and fidgeting with her driving gloves.

"Where have you been?" she asks.

She gives Jai a quick, suspicious look—Gran's gotten weird about me talking to boys, like they're all on the verge of dragging me to prom or something—then pulls me aside. Jai heads on in with a grin and a wave, and I see his father's hand clamp hard on his shoulder.

There are a bunch more kids waiting in chairs, and they're all dressed like they're going to a funeral—a very *fancy* funeral. The girls wear black dresses, the boys wear suits like Jai's. Everyone is tuning up, but a sign on the wall reads NO MAGIC, so it's just scales and random notes and handheld electronic tuners, no spells. There are warded practice rooms farther down, where I see sparks of magic beneath the doors.

"You're sure this is what you want?" Gran asks, her eyes searching my face.

"Gran, you *know* it is."

"Amelia . . ." Her hand grips my arm so tight, I worry she's about to drag me out of the hotel. "This won't be like your school, where you can play rings around everyone else."

"What are you saying, Gran?" I frown. "Are you saying I'm not good enough for Mystwick?"

Her eyes widen. "No! No, not that. It's only that . . . you're so young to already have your whole life planned out. Maybe there are other things you'd like to try first. You never know—"

"Are you going to tell me I'm not allowed to audition?" I say it louder than I'd intended, and a few people glance at us. My cheeks burn but I don't look away from Gran. "Are we really going to go over this *again?* Gran, this is what I want. This is the *only thing* I've ever wanted."

"It would mean leaving me," she says. "The school's on the other side of the country, you know, way up in the Rocky Mountains."

"Well, maybe it isn't about *you*, Gran." The words leap off my tongue before I can stop them, sharp as glass.

She looks at me a moment, and my stomach clenches. I so do *not* want to argue with her about this now, not in front of all those other kids, right before the most important audition of my life. Why can't she just tell me good luck? Or even snap at me to

29

be serious and focus, like Jai's dad did to him? At least then I'd know she *wants* me to do my best today.

Then she says, "No. It's about *her*. You think I don't know that? I know you keep her picture in your flute case."

"So what? You don't want me to be like my mom?"

"Of course I want you to feel close to her. I'm just scared of you trying so hard to be someone else that you never find out who *you* are. And Musicraft, Amelia . . . it's dangerous."

My chest pinches. "Well, just because you're scared doesn't mean I have to be."

She must see the determination in my eyes, because she finally sighs and shakes her head. "They aren't letting adults into the waiting area. So I'll be over at the restaurant, okay?"

That's it. No hug, no advice. But that's how it's always been with Gran. I stopped expecting encouragement from her years ago. Suddenly I wish I'd asked Mrs. Parrish to bring me here today, not Gran. Deep down, I guess I'd thought if I did well here, Gran would finally accept my magic and realize I'm not giving it up, not for anything.

I just wish I understood *why* she hates it so much.

Face still red, I walk into the waiting room, where it seems like a million pairs of eyes fix on me. I can't help but think they heard some of the argument, even though Gran and I were mostly whispering. Cheeks burning, I take the seat beside

Jai, who's got earbuds in, probably listening to his audition spell. There's a pair of double doors at the end of the room, where the kids go in one by one to audition for the Maestros from Mystwick.

"So many people," I say, taking out my flute and fitting the sections back together.

Jai nods, taking out one of his earbuds. "But Mystwick only takes the best of the best."

I swallow. Hard. As a distraction, I point at his dangling earbud, from which a spell is blasting at top volume so it almost buzzes like a bee against his tuxedo, all drums and wild guitar riffs.

"You're playing a rock spell for your audition?"

He laughs, but glances nervously at the corridor, where his dad is still lurking. "No, this just gets me in the zone. Besides, my dad would probably disown me if he ever caught me playing a spell that was so"—he drops his voice and does an impression of his father—"*unserious*. He says rock magic is for losers." Jai rolls his eyes.

At least his dad doesn't hate *all* Musicraft, like Gran does.

I wish I had something to listen to to get me in the zone, but I don't think anything short of a hypnotizing jazz spell would work right now. My feet bounce restlessly, like they're ready to take off at a sprint for the doors.

As if he can read my thoughts, Jai nudges me and says, "Don't worry. You'll get in. We both will." He pauses, then adds, "Or we don't. And we end up as street musicians, removing warts for a pound—er, sorry. Dollar."

"Or charming runaway chickens."

He laughs. "Never heard that one before."

I could make a living as a Novice, sure, with a little silver pin on my collar. Anyone at all can be a Novice, even without going to a Musicraft school.

I'd just be unable to join a Symphony, and I'd never get to play high-level spells. I'd forever be a beginner, never finding out my true potential. And worst of all, I'd fail my mom.

I can still remember the day I found her flute. I was seven years old, digging around Gran's attic for a sled, since it had snowed the day before. Instead, I found a slender black case, and inside it—the impossible.

A flute. *Her* flute.

I could remember her and me lying on a picnic blanket under a big tree, and her playing a spell to make the wind rustle the leaves. I could remember her polishing the flute, sitting on a faded blue couch while I lay with my feet in her lap, listening to music on the radio.

"Why do you listen to this?" I asked her. "It doesn't make any magic." Recorded music is just sounds. It has to be played live to become a spell.

"Oh, Amelia." In my hazy memories, her voice was always shifting—sometimes light, sometimes deep—but it was always kind. "There is magic in just listening, you know. And if you listen close enough, you can hear music everywhere."

Then she let me hold her flute and pretend to play it, my fingers on top of hers as she showed me the fingerings for her favorite spells. In a way, the flute and my mom are one and the same. If I hold it tight enough, sometimes I can imagine it's her hand I'm holding.

I'd thought the flute had been lost after she died.

When I'd asked Gran about it, she got upset and hid it again. I was so mad that I tried to run away from home, but I only made it as far as Mrs. O'Grady's. She was the one who told me my mom had gone to the Mystwick School of Musicraft and become a Maestro.

And that's when I decided I would do everything it took to get there too. I would find out if I was good enough to follow in her footsteps.

"Two forty-one!" shouts the woman in charge of the audition room doors, startling me from my thoughts.

"Well, here I go," Jai sighs, taking his violin from his case.

"Good luck!"

"Psh! Who needs luck?" He grins. "The Maestros like confidence, Amelia Jones. Don't forget it. Your magic is only as strong as your belief."

He gives me a thumbs-up, then disappears through the double doors to the audition room.

If it's confidence the Maestros want, then they might as well hand Jai his diploma and golden Maestro pin. I already saw him play like a master; he's got the swagger of one, too.

I look around, my eyes falling on the girl beside me, who's obsessively polishing her oboe.

"Hi," I say, with a little wave. "Where are you from?"

The girl's lips curl. "There's something in your hair."

I reach up and feel around until I find it—a fluffy white chicken feather.

These kids are all serious, well-dressed, shining. I bet their instruments cost a ton. Maybe they've had fancy tutors and all their relatives are famous and important Maestros like Jai's. I wonder if any of them have ever charmed a chicken for five dollars or ridden their bike three miles through a rainstorm just to get to their music teacher's house.

"Two forty-two!" calls the lady.

I look up to see Jai leaving. He gives a small fist pump. I guess *his* audition went well. My eyes follow him as he leaves, and I wonder if I'll ever see him again. I hope he gets into Mystwick. But then, why wouldn't he? His family is a tradition there.

And so is mine, I remind myself.

"TWO FORTY-TWO!" the voice calls again, louder, and I jolt upright, remembering that *I'm* 242.

The woman in charge of the doors waves, urging me to hurry. Her brown hair is tied into a sleek ponytail, and it swings as she shakes her head, her eyes taking in my appearance with disapproval.

"Sorry," I say quickly.

"Two forty-two?"

I nod.

"Through here, dear. Quickly, now! And good luck!"

Drawing a deep breath, I walk past her and into the next room, clutching my flute case like it's a float and I'm about to jump into a stormy, shark-infested sea.

CHAPTER THREE

Sonata in Oops Minor

THE **DOUBLE DOORS LEAD** into another ballroom, this one even bigger than the first. The floor is shining marble and my steps echo off walls paneled with mirrors. Fragments of light dance everywhere, thrown by the prisms dangling from crystal chandeliers overhead.

The place is empty except for four people sitting behind a table at the far wall, two women and two men. They watch me silently as I cross the wide open space. Three of them are wearing tuxedos, and the woman on the end is wearing an elegant black dress. Each one wears a golden Maestro pin.

It takes a century for me to reach them. Their faces are completely blank, eyes fixed on me. I feel like they can see every speck of dirt on my clothes, every bad and unmusical thought I've ever had.

Now I know exactly why those kids before me left looking like they'd learned the time and place of their own deaths.

All except Jai, of course. How had he handled these four stony-faced Maestros and still come out smiling?

And here I am with my muddy clothes and frizzy hair and no sheet music. For a minute, I can only stare at the floor, face on fire, wondering if I could get my audition fee refunded if I left now.

But then I tighten my jaw.

I didn't come all this way to chicken out. Anyway, it doesn't matter that my clothes are messy and my sheet music is burned to a crisp, or that I've never played in front of a real Maestro before.

Like Jai said: they like confidence.

I lift my chin and remind myself to breathe.

"Two-four-two?" says a grumpy-looking Maestro with more hair in his mustache than on his head.

I nod.

In front of me is a small table, and on it sits a clay pot. Leaning over, I see it's filled with dirt, and on top of the dirt rests a small acorn. There's a music stand, too, but it's not like I have anything to put there.

"Excellent, *another* flute," Mustache Man sighs, as if there are a million other things he'd rather be doing. "You have before you an acorn and ample soil. I trust our expectations are clear. Now, what piece will you be performing?"

"Handel's —"

"Speak up! We can't hear you when you squeak like that."

I clear my throat. "Handel's Flute Sonata in E minor."

My hands shake like they're made of paper. Wiping them on my jeans, I take two deep breaths before placing the silver barrel to my chin, my bottom lip lightly resting against the lip plate.

Three of the Maestros stare with flat eyes, but the lady in the dress gives me a small, encouraging smile.

The instructions on Mystwick's audition website had been vague: Prepare a healing spell, it had said, and the rest of the instructions would be made clear at the audition itself. Now it all makes sense — healing spells also double as growth spells if you know how to alter the tempo just a bit. And I've had a lot of practice with that, helping Mrs. O'Grady in her vegetable garden.

But I'd counted on having my sheet music with me. I've played the spell a hundred times, but right now, I can't even think of the first note.

Panicking, I press down and blow, producing a high, smooth note — E-flat.

It's the right one.

After that, it all comes back to me: the notes, the tempo, the melody. My fingers dance over the keys.

Handel's Flute Sonata in E minor. It starts out slow and steady, *adagio,* notes marching in an orderly line, smooth as glass.

I take my time, settling into a series of rolling measures, my upper half swaying as I lean into the music and feel each note.

As the Third Rule of Musicraft states, *With all your soul do play your part, for magic rises from the heart.* That's why recorded spells don't work. They might sound nice, but magic comes from the musician, not the music — the notes and instruments are just how you control it. And that means you have to stay focused and keep your attention on the spell, or you won't produce so much as a curl of magic. It takes your whole heart and soul to pull off a proper spell, and a good musician knows controlling your thoughts is just as important as controlling your breath and fingers.

Sweet tones turn into curls of green light and swirl through the air. Most of them, directed by my focus on the acorn, drift to the pot and sink into the soil. The magic smells like water on leaves, a rainy day in spring.

The first movement goes perfectly.

I transition into the second, picking up the tempo, *allegro.* Now my fingers begin to race, notes trilling and fluttering. And the magic changes accordingly, the green curls of light shortening into brief bursts, drifting like dandelion fluff through the air and hovering around the acorn. The longer I play, the more lights come to life, until my skin and the table and the flute are illuminated with dancing green sparks. The chandeliers overhead refract the lights until the whole room glitters, the mirrored walls reflecting endless Amelias.

Finally the acorn begins to jiggle, then splits into two pale halves as a tender white shoot pries its way free.

Growth spells are one of my favorites—they're so full of hope and happiness. Seeing the little plant burst into life, straining to reach for the sun, makes my soul expand.

I risk a quick glance up, just as the sprout begins to unfurl its first leaves, and I see the Maestros watching just as grimly as before. They don't look too impressed. Mustache even looks a little bored.

My heart squeezes.

What if I'm doing something wrong? What if I misunderstood the instructions or picked the wrong spell? What if they don't like my technique? Or what if they decided the moment they saw my muddy shoes and my chicken-poop jeans that I'm not Mystwick material?

SQUEEEEET!

The jarring note splits the air like a scream and my whole body contracts, my fingers momentarily freezing on the keys. The fragile shoot shivers in its pot.

No no no no no!

Desperately, I keep playing as if the bad note never happened. I don't dare look at the Maestros. But then I hit a wrong note, and another squeaky A, and sweat runs down my face and my neck and slimes my palms.

I keep picturing their stony expressions, especially Mustache Man, frowning at me and thinking, *Who is this weirdo? She doesn't belong here. Send in the real musicians!*

Suddenly I hear a shout from the Maestros, and I look up.

And I'm so startled by what I see that I stop playing altogether. The green motes of light all die as suddenly as they appeared, like startled fireflies.

I stand frozen in horror in the following silence, gaping at Mustache Man.

Or rather, at the *mustache.*

It has sprouted so much hair that it now hangs to his belly. He could braid it and toss it over his shoulder, if he wanted. He could string it between two trees and use it for a hammock.

By letting my mind get distracted, I lost control of the magic, and it fixed on the Maestro instead of the acorn. The growth spell *worked,* at least . . . just not on the right thing.

The other three Maestros gape at the man, who is slowly lifting his ridiculously long mustache with both hands.

Then his eyes rise to me, shiny with rage.

"Young lady," says the Maestro in the dress, "finish your spell, please."

Shaking, I raise my flute and play the last few measures, but it's too late to undo the damage.

The sprout had put out three leaves, but that last awful note had not only broken the spell—it had twisted it completely. In response, the shoot bent sideways at a ninety-degree angle, so the whole thing is now shaped like an upside-down L. The leaves droop sadly, as if heartbroken.

Kind of like how *my* heart is breaking.

I lower my flute and stare numbly.

"Somebody bring me a pair of scissors!" bellows Mustache Man. "And *you!*" He points at me. "Get out of here!"

"I—I'm sorry!" I say. "I can start over. Or I—I can play a trimming spell and fix it! Please, you'll see—"

"We've seen *plenty*," he growls, pulling more and more of his mustache up and onto the table. It coils there like a pile of brown yarn. "*Where* are those scissors?"

I'm still blinking at them, pleas gathering in my throat, as I hear the doors behind me open and the woman outside runs in and slams a pair of scissors onto the table.

Then she pulls me away by my elbow. I don't even have time to put away my instrument. I can only bundle my flute under one arm, grab my case in the other, and shuffle quickly after her.

"Wait! Please!" I shout. "I can do better, I promise!"

I'm pushed through the doors to find myself staring at the

other kids, who watch with wide eyes. Tears run down my cheeks, and a pressure builds inside my chest. I can't *breathe*.

"Two-four-three!" the woman yells.

I run through the ballroom and into the lobby, out the front doors, bursting into the sunny parking lot. Gran shouts my name but I don't stop. I just want to get as far away from here as possible. Back to the train station. Back home.

"I'm sorry, Mom," I whisper, doubling over as a sob rises in my lungs. "I tried, but I —"

The words stick in my throat. *I guess I'm nothing like you after all.*

CHAPTER FOUR

The Treehouse Blues

MY TREEHOUSE IS HIDDEN deep in the forest, out of sight of any other houses. I climb up and sit on the edge of the floor, legs dangling. After two weeks of shutting myself up in my room and crying into my pillow, I was finally pushed —literally—out the front door by Gran, who told me my "sulk-athon" had gone on long enough, and some sunshine would do me good. So I slunk off, taking my flute with me.

The world didn't end because I screwed up one audition.

It only *feels* that way.

The woods here seem silent at first, but if you know how to listen, you can hear a whole symphony, magic of an entirely different sort: wind shivering through the needles, pines creaking as they lean, squirrels chirping and birds trilling. Little white mushrooms stubble a fallen log below, beneath the long, glossy ferns that are starting to turn brown at the tips of their leaves. Looking at all the growing things around me, I'm reminded of my audition tree.

So young and fragile and hopeful, only to end up mangled and broken.

My flute case is beside me; I snap it open and take out my instrument, sliding the pieces together without even having to look.

Then, lying on my back, I stare up at the roof of my tree-house and try to think about what Mom would do.

I wish I could talk to you, I think.

Putting my flute to my chin, I begin to play.

Instead of choosing a spell, I just let the notes flow from my fingers. I close my eyes and stop thinking, and just *feel* the melody.

Usually I know what notes are coming, because I've studied the spell and practiced it a hundred times. But this time, each note is a surprise. The melody begins slow, then races faster and faster, falling like rain and then skittering upward.

Where the music comes from, I don't know. I've never tried anything like this before. Always, I've had my sheet music or memorized the spell, striving to hit each note perfectly.

But this time, it's like someone else is playing *through* me. It's like I'm crossing a foggy river, jumping from one stone before I can even see the next, landing each time with a flutter of surprise and relief. The notes rise up from the bottom of my soul and carry me along, pulling me deeper into a strange melody, asking me to follow.

I let them guide me, trusting them, and as I do, I think about my mom, laughing in her graduation gown, confident. Happy. Beautiful. Her new, golden Maestro pin gleaming on her collar. Whatever happened to that pin, I wonder? It wasn't with the flute, and Gran has never mentioned having it.

I wish you could tell me what to do.

I wish you were here.

I shut my eyes and let the music take over, until I forget how long I'm lying there on the hard floorboards, the cool wind rolling over me and the trees sighing all around. The music is instinct. It's my heartbeat spun into sound. It's a spell entirely my own. My fingers seem to play with a mind of their own, like I couldn't stop even if I wanted to.

The wind sweeps across the forest, getting stronger, rattling and rustling the trees around me, stirring my hair and leaving a trail of goose bumps up my arms. For a brief moment, my whole body feels cold.

I hear a rustle nearby, and when I open my eyes, I see rainbow tendrils of magic swirling from my flute and coiling upward. All around my treehouse is a spiraling column of pine needles and twigs and leaves caught up in the spell, a slow and gentle tornado of woodsy debris borne on the current of my music. The funnel rises to the treetops, glittering and twisting. The air smells of burned matches.

I've never seen magic like this before, made of every color, instead of the usual yellow or green or white spell. For a moment, I'm awestruck, caught up in the strange beauty of it.

Then, panicking, I break off the spell, and the bits of leaves and sticks all rain down on me. I sit up and wipe them from my face and clothes, heart pounding.

Fooling around with music is a dangerous thing. What if I'd started a wildfire?

They should add a new rule of Musicraft: *Mess around, you burn stuff down.*

A shadow crosses my face. Shielding the sun, I look up and see a butterfly drifting through the trees. It circles, then swoops toward me, wings lazily flapping.

Startled, I jump to my feet. It's like no butterfly I've ever seen before. It's white, almost as if . . . The butterfly is completely made of *paper*. Like an origami bird.

I stare in shock as it lands on my outstretched palm, wings falling still. Then, before my eyes, it unfolds itself into an envelope, sealed with a gold foil sticker shaped like a treble clef. Written in elegant letters of gold ink is my name, *Amelia Jones,* and below that is the crest of the Mystwick School of Musicraft, a harp wreathed in ivy, below a banner stamped with AUDIENTIBUS MUSICA ADEST, the school motto. *Music is there for those who listen.*

My heart sinks.

I knew I'd get the rejection letter. I just didn't expect it would come flying like a butterfly. But still, maybe it's better this way: I can get it over with. I can put Mystwick and that awful audition behind me forever.

Might as well rip off the Band-Aid, right?

But as I slide my thumb between the two halves of the paper, my heart does a flip.

For a moment, I imagine a different future, in which the words inside bring a smile to my face. In which I run into the house shouting for Gran, opening my suitcase, packing my clothes and my flute. Leaving for the big wide world and my future as a Maestro.

Finally following my mom's footsteps.

But as soon as I open the paper and see the actual words inside, it will all be over.

No more daydreams.

So I put it in the pocket of my skirt, still folded, and head home, my flute case swinging at my side. It's getting dark anyway, and maybe it'll be easier if I wait and open the letter in the morning.

All I want to do is go to bed and sleep, but Gran catches me and forces me into the kitchen.

"We need to talk," she says.

"Can we do it tomorrow?"

But she pulls out a chair from the kitchen table and points at it, relentless. With a sigh, I sit and plop my case on the floor.

Gran stands across from me, her arms folded. "I won't have you moping around this house for days on end, young lady. We need to find something constructive for you to do."

I groan and let my head fall onto the table. "Please don't say you signed me up for swim team again, Gran. You know how many times I've nearly drowned? Water and I do *not* mix."

"There must be something else that you want to do."

I lift my face. "I wanted Mystwick. That's *all* I ever wanted."

She frowns, uncrossing her arms. "Why? Why do you want to go to this school so badly?"

"Because — because I wanted to show you and everyone else that I could do it, that I could be a real musician! That I could be . . ." I pause to swallow, then whisper, "That I could be like *her*."

"Your mother."

I nod, my eyes dropping to the tabletop.

"Amelia . . ." Gran sighs heavily. "Your mother would have been so proud of you, even if you didn't go to this school. She'd tell you that you don't need to prove anything, that you're a strong, smart girl with or without Mystwick."

I scowl, my hands knotting into fists on my lap. "How would I know what she'd say? You never talk about her! It's like — it's like she never even *existed*. Even Mrs. O'Grady tells me more than you do!"

Gran turns away, shaking her head. "You don't understand."

I stand up, my fists planted on the table. "I understand that my music reminds you of her, and that makes you sad. And I understand that's why you don't want me to go to Mystwick. I understand that you're *happy* I blew my audition."

"Is that what you think?" she whispers, turning back to me.

"It's what I *know*. I know you hate Musicraft and Mystwick, but it's all I had of her, and now I don't even have that. And now I—I don't even know who I am or what I'm supposed to do! I wish she'd never gotten in that car eight years ago!"

Gran's face creases. She rubs her arms like she's cold and stares through the window by the fridge, into the murky twilight. "It wasn't a car accident, Amelia."

I freeze. "What?"

Gran sits, picking nervously at her nails. "Your mother didn't die in a car accident. I didn't tell you the truth because . . . because the truth is, I don't know *how* she died. There are still so many unanswered questions, and I wanted you to have the closure I couldn't have. So I . . . I lied, telling myself I'd set the record straight one day. But sit down, Amelia, and I will tell you the truth. Or as much of it as anyone knows. You deserve that, and I've kept it from you for too long."

I stare at her, stunned.

The story she always told me, when she spoke of it at all, was that my Mom died in a car crash. It's what I believed for eight years. Now she's telling me that was a lie? That something *else* happened, and she's kept it hidden all this time?

She picks up the flute case and sets it between us, slowly opening it so that the silver barrel glints in the light coming through the window over the sink. She takes out the photo of my mom and sighs deeply, her thumb gently rubbing the paper.

"Susan was exceptionally gifted," Gran says at last, her eyes shiny with tears. "Your grandfather and I were delighted. We gave her everything—the best lessons, the best instruments. She could play such spells . . . There was no doubt of her getting into a good school, but even we hadn't expected she'd make it to the famous Mystwick. The day her acceptance letter came was the day we finally realized how truly special our Susie was. She would become a Maestro. She would make a difference in the world with her magic. How proud we were."

Tears pricking my eyes, I whisper, "What *happened*, Gran?"

"Amelia," Gran says, looking up at me, "even with all her talent and training, your mother still fell victim to Musicraft's darker consequences. No one knows exactly what happened that night, and you were too young to remember, but all we could determine was that she'd attempted a spell beyond even her skill. She was found beside a river, the trees around her all scorched to ash. All that remained was you, perfectly unscathed, asleep in a patch of green grass amid the destruction. And of course, there was the flute. We know from the scorch marks found on it that it had to be the source of the magic that killed her. It's a wonder the thing could be salvaged."

She draws a shaking breath. "When you get into that dangerous magic, the sort Maestros play, it can have terrible consequences. The smallest mistake can have the most devastating results, and whatever your mother tried to do that night by the river, it didn't work. And it killed her."

My body goes cold. *Musicraft* killed my mom? I've heard of people getting seriously hurt or even dying from spells gone wrong, but it takes extremely powerful magic to do that kind of damage. There are some spells even the best Maestros won't attempt.

What was my mom doing the night she died? What sort of magic had she tried to work?

I guess that's what Gran meant by unanswered questions. And now I know why she has always disapproved of Musicraft—not just because it reminds her of Mom, but because it reminds her of how Mom died.

Gran rests her elbows on the table and covers her face with her wrinkled hands. There's still flour dusting her knuckles. She looks so sad that I can't even feel mad at her for lying to me.

In fact, I can't feel anything at all.

It's like I'm made of concrete, hardening in my chair. The tears in my eyes have dried up and I stare at the tabletop.

"What about my dad?" I whisper. "Where is he? Did you lie about him too?"

She shakes her head, looking angry, but not at me. "I never liked Eric to begin with. He was a wanderer, coming and going, never able to settle in one place. Couldn't even sit still long enough to marry your mother. For weeks he'd be gone, leaving the two of you alone, then showing up with piles of presents and smooth apologies. And of course, after your mother . . . well, he never turned up again at all." Then her face softens a little. "But she loved him fiercely. That's for sure."

"Was he . . . a Maestro too?"

"He dropped out of Mystwick in their senior year. He was talented, but that's all he was—lots of talent and no discipline." She stops, pressing her lips together. "It's better we never hear from that man again."

Did he have something to do with her death? I know Gran must be thinking it, judging by the look on her face. I always thought my father ran away because he was heartbroken.

But what if it's because he was *guilty?* The thought makes me feel slimy inside,

"So that's why you don't want me to be a musician," I say. "You think I'll get hurt too, like her."

"Yes, I admit some selfishness in trying to discourage you, and maybe I should have just said no from the beginning. But I realized years ago that if I stopped you from playing altogether, I would lose you entirely. So you see, that was also selfish of me." She reaches across the table and takes my hands in hers. Her eyes are nestled in wrinkles. "But your mother wouldn't have wanted you to live in her shadow. You don't have to prove anything to her or me or anyone else. Amelia, she would want you to be *yourself*."

I pull my hands away. "Well, I tried that. And it turned out my *self* wasn't good enough." I take out the Mystwick rejection letter and put it on the table. "I guess you got what you want —I'm nothing like my mom."

Gran picks up the letter. "You haven't opened it."

"I know what it says." I jump to my feet, my chair sliding noisily across the linoleum floor. "Maybe I'll sign up for swim team after all. At least *they'll* take me."

I run to my room and shut the door. Curled up on my bed, I hug a pillow and stare up at the ceiling, where years ago I hung a poster with the Mystwick crest on it. On the wall is a calendar counting down to audition day. In my closet are clothes all in Mystwick navy blue. Everything I've done was for her, and now it's all falling to pieces.

How do you just give up a dream you've had your whole life?

Gran knocks on the door. "Amelia."

"Go away."

"Amelia."

With a groan, I force myself to my feet and go open the door.

She's standing in the hallway with my flute assembled, and now she holds it out to me. The silver barrel reflects both our faces, warped into caricatures.

"Take it," she says, an odd look on her face.

"I don't want it. I shouldn't ever have picked it up in the first place. I don't deserve it."

"Amelia—"

"Maybe donate it to someone. Give it to some other, better musician. Someone better than me, who'll do Mom proud."

She starts to argue, then shakes her head. "Fine. If that's what you want. But it's going to be mighty awkward when you show up at school without an instrument to play."

I blink. "Huh?"

Gran pulls the Mystwick letter from her pocket. She's opened it up, and now she raises it to my eyes. I can't help but glance at the words, my stomach reeling.

Then I freeze and read it more slowly, start to finish.

Reaching out, I take the paper from Gran and grip it so tight that it rips a little.

Dear Miss Jones . . .

I read the letter a third time, and do not breathe even once until I reach the *Cordially, Euphonia Le Roux, Headmaestro,*

Mystwick School of Musicraft at the very bottom of the page, over a wax seal stamped with Mystwick's crest. Fixed to the bottom of the paper is a shiny purple ticket.

"Gran . . ." I look up at her, my hand starting to shake. *"I got in."*

CHAPTER FIVE

The Flight of the Purple Bumblebee

A MONTH LATER, I STAND at the end of the driveway with a duffel bag, my flute case, and a tin of cookies baked by Gran, pinching myself because I'm still not sure this day is actually happening.

I'm wearing my favorite pair of hiking boots, a brand-new pair of overalls, and a jacket tied around my waist. Gran wanted me to wear a dress, but the only one I liked is the one that I burned to a crisp, and the only other one I own is pink and lacy and I am *not* showing up at my new school looking like I just crawled off the Easter Bunny's lap.

It's so early there's still fog hunkered in the pines, and though it's light out, the sun hasn't yet risen. Everything's wet with dew. Down the road, Mrs. O'Grady's rooster is screeching to the sky.

"It's almost six thirty," I say. "What if they forgot to come for me?"

Gran grunts, like she hopes they have.

My stomach is twisted up with nerves, but mostly I'm too

excited to feel scared. I've never been further than a two-hour train ride to the city, and now I'm going halfway across the country.

"Is this how they picked up Mom?" I ask.

Gran nods. "But it was raining that morning," she adds softly. "I'll never forget."

The street is awfully quiet. All around us, in the dim morning light, the other houses sit silent and still. I start to get anxious, worrying something's wrong. Maybe the Maestros changed their minds about me. Maybe—

A tingle of music shivers through the air.

My chin jerks up. "What's that sound?"

Gran sighs. "Sounds like a church organ. Just like it did when it came for your mother."

"It's getting closer!" I shout, just as I realize the noise is coming from the *sky*.

I look up to see a storm cloud has gathered out of nowhere. It hangs right above our house, lightning snapping and thunder rolling. And over it all, the sound of organ music splits the sky, rapid, aggressive notes bursting in the air. Whoever is behind the music must be a powerful musician indeed, playing with a skill that leaves me awestruck. The cloud is clearly some sort of spell, but I can't tell who's controlling it.

Gran pulls me close, muttering under her breath, "Honestly, I don't know why a simple school bus wouldn't suffice. Always the *dramatics* with these people."

Then all at once, the cloud dissipates, and there in its place hovers a zeppelin.

"Whoa," I breathe.

Hanging in the sky like a great whale, the airship is shiny and purple, with a swirling strip of piano keys down the side under the words *Mystwick School of Musicraft.* Propellers whir on its tail and fins. The gondola underneath bristles with pipes, and they're belching golden clouds of magic with the swell of organ music.

"Teleportation spell," Gran says, to my surprise. She glances at me. "They always smell of cinnamon. Your mother told me that."

I take a sniff and find she's right. Teleportation spells are very rare and *very* dangerous. I've never even seen one, much less attempted one. Only Maestros are allowed to play them.

A hatch under the gondola suddenly drops open, and a metal ladder slides down toward us, with a man clinging to the bottom rungs. As the ladder lowers, his black tie flutters free from his crisp white collar. The cuffs of his sleeves are circled with gold bands and the front of his dark coat gleams with shiny buttons. He looks like an airplane pilot, except instead of wings pinned to his hat, there's a little silver zeppelin.

When the ladder stops a foot off the ground, he leaps down and lands neatly in front of us. "Ticket, miss?"

Still stunned by the zeppelin's sudden appearance, I hand

over the ticket that came with my acceptance letter. The man trades me back a piece of grape gum.

"For the motion sickness," he says, winking. "Are you Amelia, then?"

I nod, still speechless.

"Excellent. You can call me Jenkins." He turns to Gran. "And this lovely lady is . . . ?"

Gran snorts. "This lovely lady is the one who'll drag you by your ear into court if you let anything happen to my granddaughter."

Jenkins bows to her, sweeping off his hat and pressing it to his heart. "I assure you, no child comes to harm whilst in my care, madam. This is the safest ship in the world, you have my oath."

Then he straightens and whistles, and a tiny shape drops from the gondola's hatch. It speeds toward us before pulling up in a sweep of feathers. It's a gray parrot with a red tail, and it's got a little gold band around each claw.

"This is Captain," Jenkins says. "He'll see to your bags."

The parrot lands on his shoulder and blinks at me.

Jenkins sighs. "I *said*, he'll see to your bags. Captain, don't be rude. Can't you see this is a very important passenger?"

I could swear the bird rolls his eyes.

He takes off with a squawk, then begins to whistle. Threads

of magic curl from his beak and surround my luggage like a lasso. The bags lift into the air, and Captain flies around them, guiding them up to the zeppelin. I gape at him. I've heard that parrots and certain other musical animals can work magic, but I've never seen it happen before.

"All right," says Gran, though she still sounds doubtful. "I suppose this is it."

I'm bouncing with excitement and impatience, but before I can go, she pulls me into a massive hug. "You be careful, sweetheart. Brush your teeth. And remember, you can change your mind at any moment and come right back home."

"*Gran.*"

"And write to me every week."

"I'll *email,* Gran. Remember, I set the computer up for you?"

She makes a face. "As if I'll recall how to use that thing."

"You will, Gran. I love you."

"I love *you.*"

Pulling away, I climb up the ladder, higher and higher, till I can see over the roof of the house and across the woods. I can even see my treehouse tucked under the canopy. The wind pulls at me and the ladder sways, but I'm too excited to even be afraid. At the top, I pause to look down at Gran, no bigger than my thumb below me.

"Bye, Gran!" I shout, waving. I'm not even sure she can hear me.

Then I turn and scramble up through the hatch.

I find myself in a large open cabin with lots of comfy-looking chairs that swivel, so you can look out the many windows into the sky beyond. The floor is made of gleaming wood planks, and a big, curving desk with lots of controls and a wooden wheel is tucked into the tapered nose of the gondola.

At the back is an enormous pipe organ. An old woman is hunched over it, banging on the keys like she's playing whack-a-mole. Jenkins follows me up and sits in the pilot's seat. Captain lands on a perch beside him and begins grooming his feathers.

"Welcome aboard the Bumblebee!" Jenkins says cheerfully. "You're my first pickup. Which means you get any seat you want."

"Hurry it up, Jenkins!" yells the old lady over her organ music. "We're on a schedule!"

"We're going, we're going! Don't pop your dentures!" Jenkins yells back, then he winks at me and adds in a low voice, "Miss Myra's the best organist in the world. But don't tell *her* I said so."

"Are we going straight to Mystwick?" I ask.

"What? Not yet! We've got a full day ahead, kid." He picks up a stack of papers and waves them at me. "And a tight schedule. Next stop, London!"

Taking a seat, I strap on my seat belt and then lean to the window, looking down at Gran. I can barely make her out.

I wave furiously, grinning so she can see that this is fine, totally fine, *completely* fine, until the old lady in the back plays

63

a crashing glissando, and suddenly Gran blurs along with the whole world below the zeppelin, hidden behind a cloud of gold smoke. The house, the road, the woods—all smear together and then vanish, and suddenly the zeppelin is soaring through a whirling kaleidoscope.

Startled, I fall back, staring through the window at the stream of colors. It's like being inside a washing machine with a bunch of open paint cans.

Soon I feel so dizzy I think I'm going to throw up.

An explosion of feathers startles me and I yelp. Then I realize it's just the parrot, landing on the seat beside me.

"Gum!" it squawks. "Gum for the kiddos! Gum for the sickos!"

Quickly, I unwrap the stick and shove it in my mouth. The taste of grape bursts on my tongue, and at once the dizziness passes and my stomach settles.

The parrot bobs like he's pleased, then flies back to Jenkins.

I feel like I'm in a spaceship warping through the universe. Ahead, through the wide windshield, all I can see is a long, infinite tunnel of blurring colors. I'm falling down an endless rabbit hole into a strange new world.

This is happening.

This is *really* happening.

I'm going to Mystwick.

My mother's school, the place that has been so much in my dreams that it feels like a dream itself.

Behind me, Miss Myra attacks the organ keys, pumping out the teleportation spell that's bending the fabric of space all around us. I hope desperately that she doesn't miss a note. Who knows what would happen if she did? I imagine myself being spread out, a million pieces across a million miles, or the zeppelin suddenly appearing in the middle of a mountain or a stormy sea.

Despite the fact we're moving at probably a gajillion miles an hour, the airship feels like it's standing still. So I unbuckle and walk to the front, where Jenkins is feeding barbecue potato chips to his parrot. His feet are crossed on the dashboard.

"Well, what do you think of my magic zeppelin?" he asks.

"Why doesn't *everyone* travel by teleportation spell, all the time?" I ask. "Seems much cooler than boring old cars."

He points a thumb toward Miss Myra in the back. "Only sixteen people in the world are licensed to teleport anything bigger than a refrigerator. And soon, there'll only be fifteen." He shouts around a mouthful of chips, "How old *are* you, Miss Myra? Like, one hundred and three? Why haven't you retired yet?"

"You better not be eating food on *my* zeppelin, *Jenkins,* you moose!"

"*Your* zeppelin, Miss Myra?" Jenkins bellows. "*Your* zeppelin!? I ought to drop you off on a desert island."

"You cheeky baboon! I've been teleporting this leaky balloon all over the globe since before you were *born*."

"Leaky?" I echo, feeling a spike of alarm.

"Don't panic, kid, this thing is reinforced with more safety spells than you could play in a lifetime." Jenkins laughs and grabs the wheel of the zeppelin. "Still, you better sit down and buckle up."

I hurry back to my seat and strap in just as the zeppelin begins to slow, so hard and so fast that I'm thrown against the seat belt. In the back, Miss Myra holds a long, final note, then releases the keys with a cackle. Outside, a storm cloud surrounds the airship, obscuring any view of the outside. Lightning streaks in front of me, and I pull back, gasping as the propellers on the fins suck away the clouds.

When the storm fully clears, I press my face to the window and stare. Behind me, Jenkins opens the hatch and descends once more on the retractable ladder.

The Bumblebee is hovering over a busy street. Taxis and cars and red double-deckers blur below, while the sidewalks are packed with people. In the distance, I see a huge clock tower and a cathedral. Westminster Abbey, I think, where some of the greatest spells in the world are performed.

I'm in *London*. In a whole other *country*.

My old life is an entire ocean away.

For a moment, I'm sure I'm dreaming. I press my hands to

the window and look out across the great city. There's a river snaking beneath gorgeous old bridges, and a great big Ferris wheel that I decide I *have* to ride on one day. Ancient-looking buildings mix with modern skyscrapers, and I wonder which one the queen lives in. This is also the home of one of the greatest Symphonies in the world, the London Philharmonic, the great heroes of World War II who staved off an enemy attack by playing Baroque warding spells for three days straight.

Looking down, I see Jenkins take a purple ticket from another student. Grinning, I find a latch on the window and open it up, then lean out.

"Helloooo down there!"

The boy on the sidewalk looks up. "Hey! It's Amelia Jones!"

"Hello, Jai!"

He waves wildly. His dad is there too, and he only gives Jai a stiff handshake in farewell.

But Jai looks far from sad as he leaps aboard, his eyes wide. Looking all around, he finally settles his gaze on me.

"Amelia Matilda Jones!" he shouts again, throwing his arms wide.

I giggle. "That's *not* my middle name."

He shrugs, unbothered. "It was a guess. No—don't tell me! I'll figure it out. But look at you! You got in!"

"I got in!"

"Me too!"

"Yeah," I laugh. "I can see that."

"And we're on a teleporting purple zeppelin!"

"I can see that too!"

He whoops and does a cartwheel across the open floor. When he reaches Miss Myra, he plants himself on the bench beside her and throws an arm around her shoulders. She looks startled.

"Hello, little old lady!" Jai cries. "Look at this! An organ! On a zeppelin!"

He reaches out like he's going to press the keys. Miss Myra slaps his hand.

Laughing, Jai jumps up and runs back to me. "Isn't this great? Isn't this the *best* day of your *life?*"

"Take your seats!" calls Jenkins, sliding back into the pilot's chair. "Next stop, Taiwan!"

We do fourteen more pickups that day, and sometimes one student boards, while other times there's a whole group of them, all waiting with families at their designated pickup locations. In some places, it's the middle of the night. Each time the zeppelin comes to a stop, I gape at the surroundings: a quiet street outside Kyoto where we pick up Hana, a percussionist. I stare at the wooden houses with their curving roofs and the moon shining on a slow river winding through rice paddies behind her house.

Next is a townhouse in Philadelphia, where we add a pair

of twins: Jamal and Amari, both violinists. Their whole family has come to send them off, thirty or forty people crowding the street. We stay there the longest, because each of them has to hug each twin. When Jamal and Amari finally make it aboard, they both look a bit dizzy.

We visit Berlin, Dallas, Christchurch, and others that come and go like TV channels being flipped. Each one adds new faces to the zeppelin's cabin, until nearly every seat is taken and the air is filled with a blur of voices, all different languages and accents. They all speak English, but it's clear the one language we're all most fluent in is Musicraft, and everyone is quick to compare instruments and tell exaggerated stories of their auditions. But shy to join in the conversations, I instead glue myself to the window and watch everything like it's a dream I'm about to wake up from, and I don't want to forget any of it. I store up images of the world like they're photographs, trying to decide which ones I want to visit again. I want to stand in those streets and close my eyes and just *listen*. Is this how my mom felt on her first trip to Mystwick? Did she travel to any of these places and listen to the music of these faraway cities?

I feel like with each passing hour, I'm getting closer and closer to her, as if she might actually be waiting at Mystwick for me. Like she's been there all this time.

We take a brief lunch break on a beach in Acapulco where Jenkins buys us the best tacos I've ever eaten in my *life*. We make a picnic of it right there on the sand, getting salsa all over our clothes, and Miss Myra nearly explodes when she sees the mess we make of ourselves. But Jai gives her his churros and flashes his ear-to-ear smile, and she softens.

Finally, as we're drifting through the endless kaleidoscope tunnel, Miss Myra pounding on her organ keys, Jenkins gets on the announcement system and says, "Next stop, the Mystwick School of Musicraft!"

I'm half-asleep, my head propped on the window, but when I hear that, I join everyone else in a cheer. Jai does another cartwheel, but there's not enough space now and he crashes awkwardly into the two violinists from Philadelphia, who yell at him to cut it out. I think we're all on a bit of a sugar high, thanks to Captain continually bringing us as much grape gum as we want. And everyone's starting to get edgy; a few people put headphones on. You can only listen to the same loud organ spell so many times before you start to go a *little* loopy.

Jai plunks down beside me, grinning. "We're almost there. Are you excited?"

I laugh. "Of course!"

"You have to *shout* it! Like this!" He spins in his chair and beats on his chest. *"I am the champion of the woooooorld!"*

As the yell rips from Jai's throat, Jenkins spins the airship's wheel, and the Bumblebee comes to a shuddering, clunking halt,

Miss Myra's organ wailing. Jai is thrown forward, smashing his face into the window.

"I'm okay," he says, blinking. "I'm *o*-kay."

But no one's paying him attention. Instead, we're all stuck to the windows, staring down as the zeppelin descends over forests of white trees with yellow leaves. Aspens, I think. In the distance, the Rocky Mountains jut against the evening sky. Even with a magic airship, it's taken all day to pick up the kids, and my stomach's growling for dinner.

Finally, Jenkins calls out, "Welcome to Mystwick!"

And there it is.

The Mystwick School of Musicraft sits high in a vale beneath jagged snow-capped peaks. The main building is enormous, five or six stories tall. It's like a fairy-tale castle and a log cabin all in one, and the setting sun reflects on the windows, making them seem as if they're on fire. They overlook a small lake that has fountains sprouting from its center. To the right and left of the main building are more log-cabin-style structures, each several stories high. It reminds me of pictures I've seen of luxury ski resorts, only without the chairlifts crooking their way up the mountain. The whole place glitters in the fading light of day, golden walls and diamond lake and dark forest beyond.

We climb down the ladder, everyone yawning after the long day but still looking excited. Captain perches on the dash, croaking, "Have a nice life, have a nice life!" at each of us as we walk by, until Jenkins reminds him he's supposed to be transporting luggage. Then Jenkins takes out a fife and plays a transporting spell to lower down Victoria, a guitarist in a wheelchair. She waves at the rest of us as she floats down and reaches the ground first, borne on a cloud of glittering gold light that pours from the fife.

When my foot touches the ground, a thrill runs through me. My heart pounds like a drum.

After years of dreaming, I'm finally *here*.

CHAPTER SIX

Nocturne, Nocturne, Who's There?

WE GATHER ON THE SLOPED LAWN in front of the main building, surrounded by luggage and instruments. The sun has set, and now shadow begins to creep over the campus. Hearing a distant, low growl of thunder, I look up but see no clouds. Still, I untie my jacket and pull it on.

Jenkins is the last one off the ladder, and as he jumps down, a woman comes running toward us. She is small and primly dressed, with very short blond hair and an expression of fury, like an angry little fairy.

"You're late, Mr. Jenkins!" she says, all out of breath. "The other zeppelins landed hours ago. You've got to stop chatting at every pick-up! And don't tell me you landed for tacos *again!*"

Jenkins grins and holds out a wrapper to the woman. "Brought you one, Miss March. I know you like extra guacamole."

She scowls but takes the taco. "Don't think this lets you off the hook." Shaking her head, she turns to us kids. "Come, come, students! You've missed dinner, thanks to your *incompetent* pilot. There's still some left, if a little cold. Hurry now!"

We follow her up the grassy hill, dragging our instruments.

"Farewell, young musicians!" Jenkins calls out, holding on to the ladder as it rises back into the zeppelin. He waves grandly, his hair fluttering, and adds, "And farewell to you, Miss March!"

Miss March rolls her eyes, but I notice spots of color in her cheeks.

"I think somebody has a little crush on the zeppelin captain," I whisper to Victoria, who rolls beside me.

She giggles, then stops her wheelchair to look up.

Miss March brings us to a halt in front of the main building, which has the words *Harmony Hall* over the front doors. It has a peaked roof and huge timber walls and lots of windows. Six giant logs rise vertically to support the front overhanging roof, each one carved with spiraling music notes. On either side of the door, wild horse statues rear up, wooden manes and tails flowing with lifelike detail.

A huge banner above the doors shouts: WELCOME, NEW STUDENTS!

And in smaller letters under that: AUDIENTIBUS MUSICA ADEST.

I stare at it, my heart fluttering. I'm half-afraid to blink, in case it all were to vanish.

"Children, gather around," says the woman. "I am Ellie

March, the dean of students. We're currently putting together dinner for you. Give us fifteen minutes and everything will be ready, I assure you. In the meantime, wait here and, um . . . enjoy the view. I'll be back shortly for you. Oh dear, oh dear, day one and already a crisis!"

She hurries inside, leaving us standing on the front steps.

Swinging my flute case at my side, I turn and survey the lake, the trees, the mountains beyond. The school buildings are arranged in a semicircle around the water, all timber-framed like Harmony Hall, except for what looks like a glass concert hall on the other side of the lake. I spot a soccer field and a gym, and what might be an indoor pool. And there are statues everywhere, of Composers and Maestros both past and present. Bach and Mozart stand nearby, looking solemnly out at the mountains, and I turn and find the serious stone face of Toru Takemitsu frowning down at me, a plaque at the base of the statue telling of his great achievements and most famous spells.

The sky is fading from red to violet, the buildings growing indistinct in the shadows. I breathe in deep, relishing the cool clarity of the air, though I know I'm going to need to adjust to the altitude before I attempt any long spells.

Closing my eyes, I listen for the school's music. It's soft and whispery, an easy nocturne of murmuring voices, chilly mountain wind, the lake lapping below, and a distant owl's low hoot.

The other kids seem too excited to stay still, and a few wander down to the lake while the rest spread across the nearby grass, looking around. Jai climbs onto the statue of Mozart and plays air guitar, and Hana yells at him to get down before he gets us all in trouble.

I figure it won't hurt to take a look around. I'm itching to explore, and anyway, Miss March *did* say to enjoy the view. So I slip away and follow a stone path that goes around Harmony Hall. I pass more stone Maestros on the way, and there's just enough light to make out their names: Fanny Mendelssohn, Solhi al-Wadi, Samuel Coleridge-Taylor, and many others.

I feel a sudden chill and shiver. Maybe I should go back. It's pretty dark over here, and I don't want to get lost on my first day. I start to turn around — then hear a soft voice.

"Amelia . . ."

Surprised, I turn a bend in the path and find myself standing at the edge of the forest. To my left is a large amphitheater, bleachers and stage all sunken into the grassy ground. There's no sign of the person who called my name. Maybe it was my imagination.

Suddenly a wind pours in from my left, and all the trees start to sway and rustle.

I gasp.

When the wind rushes through their leaves, they don't sound like regular trees at all. Instead, the noise they make is like an orchestra tuning up. Violins humming, flutes and oboes trilling, groaning cellos and twanging harps and deep, deep tubas. The music is faint, like listening to a recording at the lowest volume, but there's no mistaking that it's completely magical. And in the canopy, among those swaying branches, the faintest golden dust swirls.

These are no ordinary trees.

Then the wind dies down and the trees go silent. They leave a hollowness inside me, a yearning to listen to their music for hours and days and years. I've never heard anything so beautiful or strange.

"Amelia . . . play for them, Amelia . . ."

Is it . . . the *trees* talking? Play for who?

Then I laugh uneasily at my own ridiculous imagination. Trees don't *talk*.

Of course, they aren't supposed to make music either.

And before I half know what I'm doing, I've taken my flute from its case. I feel like I'm trapped in a spell, my brain all fogged up.

"What should I play?" I whisper.

The trees don't answer. But the wind blows again, harder this time, and the leaves sing in response. Listening very close, I can pick out a melody, so soft and faint I might be imagining it.

It's a spell I know well: Pachelbel's Canon, a summoning spell, meant to move an object from one place to another. But what would *trees* need to summon?

After a moment of hesitation, I play along. The notes rise from my flute in glowing yellow streamers, coiling and fading. Slow and measured, the same eight notes repeating over and over, a melody with no clear end.

Is it my imagination, or are the trees echoing the notes back to me, harmonizing with my flute?

My arms break out in goose bumps.

When the wind dies down and the trees fall silent, I hold the last note of the spell, then lower my flute. The air around me feels charged and tight. But as the music fades, everything relaxes, until it seems it was all just my mind playing tricks.

I pack up my flute and hurry to the front of the school. I'm probably not supposed to be back here. And I definitely don't want to start my year at Mystwick with detention — if they even have detention. I'm beginning to think this place will be nothing like my old school.

Back in front of Harmony Hall, I see I've returned just in time. The other students are heading in, with Miss March waving them through the main doors. I jog up and slip in line behind Amari.

"Come in, come in," Miss March says. "Check in with Miss Noorani on your left, then head through the back door to dinner. Hurry, now!"

We walk into a grand foyer with wood floors and a huge fire-place against the back wall, surrounded by couches and tables, all in warm tones of red and brown and deep purple. Iron chandeliers hang above, and the columns supporting the high ceiling are carved like real trees. In one corner sits a huge, gleaming grand piano, and even though I'm not great at piano, I still sigh with awe when I see it. Above us, three inner balconies overlook the common area. The entire front wall of the hall is made of huge windows, giving incredible views of the lake and mountains.

Standing on a large rug with music notes all over it, I turn a full circle and take everything in, mouth gaping. I listen to the sounds of the students' shoes squeaking on the floor, their soft conversations, and from one of the upper floors, the low tone of a cello.

Just as I expected: perfect acoustics. I bet every room in this school has perfect acoustics, bouncing sound around until it's as pure and sweet as it can be.

"Ahem," says a voice. "Name?"

I turn around, startled, to see everyone else has finished checking in.

I recognize the woman, Miss Noorani, from my auditions. She's the one who smiled at me . . . until I ruined everything. For a moment, it all rushes back—the bungled spell, the mustache man staring angrily at his sudden bounty of facial hair, the poor little tree twisting sideways.

And I wonder: What did the Maestros see in me? What about me made them overlook the disastrous audition? The questions have been buzzing in my mind ever since I got the acceptance letter, but I haven't had the guts to really think about them.

I almost ask Miss Noorani, but then my courage fails. She doesn't seem to recognize me.

But when I tell her my name, she gives me a startled look. "Did you say *Amelia Jones?*"

"I have my letter." The paper is soft and wrinkled from me unfolding it so much—as in, twelve times a day and a couple times at night, when I woke up thinking it must all be a dream.

She takes the acceptance letter and scans it, her brow furrowing. She looks at me again, then down at the papers on her desk.

My stomach starts to sink.

She purses her lips, then turns and beckons to Miss March.

"Take the others on to dinner," she whispers. "I'll look after this one."

Uh-oh.

Something is wrong.

Miss March rounds up the rest of the group and leads them to an open set of doors, through which I can smell the unmistakable aroma of pizza. But my hunger seems to have vanished. I don't think I could eat so much as a pepperoni.

Miss Noorani picks up a viola, tucks it under her chin, and plays a quick summoning spell that I don't recognize. Then, giving me a tired look, she says, "Follow me, dear, and we'll sort this out."

I nod woodenly.

Miss Noorani leads me through a door and down a hall-way, then up a shining spiral staircase. My steps get heavier and heavier. My flute feels like it weighs a ton. I can't even begin to wonder what the problem is, because if I do, I think I might throw up. So instead I just watch my feet.

We stop in front of a large door on one of the inner bal-conies and find three more Maestros waiting there. I recognize them all from my audition: the mustache man, a tall, skinny man, and a short, muscular woman with braided hair.

"Miss Noorani, we are all exhausted from chasing new students," says the skinny one. "I hope this is important."

"Yes, with all the chaos I almost didn't hear your summoning spell," says the lady with the braids, in a strong accent. German, maybe? "What's wrong?"

Miss Noorani puts her hand on my shoulder. "I'm sorry for pulling you all away at such a busy time," she says. "But I wanted you to meet Amelia Jones."

The three Maestros stare.

"Amelia Jones?" echoes the skinny one. *"Amelia Jones?"*

"Why is he saying it like that?" I ask Miss Noorani. "What's wrong with being Amelia Jones?"

Oh no. Did Gran change her mind? Did she call the school and demand that I be sent home?

"Amelia," Miss Noorani says, "these are the deans of

Mystwick." She introduces them—the skinny one is Mr. Walters, Maestro of brass; the German one is Miss Becker, Maestro of percussion; and the mustache man—his facial hair a lot shorter than it was the last time I saw him—is Mr. Pinwhistle, Maestro of woodwinds.

Wonderful. He *would* be in charge of flutes.

"I, of course, am Maestro of strings," she adds. "Now, why don't we all go into the office and see what the headmaestro has to say?"

Day one, and I'm already being sent to the principal's office.

Miss Noorani gestures to the big door behind us. The others nod and head toward it. None of them look annoyed anymore that they were called away—worse, they look grim. Like my arrival is the worst news they've had all week.

What is going on?

The door takes us up another staircase to a big office. A window on the back wall overlooks the forest beyond, where I played my flute earlier. It's mostly dark now, and I hear a strange, musical humming that I can't trace to any source.

At the center of the room is a desk lit by a stained-glass lamp, and behind it sits the most elegant woman I've ever seen. She has warm brown skin and a heart-shaped face. Her hair is twisted in a tall swoop like a piece of art. She's working at a computer, the blue light of the screen reflecting on her glasses, and there is a cello propped behind her.

She looks up as we enter, taking off the glasses and blinking at me, then at Miss Noorani. Something jumps from her lap—a sleek, spotted cat with yellow eyes. It runs around the desk and rubs against my legs. I realize it's the cat who's humming, repeating a low, simple melody deep in its throat. Faint wisps of gold magic curl around its whiskers and then fade away.

A musicat!

I've only ever read about the rare species, which, like Jenkins's parrot, is one of the few types of animals capable of working magic. Leaning down to pet the cat, I hear a cough from Miss Noorani, who shakes her head at me.

"Better not," she says. "Wynk tends to purr when you pet him, and his purring has a rather . . . somnolent affect." She pauses, then adds, "It makes you fall asleep."

"Oh." I withdraw my hand, and settle for watching the musicat as he slithers between my legs and moves on to rub on Mr. Pinwhistle, who grumbles irritably.

The woman at the desk ignores all of this, instead asking, "What's wrong, Lila?"

"A bit of . . . confusion, Mrs. Le Roux." Miss Noorani hands her my acceptance letter.

I stand very still while Euphonia Le Roux, headmaestro of the Mystwick School of Musicraft, reads the letter that bears her own signature at the bottom. She takes her time, until the other Maestros start to fidget. Wynk hums and licks his paw.

Finally, Mrs. Le Roux lowers the letter with a long sigh.

"Amelia Jones," she says. "Well, this *is* a development."

I look up at her pleadingly. "Can someone please tell me what's going on?"

Mrs. Le Roux stands up and circles her desk. She folds her arms, my letter pinched between her fingers, and studies me like I'm a dog that sat up and asked her for the weekly forecast.

"Miss Jones, I'm sure you understand that each year we audition thousands of students all over the world."

I nod. Will she just get to the point?

"Because we see so many children, it's inevitable that we usually see several with the . . . same name."

I suck in a breath, as the floor seems to fall out from under me. I understand at once what she means.

That letter was never mine at all.

This was all a huge mistake.

Because I'm the *wrong* Amelia Jones.

CHAPTER SEVEN

The World Tuned Upside Down

THE ROOM SEEMS TO SPIN. I concentrate very hard on not throwing up on the headmaestro's expensive-looking shoes.

"Perhaps I ought to explain further," she says. "You see, a young lady also by the name of Amelia Jones—a remarkable pianist of uncommon skill—entered our Los Angeles auditions two months ago. Then, a few weeks later, she embarked on a yachting trip with her parents in the Maldives. Tragically, a storm capsized their boat and everyone on board was lost."

"Oh," I say in a very small voice. "That's terrible. That poor girl."

For a moment I forget all my worries and instead imagine this other Amelia Jones, terrified for her life as waves crash all around. While I was worrying about my audition, she was *drowning*.

"This occurred the same day the Mystwick acceptance letters were sent out via a finding spell," Mrs. Le Roux explains. "And I imagine when this letter"—she waves the paper that I've treasured like gold—"was unable to find Miss Jones—uh, the *other* Miss Jones—it found you instead."

"A terrible misunderstanding," says Miss Noorani. "Made possible only by the most extreme of circumstances."

I don't know what to say. I can hardly think straight, but I know what this means.

I'm only here by accident. I was never *supposed* to be here at all.

I should have known. I should have seen this coming a million miles away. After the audition I had? Why *would* they want me?

My face flushes with embarrassment that I had ever imagined I might be good enough for this place. All those years devoted to a single dream, only to have it taken away from me *twice* in one summer. First, the disastrous audition, now this.

I can't even begin to think about how I'll tell Gran.

But then . . .

My heart skips a beat, and I curl my hands into fists.

Why should I have to tell her anything at all? Why *should* I have to go home?

I came all this way, and I know, I *know* I can be good enough. Maybe not now, but if they just let me try, I could get better. I could be what they want me to be. I could do or become *anything* if it meant being a part of Mystwick.

This is the first time in my life that I've felt this close to my mother. It's like her presence is here, in the walls and in the trees and in the light glittering on the lake. This was the place she loved best, and if there's anywhere in the world I will discover more about who she was and who I am, it has to be here.

I look the headmaestro in the eye.

"If the other Amelia Jones isn't coming," I say, "then that means there's an available spot."

In the silence which follows, Mrs. Le Roux winces.

"Well," says Miss Noorani, hastily stepping in, "that's true, but . . . that spot is technically for a pianist, not a flutist, and besides, there is a waiting list."

"And you're not exactly at the top of that list," grunts Mr. Pinwhistle. His hands goes to his mustache. "I remember your audition, young lady. And I don't remember many auditions. Disastrous! One of the worst I've seen."

I swallow hard. "I can do better, I promise. Just give me a shot. I'll prove I'm good enough."

"That's not how it works," he replies. "Mystwick has a reputation for finding the very best, most talented young musicians in the world, and you are not—"

"Mr. Pinwhistle, that will do," Miss Noorani cuts in. "Amelia, I'm sorry, but this is out of our control."

I start to feel tears, but I blink them away. I will *not* cry in front of them. I won't let them think I'm a pathetic crybaby, in addition to being the worst audition they've ever seen.

"Aren't you all in charge of this school? Why can't you just let me *try?*"

"This school has traditions that have been here far longer than us," says Mrs. Le Roux in a stern voice. "It has functions we cannot control."

"Such as those annoying humfrogs in the lake," says Mr. Walters.

"And the squeaky doorknob in my office that's always spelling itself shut and locking me in," grumbles Mr. Pinwhistle.

"And the echo trees," adds Miss Becker.

"And the order in which students are granted acceptance to the school," finishes Mrs. Le Roux.

Something niggles at me. I frown, looking out the window at the forest. "The echo trees. Is that what they're called?"

Miss Noorani arches her eyebrows. "You've seen them?"

"I heard them too," I say sadly. "They're like living music. We played Canon together."

The Maestros all stare at me.

Mrs. Le Roux presses her hand to her lips.

"You played a spell with the echo trees?" she asks in a very soft voice.

I shrug. "They asked me to. Or *someone* did. I heard a voice telling me to play for them. So I did. I'm sorry if I wasn't supposed to."

I'm not really sorry, though. If that's to be my only good memory of this place, then I'm not sorry at all. Maybe I'll sneak back there and play again.

What can they do? Kick me out twice?

All the Maestros are looking at me like I just admitted to some terrible crime. I didn't hurt anything, did I? It was just a little music.

"To be clear," says Miss Noorani, "you played Pachelbel's Canon in D at the edge of the Echo Wood?"

"I said I'm sorry," I mumble.

They look at each other, then back at me.

Then Mr. Walters says, "Do you think . . ."

And Miss Noorani replies, "We have to check."

I look at each of them, confused. "What did I do?"

But it's like no one hears me. They turn to each other instead.

"This is completely unforeseen," Mr. Pinwhistle says. "The whole situation. It's unprecedented!"

"Yes," replies Miss Noorani. "But this *is* a school of Musicraft. Our mix-ups generally do have odd and unpredictable consequences."

I guess I'm the odd and unpredictable consequence she means.

"Well, we'd better see what the damage is," sighs Mrs. Le Roux.

Mr. Pinwhistle, Mr. Walters, and Miss Becker excuse themselves in order to get back to the other students, after making Miss Noorani promise to fill them in later.

Fill them in on *what?* I want to ask.

Miss Noorani and Mrs. Le Roux lead me out of the office and down the stairs. We stop at another door, this one locked tight. Mrs. Le Roux opens it with a large key, and then we're walking onto the grass behind the school, near the amphitheater I saw earlier. Ahead, the Echo Wood waits in silence and darkness. The air is much chillier than it was when the zeppelin arrived, and I shiver, despite my jacket.

"I don't understand what's wrong," I say. "I didn't mean to—"

"Hush now," orders Mrs. Le Roux. "We will see what we will see. Miss Noorani?"

Miss Noorani nods and holds up her viola, striking a quick tune that produces three bobbing spheres of blue light. One hovers over each of our heads, lighting the grass around us as we walk.

When we reach the edge of the trees, the Maestros begin looking all around. They walk this way and that, illuminated by their glowing blue light-balls, while I stand there like a dummy with no idea what they're doing. I hug my flute case and wait, tapping one foot. Whenever I move, my little light moves with me, casting dancing shadows all around.

Overhead, a gentle breeze curls through the canopy, and the

faint music hums and then fades, like violins testing their strings before falling silent. A brief dusting of magic lights the trees then dissipates.

Then Miss Noorani shouts, "Here!"

Mrs. Le Roux and I hurry over to where Miss Noorani is pointing at something on the ground. I don't see it until I step around her—and then I gasp.

"Recognize this?" she asks me.

I nod, unable to believe my eyes. "That's . . . my audition tree."

I'd recognize it anywhere. It's a little taller than it was six weeks ago, yet it's just as crooked, stuck forever in a low bow. But it looks healthy, even if it is shaped funny. It has more leaves now, and they're green and glossy, shining in the blue lights suspended over us. The soil around it is fresh and damp, like it was just planted there.

"It's an echo tree?" I ask.

"Yes," replies Miss Noorani. "Echo trees are special. They thrive on music."

"But most important of all," adds Mrs. Le Roux, "they protect the school and everyone inside. You see, their natural music is Canon, a summoning spell. Many people think Pachelbel Composed it, but really, he only *recorded* it after discovering a grove of these trees. And when you change a summoning spell to a parallel key, in this case, D major to D minor—"

91

"—it reverses and becomes a repelling spell," I whisper. "The trees change key?"

"Yes, the moment any unwanted visitor sets foot in the forest, they're repelled." She reaches out and puts her hand against one of the bigger trees, smiling up at it. "Better than any *electric* security system."

She says *electric* like it's an affront to magic.

"So . . . how did *my* tree end up here?"

"You put it there yourself." She points to a building I'd not noticed before, a large greenhouse that reflects the moonlight.

We walk over to it and find the door hanging open. Inside are rows and rows of shelves, and on the shelves are a lot of small pots, each holding a little echo tree. I notice right away that most of them are very straight and perfect, the way little echo trees ought to look.

Not at all like mine.

Miss Noorani hunts down the shelves until she finds an empty spot.

"Here it sat," she said, "until you played the trees' summoning spell. Then it would have flown out and planted itself with the other trees."

"Tomorrow," says Mrs. Le Roux, "we will hold a grand Planting Ceremony, in which all the new students will add their trees to the Echo Wood."

Miss Noorani nods. "Every tree in the forest represents a student of Mystwick, most of them long since graduated."

So . . . somewhere in this forest is a tree planted by my mom.

"What about the rest of these little trees?" I ask. "There are a lot more than a hundred here."

"Well, we never throw them out until we're certain who will be in our new class. There are often a few dropouts just before the term begins. That's why we don't send rejection letters till next week."

"Which is why I never got one," I mutter. "Well, unless you're going to rip up my tree, I guess at least a part of me will always be here. That's something, anyway."

The Maestros exchange a long look, and then Miss Noorani takes my hand in hers.

"Amelia," she says softly, "I don't think you understand."

"Understand what? I know I have to go home."

She shakes her head. "Like we said earlier, not everything in this school is ours to control. By planting your tree in the Echo Wood, you've come under the forest's protection. If you leave the school now, your tree will wilt and the protective barrier around the campus will weaken, making everyone inside vulnerable. There are only two ways to safely leave Mystwick for good — by graduating or by being expelled, either because you chose to drop out or because you broke enough rules."

Mrs. Le Roux nods. "And expulsion is a difficult process. It takes an entire orchestra of Maestros playing very complicated and taxing spells to forcefully remove a tree from the wood. We only do it when absolutely necessary, for it causes a great deal of strain on both us and the forest."

I lick my lips, my heart seeming to stand still. "So . . . what are you saying?"

"I'm saying, Amelia Jones, that accident or no, you're a part of Mystwick now. And you're not going anywhere."

"I'm . . . not?" I suddenly feel lighter than air, like I could float right up into the sky.

"At least not yet," Mrs. Le Roux adds, and my stomach sinks a little. "I will make a deal with you, Miss Jones. I will give you two months, in which you will participate in all your classes and activities as if you were a normal student. And at the end of those two months, if you pass an exam I myself will administer, then you will be allowed to stay on. For good. But fail that exam, and you will be expelled, so that another, worthier student might have your place."

She exchanges a look with Miss Noorani, who nods in agreement.

"Well?" Mrs. Le Roux says, extending one elegant hand toward me. "Do we have a deal?"

I stare at her hand a moment.

But I already know I don't have to think twice about my answer.

If it's a perfect musician they want, then it's a perfect musician they'll get.

I shake the headmaestro's hand.

CHAPTER EIGHT

Requiem for a Roommate

THE GIRLS' DORM IS a long timber-frame building overlooking the lake, with a wide front porch lined with rocking chairs. Miss Noorani escorts me there, where all the other seventh-grade girls are settling into their rooms. We stop outside the door, and I can hear giggling and shouting inside.

"If you need anything, ask for Phoebe. She's your senior captain." Miss Noorani gives me a black bag. "I found a uniform and shoes that ought to fit, and here is your room key. Oh, and the cafeteria will send over a sack dinner for you soon, since you missed the evening meal. Good luck, dear!"

She hands me a little wooden whistle with three holes in it. It's the oddest-looking *key* I've ever seen.

Drawing a deep breath, I head into the dorm.

At least the Maestros are keeping this between me and them. The other students never have to know that I *accidentally* got accepted into Mystwick. I just have to blend in for the next two months, focus on my studies, and all of this will blow over.

This may have started as a big mistake. But I can fix it, if I can just stop being the Amelia who screwed up her audition, and instead become someone better. More talented. More disciplined. More like the other students. I'll practice every single hour of the day. I won't miss any classes. I'll do every extra credit assignment.

I am *not* going to give them a single reason to expel me.

From here on, Amelia Jones will be known as the Perfect Student.

Inside the dorm, I find a scene of chaos, girls running up and down the hallway, dragging suitcases, yelling for dibs on showers. Quietly, I take my key and go from door to door, listening to the others squeal when they find the doors their whistles open. Victoria and Amari discover they're roommates and immediately start planning how they'll decorate their room.

An older, blond girl who must be Phoebe sees me standing in the hallway like a dummy, my eyes wide and probably looking totally overwhelmed. She looks pretty worn out herself, her cheeks flushed and her ponytail half fallen down.

"What's your name, guppy?" she asks in a tired Australian accent.

"Amelia," I say, my voice little more than a squeak under all the noise. "Amelia Jones."

"Right, then, you're down at the end in the —"

"What did you say?" hisses a voice right behind me.

I turn around and see a girl standing there, wearing a blue

dress, her black, silky hair cut to her shoulders, framing her dark eyes and narrow face.

"Um—" I start.

The girl's hand darts out and grabs my shoulder. *"What did you say your name was?"*

"Uh . . ." I swallow hard, not sure why my stomach suddenly feels like it's flooded with scrambling mice. "My name is Amelia. Amelia Jones."

The girl sucks in a breath and her eyes fill with tears. Bewildered, I step back, bumping into Phoebe.

"Hey," Phoebe says, staring in shock at the girl. "C'mon, now, no tears on day one. Little early to be homesick, don't you think?"

"I thought—" The girl's face is very pale. "When I heard that name, I thought it was—"

With that she turns and runs out of the dorm altogether, pushing through the other girls.

Phoebe sighs. "What the heck was that about?"

Another student answers, one of the ones the girl pushed on her way out. I remember this one from our zeppelin, and because her name alliterates: Claudia the clarinetist from Canada. "That was Darby," she says. "I didn't think she'd still come to school, not after what happened to Amelia Jones."

"What?" I whisper.

"Everyone at dinner was talking about it," says Claudia. "She

98

and Darby were best friends. They used to go to the same Musicraft camp as me, and they were always together."

"Oh, right," Phoebe says. "I heard about that girl. She was some kind of piano prodigy. Real sad story."

Immediately I feel sorry for the girl in the blue dress. I can't imagine what it would be like to lose your best friend, and only a month ago. They were supposed to come here together.

No wonder she looked at me like I was a ghost.

I groan and rub my face.

"So . . ." Phoebe pats my shoulder awkwardly. "Two Amelia Joneses. Weird coincidence. You all right, then?"

"Yeah . . ." I look down at my shoes, feeling like a total fraud. Maybe it's not my fault, but it *is* true that if she hadn't died, I wouldn't even be here at all. As far as any of the other kids know, I got here the same way the rest of them did: by being a good musician. Though Claudia *is* giving me a suspicious look. I quickly turn away, before she can see the guilt in my eyes.

Phoebe shows me my room, which is at the end of the hall, the door shut. There are two silver nameplates nailed to it, one blank, the other with the name *Hamako Bradshaw*. Leaving me to it, Phoebe goes to check on the crying girl.

Taking a deep breath, I raise the whistle to my lips and blow, covering each hole in slow succession the way I've seen the other girls do, producing three smooth notes: C–E–E♭. It's a haunting little tune, but I hear a click and look up to see the door creaking

open in response, and on the blank nameplate, letters material-
ize: AMELIA JONES.

I look at my own name uneasily and wonder if it even *is* my
own name. Or was this room also meant for the other Amelia?
Am I just inheriting an entire life that was never supposed to be
mine, from a spot at this school to the pillow I'll sleep on?

With a little shiver, I step inside and look around. The space
is long and narrow, with a bed on either wall and a desk at each
end. A sign reads PRACTICE IN DESIGNATED ROOMS ONLY!
ABSOLUTELY NO MUSIC IN THE DORMS! Noting an old
scorch mark on the ceiling, I wonder how many people set fires
or unleashed floods in their room before they had to make *that*
rule.

My duffel bag is waiting on the floor. Beside it sits a suitcase
— expensive, black, and polished — along with two instrument
cases, one for an oboe and another I don't recognize. Snooping
outright, I peek inside and see a kind of wooden flute. Some
students, I learned on the zeppelin, bring secondary instruments
that they get special tutoring with. Whoever Hamako is, she's
clearly very talented.

I run my hands over the desks, feeling the grooves and dents
from generations of students bearing down too hard with their
pencils. Opening the bag Miss March gave me, I take out my very
own Mystwick uniform. I unfold the sweater vest with the school
crest on the front; it's just like the one my mom was wearing

in her graduation picture. Holding it now, I can almost feel her standing behind me. Which room was hers? Did she have a view of the forest or the lake? What if she even had *this* room?

I stand up and go to the window, staring at the water, beginning to smile.

Maybe I didn't get here the same way as everyone else, but I'm *here*.

All I have to do is prove I deserve to stay.

"You've *got* to be kidding me," says a voice.

I whirl around, startled.

The girl from the hallway, Darby, is standing in the door, her gaze boring into me and her whistle-key glinting in her hand. Her eyes are still red from crying.

"Um, hello," I say. "I'm not sure you got the right room."

She jabs her finger at Hamako Bradshaw's nameplate. "Darby's my *middle* name. So. You're the replacement, then?"

My heart jumps into my throat. "W-what?" How does she know my secret already? Am I *that* guilty-looking?

"My replacement roommate," she says flatly. "Since my original one *died*."

"Oh," I say weakly, only a little relieved. "Uh . . . I guess so."

So I didn't just take the other Amelia's dorm room.

I inherited her roommate too.

CHAPTER NINE

A Perfect Harmony

I'M AWOKEN IN THE MIDDLE of the night by a blast of trumpets.

Startled, I jolt out of my narrow dorm bed and fall to the floor, tangled in my blanket, eyes gritty with sleep.

"What the heck?" groans Darby.

It's pitch-black outside, and the only light comes from Darby's alarm clock, which reads 5:30 a.m. In its green glow, I can make out her vague form as she sits up.

"It sounds like a marching band," I say. "Or . . . a marching *orchestra?*"

She just grunts.

I stumble to the window and see a group of people standing on the grass by the lake, lit by the blue light curling up from their instruments. Fog drifts on the surface of the water, and the moon is low behind the trees, full and shining.

It's the Maestros, not just the four I met at auditions, but a whole orchestra of them, probably all the teachers in the school.

Their illusion spell sends fireworks zinging into the air, where they burst with big, colorful pops. The music is loud and robust, a crashing cacophony of notes that quickens my pulse and startles the sleep from my eyes. Trombones and trumpets and strings, cymbals and tubas, a man with a huge bass drum that sends deep rolling booms across the grounds. Even the cellists and bassists walk along, their instruments in harnesses against their chests.

I press my hand to the window and feel the vibrations of each resounding beat, shivering up my arms and echoing in my rib cage.

I turn back to Darby. "What in the world—"

A pounding on our door makes us both jump. Before we can move, it's thrown open and Phoebe fills the doorway, clutching her clarinet case.

"Grab your instruments, guppies!" she shouts around the reed jammed between her lips. "You have thirty seconds to meet us outside!"

"What?" Darby gropes for her oboe case. "But—"

"Move!" bellows Phoebe. Then she's gone, banging on Amari and Victoria's door.

We don't even have time to change. I trip over Darby's flute case and knock it over, and she yelps and grabs it, glaring at me.

"That's a family heirloom!" she snaps, as she tucks it safely under her bed. "My *great-grandfather* played this shakuhachi!"

"I'm sorry!"

She pushes past me, muttering under her breath in Japanese.

Bleary and stumbling, Darby and I make our way down the hallway with dozens of other bewildered, pajama-clad seventh-grade girls. I bump into one lugging a cello and mumble an apology.

"This is ridiculous," says Claudia, the clarinetist. "Our first orientation class isn't until nine. This is inhumane!"

"Your *breath* is inhumane," Hana retorts, wrinkling her nose. "Point it in another direction, please."

Claudia glares at her.

"Wasn't there supposed to be some sort of ceremony this morning?" asks Rabiah.

"The Planting Ceremony," I say, remembering that the head-maestro had mentioned it.

Outside, we see the boys coming from their dorm across campus, just as confused as we are. Some of them aren't even wearing shirts, hugging themselves in the cold air. Their dorm captains lead the way with flashlights.

I spot Jai and wave, and he waves back excitedly. His matching pajamas have music notes all over them. The light from the Maestro's fireworks illuminates his face: blue then red then green.

The Maestros start marching across the lawn, still playing their spell, while we students look at each other, shrug, and fall in line behind them. Fireworks pop and crackle above us, reflecting off the windows of the buildings. The dorm captains herd any slow students into line and help the double bassists and tubists with their heavy cases.

We walk for a few minutes in the dark until we finally come to the Echo Wood and the amphitheater behind Harmony Hall. The greenhouse is behind us. Everything is dim and foggy, but the sky is faintly gray now. It'll be morning soon.

The Maestros gather on the stage while the captains sort us into roughly equal groups: strings, percussion, woodwind, and brass. Some instruments are already set up and waiting for their students — the pianos, drums, xylophones, and other large pieces. I find myself sitting between Claudia, with her clarinet, and Darby, with her oboe.

Then my attention is drawn away by the Maestros, who finish their spell with a mighty crescendo, sending up a dizzying spray of fireworks. We all stand up and cheer as the sparks dance and fade around us. Only Darby stands in silence, her face flat.

Miss Noorani then plays a soft melody on her viola, and behind us, a long row of fire suddenly shoots from a curved channel above the bleachers, just a foot away from me. Several students cry out, startled, but the fire doesn't give off heat. I hold a hand into the flames, watching them lick my palm. The fire illusion smells sweet, like vanilla.

"What are you *doing?*" Claudia hisses.

I withdraw my hand, showing her that it's unharmed. "It's just an illusion. Not real fire."

The flames illuminate Mrs. Le Roux as she steps forward. She is dressed in a long burgundy gown, her lips painted to match. Her hair is twisted into a bun and spiked with long feathers, and gold earrings brush her shoulders. Her musicat, Wynk, is at her side, licking his paw and watching us with glowing yellow eyes.

Miss Noorani finishes her spell and lowers the viola.

"Students of Mystwick," begins Mrs. Le Roux, in her deep, soothing voice. Firelight glints on her earrings and the rings on her fingers. "From all over the world you have come, bringing your own unique music to add to our symphony. We hope you will come to think of this place as a home."

There are tears in my eyes. I brush them away, before anyone can see. Stupid, crying at some rehearsed speech, I know. But I think of my mother standing here years ago, hearing this same speech under these same trees, and something in me crumbles.

I've never felt this close to her since she died. Ever since I went to live with Gran, it's like I've been searching for some way to reach Mom, and now, for the first time, I feel like she's here. It's almost as if she's standing right beside me now, as if I could reach out and touch her.

I may have gotten here by accident, but I'm going to fight to stay. I'm going to fight like I never have before.

Miss Becker begins a tight drumroll, which ends when another Maestro clashes a pair of cymbals. Then Mrs. Le Roux raises her hands.

"Welcome, Aeros!" She gestures to us woodwind instruments, and the kids around me let out whistles. I join in, following their lead.

"Welcome, Percussos!" The percussionists stomp their feet in a thunderous roar, and when Mrs. Le Roux calls on them, the Chordos (Jai's group of string instruments) make a buzzing sound, and the brass players—or Labrosos—give loud whoops, like a gang of monkeys, until the rest of us roll our eyes and shout at them to shut up.

"These are the four classes that comprise our student body," Mrs. Le Roux says, smiling as we settle down, "and your classmates are your brothers and sisters. There will be times when magic demands everything from you. It is then you will look to each other for strength, for as the Fourth Rule of Musicraft states . . ." She holds out a hand to us expectantly.

In unison, we say, "The more who join into the spell, the greater will its power swell."

She nods. "We, your Maestros, are here to guide you, but it is the students on your right and your left who will be your support and strength. The friendships you forge at Mystwick will endure for the rest of your lives."

I glance at Darby.

She stares hard at Mrs. Le Roux.

The headmaestro gestures to Miss Noorani and Mr. Pinwhistle and the others, who step forward and ready their instruments.

"The great echo trees behind me represent every student who has gone before you, as well as your teachers here at the school, and now you'll add your own trees to the forest. Join together in a rendition of Canon in D Major, and think of your own echo trees taking root in the wood, making you forever a part of this place and the Mystwick family."

She flicks a hand, a Conducting baton appearing from her sleeve. Everyone scrambles to take out their instruments, quickly tuning up. No one has told me whether or not I should play, given that my tree is *already* planted.

I hold my flute uncertainly, face warming, until I hear a soft cough behind me. Turning, I see Miss March, the lady who met our zeppelin last night.

"You too, Amelia," she says. "This spell is for all who have a place in the Echo Wood, and you are part of its music now too."

I smile and nod, and try to believe her.

Finally, Mrs. Le Roux nods to Miss Noorani, who raises her viola and draws her bow over the strings. The eight solemn notes of Canon sound out, rich tones made eerie by the darkness.

Then Mrs. Le Roux turns and motions for us to join in.

One by one, the other kids slip into the spell. I wait a few breaths, then add my flute's silver tones to the rest.

We've never played together before, and I think most of us had never even *met* each other till yesterday. But Canon in D is one of the most basic of summoning spells, so we make it work with Mrs. Le Roux guiding us along. Though she isn't playing an instrument herself, as Conductor she is the heart of the spell, knitting all our magic threads into a whole, making sure we play together. Conducting is an entire skill unto itself, and not many musicians have it.

I manage to keep up, but I start noticing the other flutists begin to thread complicated runs and trills into the spell. Watching them, I start to get nervous.

I told the Maestros I could prove I belonged here.

But that was before I realized how *good* the other students are.

Some, like me, follow Miss Noorani with the melody, but many break away to add their own harmonies and counter-melodies, showing off their dexterity and creativity. Several of the strings players lift their bows and instead pluck notes or tap rhythms. The pianists make use of the full range of their keys. A few students go high and sweet, jumping octaves, while those with bass instruments provide a deep, resonating foundation. No showy trills from me—I won't be the one who ruined the entire Planting Ceremony by getting my fingers all twisted up. I'm not even sure I could manage some of the gymnastics the other flutists are doing with their fingers. So I focus on Mrs. Le Roux's baton, following the simple melody.

And if anyone gets *too* creative, Mrs. Le Roux reins them in with a look and a small, disapproving tilt of her chin. Somehow, she keeps everyone under control and in sync, and though we sound a bit messy at first, the spell begins to even out as each of us finds our place and tempo.

Then, it's as if everything clicks, and our individual spells merge into one. All our instruments weave and blend together, until goose bumps run down my arms at the beauty and immensity of the combined sounds.

The melody is every spell's heart, giving the magic structure and direction. It's the most important part of any piece. But beneath the melody are harmonies, adding strength to the spell. One flute playing alone might move a branch, but a five-piece ensemble might move a tree. A full orchestra of Maestros could move a *forest*.

It isn't long before the spell begins to work, and magic rises all around us.

I've never played with an orchestra this big—just the small Musicraft classes back at my old school. So I'm not prepared for the brilliance of the light that springs from our instruments. It's like watching a fireworks display.

No, scratch that—it's like *being* a fireworks display.

In golden curls and yellow spirals and twisting threads the magic rises, shimmering before fading into the air. From the students who add complicated scales and arpeggios to the harmony, the lights peel away in tight curly strands. From the slower notes, like the ones my flute is producing, they rise in smooth streams. The percussionists give off bursts of color, crackling balls of light that dance over our heads. Wisps of magic curl around Mrs. Le Roux's baton and hover at her shoulders like curious butterflies.

I've never seen *anything* this beautiful. It makes my chest ache. And to top it off, the sun begins to rise behind us, its fiery glow spreading across the forest canopy.

Sensing movement above, I look up and see little pots floating overhead.

The echo trees!

As if suspended on invisible strings, they glide through the air and dip to the ground behind Mrs. Le Roux and the other Maestros, who are playing along with us. There's one for each student, summoned by their music. They pop out of their pots and burrow into the earth.

I manage to spot my little tree — it's not hard to recognize, as it's the only one jutting at a right angle halfway up. Quickly I look away, as if someone might guess that the crooked tree is mine. My cheeks warm with embarrassment at how ridiculous it looks alongside all the others.

But at least it's *there*. And right now, it's the only reason I'm standing here.

This has to be the most incredible thing I've ever seen: over a hundred individual summoning spells merging together into one great protective ward, like many threads woven into one fabric.

At last, the spell reaches its end and Mrs. Le Roux drops her hands, signaling for us to lower our instruments.

Only in the silence that follows do we hear the echo trees singing, faint and mellow, that sound like instruments being tuned. For a minute, we all listen in awe.

I hear a loud sniffle, and glance aside to see Darby with tears in her eyes.

"Hey," I whisper, reaching out to touch her shoulder. "Are you okay?"

She gives me a scowl and pulls away, and I grimace, remembering that even looking at me probably reminds her of *her* Amelia. I've got to be the last person in the world who could make her feel better.

"Musicians," says Mrs. Le Roux, raising both hands toward us. "Welcome to Mystwick."

We walk back to the dorms through a thin layer of fog, as the rising sun chases away the morning chill. The Maestros have disappeared. Our captains walk together, flirting and laughing with each other. A couple of kids start calling dibs on showers.

Then Phoebe whistles sharply. We all gather around her and the other seniors. They're grinning—and not in a nice way. More like a hungry, sneaky way that immediately puts me on my guard.

"Listen up, guppies!" she says. "Now that the boring stuff is over, it's time to *really* initiate you into the Mystwick family. This part *is* fully optional, but you should know . . ." She drops her voice so we all have to crane to hear her. "Every student who wimped out in the past eventually met a grisly death."

Someone in the back gives a frightened squeak.

Claudia rolls her eyes. "That's a lie."

"Is it?" Phoebe looks straight at her, eyes narrowing, and Claudia pales.

"What are we supposed to do?" asks Jai eagerly.

Phoebe grins. She holds out a finger and points it like she's playing eeny, meeny, miny, mo. In a singsong voice she says, "You have to face your deepest fears, unearth your darkest secrets, and . . ." Her finger lands on me. She tilts her head. "Can you swim, shorty?"

I blink. "Wh-what? Yeah, but why—"

She suddenly bursts forward, throws me over her shoulder, and then runs down the hill toward the lake.

I'm so startled I can't even struggle. As I bounce on Phoebe's shoulder, I gape at the other students. Without slowing, Phoebe pounds across a little dock, skids to a halt, then shouts, "Welcome to Mystwick, guppy!"

Then she pulls my flute case out of my hands and tosses me into the lake.

I hit with a splash, and that water is *cold*. It closes over my head and pulls me under.

Sinking in a cloud of bubbles, I feel a sudden burst of panic in my chest. My muscles seize up and my lungs squeeze tight like the water's electrified. The deeper I sink, the darker it gets, until I can't even see my own hands.

A strange memory takes hold of me: dark water, my hands —too small, the hands of a child—reaching, reaching, for something I can't quite grasp. A swift current sweeps me down, down into black murky depths.

It's a memory I didn't even know I had.

And now it fills me with fear and panic and desperation.

As I claw my way upward, my lungs squeeze and my head reels. I know how to swim, but I still feel like I'm drowning. Like the water has got me in its teeth and it's not going to let go. I fight against it, a scream locked in my mind.

Then, finally, I break through the surface, sucking down air and finding myself in a beam of sunlight. The dark memory fades away.

Gasping, I start paddling back to the dock as fast as I can, but then I see a flood of students running toward it. I shriek and dive under as they all jump over my head, flipping, falling, and cannonballing into the water. When I pop back up, almost all the other seventh graders are splashing and swimming around me, squealing at how cold it is. Phoebe helps Victoria into the water, and then the captains jump in, whooping, looking for seventh graders to dunk.

Pull it together, Amelia.

Maybe that wasn't a memory at all. Maybe it was just a moment of panic from the surprise of being chucked into a freezing lake. Still, it takes a few minutes before the shakiness leaves me. The lake starts to feel a little warmer, and the rising sun turns it to liquid gold. I try to enjoy the swim, basking in the beauty of the setting.

I'm determined to enjoy this day, no matter what.

But then I see Darby sitting on the dock, by Victoria's empty wheelchair. Darby's legs dangle over the side, and she watches her reflection as if the rest of us aren't even here.

I know she's thinking of Amelia Jones.

My gut twists. I didn't even know the other Amelia Jones existed until yesterday, but we are connected in such a big way. We have the same name, and I have her acceptance letter. I'm even rooming with her best friend. It's like I took over the life *she* was supposed to have.

I wonder what Other Amelia would think of me taking her place. I wonder if she dreamed about this day for as long as I have. And I realize then that if it would bring that other Amelia back, I'd give all of this up in a heartbeat. It belongs to *her*, not me. I didn't earn this. She did.

But I've never heard of a spell that can bring back the dead.

CHAPTER TEN

A Tough Octave to Follow

LATER THAT DAY, the older students start arriving. The Mystwick campus, which had seemed so huge and empty and quiet, now fills up with noisy kids who call out to each other, greeting friends they haven't seen all summer. They walk around like they own the campus, knowing exactly where to go and how to get there. I, on the other hand, feel like an *actual* guppy, flitting between schools of much bigger, louder fish. But that's okay, because all I want right now is to blend in until the Maestros can't possibly tell me apart from everyone else.

The perfect Mystwick musician.

It helps that we all wear the same uniforms: navy blue skirts or pants, white knee-high socks, the blue cardigan with the Mystwick crest on the front. Though my uniform doesn't quite fit right. They must have guessed at my measurements, or maybe they were meant for the *other* Amelia. The clothes are all too big, so I have to roll up the sleeves of the cardigan. And the shiny black shoes they found for me were too small, so I'm still wearing my old scruffy hiking boots, since standing to play flute for hours each day requires comfy footwear, and I'm not sure who I'm supposed to ask for new shoes.

To escape the chaos after our orientation classes end, I go to the library. It's a three-story building completely made of glass, so it reflects the forest and mountains on every side, blending into the landscape. The moment I set foot through the doors, my whole body relaxes.

I can tell at once that this library is going to be my favorite place at Mystwick.

On the first floor is regular books, and there are *tons* of them. I walk up and down the aisles, taking out everything I can find that might help me pass Mrs. Le Roux's test, and a few just for fun. My favorites are stories about Musicraft, of course: adventures about spells gone wrong, biographies of famous Maestros, histories of musical incidents that changed the world—like when the Allied Military Symphony defeated the Axis Powers in World War II, or when Leif Erikson, the Viking, found North America by playing a spell he learned from a raven, or how the ancient Japanese used elemental magic to raise typhoons that repelled the invading Mongolians.

When my arms are so full of books I can hardly see over them, I pause and look around. "Where are the spells?"

Hearing a laugh behind me, I turn to see Miss March pushing

a cart of books. So she's the dean of students *and* the librarian, it seems.

"Go upstairs," she says. "You'll see."

I leave my stack of books on a table, where I'll pick them up on the way down. Then I race up the stairs.

And find myself in paradise.

Spells upon spells upon *spells*.

The entire second floor is devoted to them.

For a whole minute I just stand and gape like a stunned frog. Rows of shelves hold books of spells, spells on loose paper, spells rolled into little scrolls and tied with string, spells of every color and type, some modern, some hundreds of years old. Classical and jazz and rock and folk and genres I've never heard of. Spells for full orchestras and solo spells for instruments of every imaginable type. I've never seen so many in one place.

I had no idea so many *existed*.

When I can finally move my feet, I roam around, touching them like they're made of the most fragile glass. I could spend a lifetime on just one shelf. There must be a spell in here for *everything*. And they're just waiting for a musician to come along and bring them to life.

Maybe if I fail out of Mystwick, they'll let me stay as a janitor or something, and pay me in library loans. I'd do anything just to never leave this building again.

"Amelia Bethany Jones!" says a voice. "You know, I guessed you were a library kind of person."

I turn and see Jai walking over, his violin case slung on his back by its long strap. "It's not Bethany. And what's wrong with libraries? *You're* here."

"Yeah, but not for books."

"There are *thousands* of spells here!"

He sighs and looks around. "And I just know they're going to make us learn them *all*."

"Don't you *want* to?" I take a deep breath and suck in that wonderful papery smell. "I'm never leaving. Never ever ever *ever*. You'll have to drag me out of here with a forklift."

He groans. "I'm going up to the third floor. Are you coming?"

"Are there more spell books on the third floor?"

"Better," he says. "There's a computer lab. And *internet*."

This is the first I've been able to contact Gran. Before I left, I made her an email account just for this purpose. I write her a quick message, telling her I'm fine, and how beautiful it is here, and about the echo trees.

I *don't* tell her about the other Amelia or the mixed-up acceptance letter or my deal with Mrs. Le Roux . . . or that my staying here is all due to some mysterious voice. No one else has mentioned hearing the echo trees talk to them, so I'm not sure it'd be a good idea to bring it up again, especially not to Gran. I'm pretty sure I just imagined the whole thing anyway. As I see it, there isn't anything she can do to help me, and if she thinks I'm in trouble, she might even make me come home.

What harm can come from waiting until *after* my two-month test before coming clean?

After sending the email, I glance at Jai's computer to see he's engrossed in music videos of rock concerts, with musicians playing so hard their drumsticks break and their guitar strings snap. Rock spells usually produce illusion magic, so the air around them sparks with glittering shapes: dragons and horses and ocean waves, entire stories told through Musicraft, better than any movie. Jai watches like he's entranced.

"You taking a rock class?" I ask.

"Huh?" He looks up like I startled him, then shakes his head and quickly closes the window. "Yeah, right. My dad would only *die of embarrassment* if he caught me in a rock class."

Sighing, he opens a zombie game instead and leans low over the keyboard, his tongue sticking out as he chops heads and limbs with a pixelated machete.

Shaking my head, I open the internet and go to a website where people share Musicraft videos. Then I hesitate, my stomach squeezing.

For a minute, I think maybe I'm not brave enough.

But then I type quickly, before I can change my mind, and hit Search.

She comes up right away: tall for her age, long dark hair, and absolutely *perfect* posture.

The other Amelia Jones.

There are tons of videos of her playing piano, and they all have thousands of views. Amelia Jones playing in Vienna, Amelia Jones playing for the president of the United States, Amelia Jones winning a TV Musicraft competition.

She wasn't just good. She was a *legend*.

I'd probably have heard of her too, if I watched more TV, but I was always so focused on practicing I never had much time for it. But even still, her face is kind of familiar, and I think I've seen her on magazines at the grocery store checkout lines.

There's a pair of headphones by the computer, and I pop them on and then play one of the videos.

Three minutes later, I realize the video ended thirty seconds ago and I'm still sitting in shock.

The other Amelia was good. Like, really, *really* good. No wonder she got accepted into Mystwick. She played better than most adults, even as well as most Maestros. And though piano seemed to be her specialty, she could play *dozens* of instruments, all of them with the same level of perfection. There's a video of her playing a spell that fills an entire auditorium with light, and another where she plays in a hospital ward for a sick little boy. In minutes, he jumps out of his bed, fully healed. It seems her specialty was healing spells, curing people who everyone thought were beyond hope.

What would it be like, to have that kind of power? To be loved by so many people?

I scroll through the comments.

"Angel!"

"Prodigy!"

"A gift from heaven! The best young pianist in the world!"

Farther down, there are newer comments, which take a different tone.

"I'm still in shock. I can't believe she's gone! It's so unfair."

"I heard it was murder."

"They say they never even found her body."

Those comments make me feel sick, so I go to close the window.

But then my eye snags on something that makes me pause. I click it, and the screen fills with another video of Amelia. But this time, instead of a grand concert hall, she's in a living room, dressed in pajamas. She's playing some kind of illusion spell on a white grand piano. Every few seconds she looks up at someone across the room and laughs, but I can't see who it is. Finally, the camera moves just slightly to get a better angle of Amelia's face, and then I see her.

Darby.

She's also in her pajamas, so I guess they were having a sleepover or something. And Darby is waving a baton, like she's Conducting Amelia. The illusion spell is focused on *her*, making her hair turn all different colors.

I stare at the Darby in the video. She seems like a whole different person—happy, fun, even silly. She makes a goofy face, and the two laugh their heads off without Amelia ever missing a note. She follows Darby's direction, playing faster and slower. Finally, the video ends with the pair of them standing on the piano bench and taking bows. Judging by the date on the video, it was taken just a few months before Amelia died.

Letting out a shaky breath, I realize Jai is watching. Meanwhile, his game avatar is getting mauled by zombies.

"I remember her now," he says. "That's why your name sounded familiar to me at the audition. She was good."

"She was *beyond* good," says another voice.

We both turn, and my stomach drops.

Darby stands there, holding her shakuhachi case and a book of Japanese illusion spells.

I want to say something, anything to make her feel better. After seeing what she was like before the other Amelia died, I now know how much she must be hurting. How much it changed her.

I know what that feels like. I know what it is to wake up in the morning and think everything is okay, everything's normal, and then you *remember.* You remember who is missing, and your stomach drops and the world turns gray and you want to smash your face into a pillow and scream. I want to tell her that even eight years later, I still feel that way sometimes.

But before I can think of what to say, Darby whispers, "She was the best there was."

With a sigh, she turns and walks away. She passes a table where Claudia and Victoria and some other seventh graders are sitting, and they whisper as she goes by. Claudia's running some sort of gossip ring, and loves to tell anyone who'll listen about the tragic death of the other Amelia Jones, as if *she'd* been the girl's best friend.

"Hey Darby!" Claudia calls. "Come sit with us!"

But Darby ignores them and goes down the stairs, looking angry.

Turning back around, I prop my head in my hands. My stomach has sunk to the floor.

"I shouldn't be here," I say to Jai.

He tilts his head. "What are you talking about?"

I let my hands fall to the desk, but can't quite look him in the eye. A part of me wants to tell him the truth — that my being here is just a huge mistake — but even thinking about it makes my ears burn. If everyone found out about my secret, they'd all look at me differently. Not like I was one of them, but like I was a fraud. And coming from Jai, that look would hurt most of all. He's my first friend here, and I don't want to lose that.

All I have to do is pass Mrs. Le Roux's test in two months, and then it won't matter anymore. It'll be like I got in the same way as everyone else. I just have to make sure no one sees through me till then, not even Jai.

"I just . . . don't want to mess up. You know, like at the hotel."

"Ah. Well, just avoid drying spells, then." He shrugs, his fingers jamming the keys as he navigates a zombie-infested street. "Or you'd probably burn down the whole school."

I punch his arm, and he yelps like his bones are broken and falls to the floor.

"Amelia Jones has slain me!" he moans. "Have pity, have pity! I'm just a poor boy from a poor family!"

The kids behind us all shush him angrily, and Jai stands and directs an elaborate bow in their direction, basking in their glares.

"Ah, my fans," he sighs, sliding back into his chair. "It's tough being loved by so many."

"Dork."

"That's *Mr.* Dork to you, Jones." Jai grins and goes back to playing his game.

I nibble my pencil, thinking about the other Amelia, trying to imagine what she was like, not as a celebrity or a miracle worker, but just as a *person.* The way Darby knew her. I wonder how she would have fit in here at Mystwick. Something tells me that even here, with all these super-talented kids, she'd have stood out. A big fish in a little pond.

But I feel like I'm being swallowed up. Back home, I never felt that way. I could play every spell Mrs. Parrish put in front of me, I was always ahead in Musicraft class, and I practiced twice as much as everyone else. I'd thought I was *good*.

Now, I'm not sure what I am, or what I have to do to fit in. This is harder than I'd ever dreamed it could be. And it feels like every move I make, I've got the Maestros watching over my shoulder and taking notes. *Is she good enough? Is she Mystwick material? Or is she just a mistake to be erased?*

But even more importantly, it's like I can feel my mom watching too, asking the same questions.

CHAPTER ELEVEN

Gone with the Woodwinds

THE NEXT MORNING, school officially begins. My first period is homeroom, which I share with the other wood-wind students, or *Aeros*. I get lost in Harmony Hall looking for it, and when I finally arrive at the right place, most of the kids are already there, talking and laughing. The room is long and the walls are sculpted for optimum acoustics. A picture window gives a view of the mountains and the lake. The other wall is lined with clear, fully enclosed cubicles, sort of like old-fashioned telephone booths, that I'm guessing are sound-proof for individual spellwork. Every desk has an apple on it, which I take to be a nice, welcoming gesture by our home-room Maestro, who is apparently not yet here.

There is only one desk still empty, at the very front of the classroom, beside Darby.

"Hey," I say, trying to be as cheery as possible. "You were up early this morning."

By early, I mean the crack of dawn. Darby was gone before I even woke up, her bed made up so neatly it would make Gran cry with happiness.

She just gives me a little nod and stares at her desk.

Claudia wanders over and snickers. "Nice shoes, Jones. Or can I even call them that? You some kind of construction worker back home?"

I yank my feet under my chair, but it's too late to hide my scruffy boots. Looking around, I notice all the others are wearing the same shiny uniform shoes. Not a scuff of dirt on any of them.

"Cut it out, Claudia," Darby snaps, surprising me.

Claudia laughs and picks up Darby's apple, tossing it lightly and catching it again. "You know, it's weird, isn't it? You and Amelia—the *other* one—were supposed to be roommates, and then you get some other Amelia Jones instead. Seems like an odd coincidence."

"Yeah," Darby says softly. "It does."

I swallow hard and lower my face, as a hot, rashy feeling sweeps from my cheeks to my toes. My hands squeeze together between my knees.

Everyone is still talking when our Maestro arrives. Mr. Pinwhistle glares around at us, then stomps in, slamming his large bassoon case onto his desk at the front. Claudia quickly slides back into her chair.

"I will have silence!" he says. "And when I enter the room, you will greet me with respect."

"Yes, Maestro," a few people mutter.

"What?" he says, holding a hand to his ear.

"YES, MAESTRO," we all shout.

He grunts and sits heavily, his chair creaking beneath him.

"Let's get one thing straight," Mr. Pinwhistle says, slapping his desk. "This is not some artsy-fartsy Musicraft camp where we sit around talking about how music makes us *feel.* Mystwick is for serious musicians and serious magic. There will be no crying, whining, excuses, eating, cheating, tardiness, talking out of turn, passing notes, vandalizing school property, chewing gum, stupidity, laziness, late homework, *or* bathroom breaks."

I'm not sure that last one is entirely legal to ban, but I don't think now is the best time to bring it up.

"At the end of each week," Mr. Pinwhistle says, "you'll be listed according to chair, based on your performance in class and on homework." He smacks a finger on a chart by the door, where all our names are written on little cards. I notice there are twenty-six slots instead of twenty-five, and wonder if anyone else notices that an extra flute was added to the class. I sink a little lower in my chair. "First chair to last. Oh, and did I mention? Last chair gets double homework."

I stifle a groan. He may as well go ahead and hand me my assignment. I heard these kids play during the Planting Ceremony, so I know what I'm up against.

Still, I'd rather play a million extra hours of practice scales than be expelled.

Mr. Pinwhistle hands out spells to each of us, based on our instruments. Mine is an etude called *Barcarolle,* by Friedrich Burgmüller, which I've never heard of before, but it doesn't look too difficult. It's a yellow spell that's supposed to "peel, unwrap, or open" an object.

I glance at the apple on my desk.

"Now, as any *toddler* can tell you," growls Mr. Pinwhistle, "there are four types of spells. What are they . . ." He looks around until his eyes land on me. "Jones?"

Everyone stares at me. Claudia's eyes burn into me from one side, and Darby's from the other.

Ears burning, I sit up straighter and say, "The four types of spells are green, yellow, blue, and white"

"And who will define *green* spells for us?" He nods at another flutist in the back. "You—who are you?"

"I'm Jingfei." The girl stands up and says in a clear voice, "Green spells are also known as bio spells. They work on living organisms: people, animals, plants. They affect biological processes, healing or causing growth, or inflicting pain and withering."

Mr. Pinwhistle grunts, nods, and turns to another student. "And yellow spells?"

"They let us move things," the boy says quietly.

Mr. Pinwhistle sighs. *"Name?"*

The boy's cheeks turn red. "Collin Brunnings."

"Collin Brunnings," mutters Mr. Pinwhistle, going to the chart by the door. He finds Collin's card and moves it into last place. Everyone falls very quiet.

I sit up a little straighter, trying not to grin. At least it's not *me* in the last spot.

"In *this* class, Collin," growls Mr. Pinwhistle, "we will be *specific* in our answers. So who can tell me what yellow spells do — specifically?"

Claudia raises her hand. "Yellow spells, or *kinetic* spells, manipulate objects. They summon, repel, levitate, ward. They can even teleport, but those are very hard to play and can end in disaster if you mess up. You have to have a special license for teleportation spells."

The rest of the answers come quickly as Mr. Pinwhistle calls on other students. This is all basic stuff. Even so, I take notes furiously, making sure to be *very* specific.

"Blue spells are elemental," says a girl named Aya. "They let you call up wind or fire, and affect the weather. They can also be illusion spells, because they conjure light and darkness."

"White spells influence the mind," a boy named George

explains, as he pushes his glasses up his nose. "They're also called *mental* spells. They can charm and enchant, put you to sleep or fog your memory. And they let some people see the future."

"That's not true!" Claudia cries out.

"It is! My grandmother knew a spell that could—"

"Enough," grumbles Mr. Pinwhistle. "It's true *some* musicians can use certain spells to discern events to come, albeit these so-called visions are usually murky and unreliable."

Darby pipes up softly, "Some people believe in a fifth kind of spell—black spells."

Everyone turns to stare at her.

Mr. Pinwhistle makes a noise in his throat like he has something stuck there.

"They let you talk to ghosts," Darby goes on. "Or resurrect the dead, steal souls, stuff like that."

"Like the Necromuse!" says George. "He uses black spells!"

Everyone whispers, and a few kids look frightened.

"What's the Necromuse?" I whisper to George, whose desk is behind mine.

He leans forward and replies, "Your worst nightmare, Jones."

I roll my eyes. "Very helpful, thanks."

Mr. Pinwhistle's face has turned red. "Miss Bradshaw, we at Mystwick do not trade in fairy tales. There are no such things as

black spells, and attempting them here will result in severe consequences. Now, we'll speak no more about that." He slaps Darby's
card into the last-chair slot, bumping up Collin Brunnings, who
lets out a relieved sigh.

Huh. I lean back in my chair, tapping my pencil to my lip.

If there's no such thing as black spells, why would it be
against the rules to try them?

Mr. Pinwhistle gives us a few minutes to tune up, then splits
us into two groups. The first group heads into the little cubicles
with the clear plastic walls, while my group waits for our turn.
I watch curiously as the students in the cubicles play over their
apples, which they place on little clear shelves inside. I can't hear
a single note from any of them. Those walls must be thicker than
they look. Each cubicle fills with sparkling motes of green light,
the magic bouncing around in the small spaces.

Behind me, George whispers, "Can you imagine *farting* in
there?"

He and the boys around him crack up until Mr. Pinwhistle
makes a growling noise.

Darby finishes first, holding up her perfectly peeled apple,
but she doesn't smile. Mr. Pinwhistle nods with satisfaction and
moves her up two chairs, putting Collin back in last place.

Finally, it's my turn. I shut the cubicle door and prop the spell
on a stand in the corner. The apple goes on the shelf. Before I

start, I hold my flute in position and practice the spell silently, clicking the keys and hearing the notes in my head. Once I'm sure of the melody, I begin.

But I only get three notes into the spell before the sheets in front of me suddenly slip off their stand, falling to the floor.

My heart jumps into my throat. I grab them up and replace them, then pick up where I left off.

Again, I barely even start playing, and the pages *leap* off the stand.

I glance around to see the students in the other booths aren't having any trouble. There isn't an air vent in here, or any other way a draft might have blown in. And I hadn't gotten far enough into the spell yet to produce any magic. Weird. Quickly setting up the papers, I try again.

This time, a gust of wind rushes around the booth, sweeping away the papers and pulling at my hair and clothes. I shout, grabbing at the sheets, and end up knocking my funny bone on the door handle. Yelping with pain, I throw out a hand for support and knock my apple to the floor. The pages rush all around me, beating at me like enraged birds. Shrieking, I bat them away with one hand and try to hold down my skirt with the other as the wind rushes around my legs.

The door flies open, and the wind dissipates.

Mr. Pinwhistle is standing there, face red. I realize all the other students have finished their spells, and are sitting at their desks staring at me, as my spell sheets gently drift to the floor and my apple rolls out. Mr. Pinwhistle stops it with his shoe, then picks it up and holds it between us. It's covered in dark bruises, and not so much as a sliver of the peel has been removed.

I stare at it, then him, at a loss for words.

What just *happened?*

It wasn't my playing that started that wind. It's almost like someone was playing a trick on me. But it doesn't make sense —I was alone in there, and no other spells could have worked *through* the soundproof walls.

Mr. Pinwhistle looks disgusted. "Miss Jones, if you aren't going to take this seriously, perhaps you should reconsider why you're here at all."

"But didn't you see that—"

"Sit *down,* Miss Jones."

A few people snicker, and it's clear they thought *I* was the one making the wind, or maybe it just looked like I was being clumsy, dropping my papers everywhere.

"What a tragedy," Claudia says.

I don't know what to say to Mr. Pinwhistle. I can tell arguing will only make things worse.

So I mumble an apology, promising not to do it again, even

though I didn't *do* anything. Someone booby-trapped the booth or something. I have no idea how, but I do know who used it before me: Darby Bradshaw. I watch her closely, but she isn't even paying attention to me. She's just staring at her desktop. Is that a sign of guilt? Does she suspect my secret?

Mr. Pinwhistle firmly plants my name at the bottom of the chair list, and there it remains until the end of class, when he calls me to his desk.

He wasn't kidding about the extra homework part.

That evening, what little free time I have left after all the extra work I had to do, I spend in the library. It's not so busy now, because most of the students are hanging out in the gym or common areas. And I guess it's still early enough in the year that people aren't cramming for tests.

I try to call Gran from the library phone, but just get her voicemail. My throat closes up when I try to speak, and I only manage to squeak: "Hi Gran, it's me, I'll call again later."

I send her another email instead, and find it's much easier to lie that way.

This place is amazing! I write. *I've made so many friends and am doing really well in all my classes. There's nothing to worry about, not a single thing! Everything is totally fine.*

After a moment's thought, I erase the last two sentences,

imagining Gran's nose wrinkling up as she squints through her glasses, reading between the lines.

I miss you a lot, I write instead. *The banana pudding here isn't half as good as yours. Anyway, better go—lots of homework! Love, Amelia.*

After sending the email, I go downstairs. I have to find something to do a report on for my literature class, and end up in the fairy-tale section.

My fingers trail along the spines. *The Little Siren. Snow White and the Seven Drummers. Aladdin and the Wonderful Lute. The Pied Piper of Hamelin.*

I can't stop thinking about the spell I flubbed in homeroom, and that stupid apple rolling over the floor. And the rest of my classes today drove home one undeniable fact: I'm not as good as these kids are. Maybe with a lot of practice, I *could* be, but can I really improve that much in just two months? Am I wasting everyone's time by even trying?

What if I'm just fooling myself, and should give up now?

Then my fingers pause on a slender blue book: *The Magic Flute.*

I take down the book and crack it open, recognizing the illustrations, because it's the same edition as the one I have at home. It's the story of a prince and an enchanted flute that could transform sadness into joy, and how he rescued his love by playing the most wonderful spells. When I was smaller, I used to read this one over and over, until I could repeat whole sections from memory. But as much as I love this one, I need something longer for my book report.

I start to close it, but then a card slips out the back. I bend over to pick it up — and freeze.

It's one of those old cards people used to write their names on when they checked out a book. The list is old, because everything's done with barcodes now; the dates are all from twenty years ago. But it's not the dates that catch my attention.

It's the name that practically leaps out at me: *Susan Jones*.

I gasp, staring at the little card like it's a million-dollar bill.

She checked it out seven times.

Like it was her favorite book, too.

My hands start to shake. I sink to the floor, cradling the book, gripping it until the pages crinkle. *She* held this. She read it, over and over. She came to this spot, took it off this shelf, stood right here. I turn through every page, in case there are any other signs she left behind, but all I find are smudges left by dirty fingers. They could be anyone's.

I slowly close the book, staring at the worn cover and imagining it in her hands. I can feel her so intensely at that moment that it's like her arms are around me.

And I realize I can't give up.

Because if I do, I'll spend the rest of my life never knowing who I really am—am I my mother's daughter, or am I my father's? Do I stick by my dreams, or do I run away when things get hard, the way *he* did?

If I get expelled from Mystwick, let it be because I wasn't good enough.

Not because I was a coward.

CHAPTER TWELVE

The Second Rule of Musicraft

O N OUR FIRST FRIDAY MORNING, all the seventh graders gather in the main auditorium, called the Shell. It's the huge, vaulting concert hall at the far end of campus, shaped kind of like an armadillo shell. The whole seventh-grade class fills up only one small section of the seats. In front of us is an enormous stage, dark except for a lone spotlight shining down on a microphone stand.

I slump in my seat, yawning from staying up late to study my homework. I sat for hours in the dorm's shared bathroom, feet pulled up on the toilet seat so no one would notice me and make me go to bed. But my first week of classes proved one dire fact: I am very far behind my classmates. They play on a level I didn't even know kids my age *could,* and if I'm going to catch up and earn my place here, I can't waste time *sleeping.* So I'm tired and cranky, and my feet are sore from being squished inside my tiny shoes all week.

At the end of the first day of class, I shoved my old boots deep into the closet. If being the perfect Mystwick musician means curling my toes all day and hobbling a bit when I walk, so be it.

Mrs. Le Roux herself walks out. I haven't seen her since the Planting Ceremony. Today she wears a bright, multicolored caftan. A gold comb in her hair sends up a spray of feathers that sway as she crosses to the microphone.

"Good morning, students. Today's lesson is one of the most important you will learn here," she says.

I sit up straighter. If it's important enough that they'll call a full assembly *and* Mrs. Le Roux, I better not miss a word.

"I know you've all heard the Rules of Musicraft over and over again."

We all groan, nodding.

But Mrs. Le Roux doesn't smile. "Unfortunately, sometimes we can hear a thing so many times that it begins to lose its meaning. Tell me, students, what is the Second Rule of Musicraft?"

Together we recite: "Lest you be doomed by your own art, always finish what you start."

Mrs. Le Roux nods seriously. "We all know what this rhyme means: that it is *very* dangerous to leave a spell unfinished. An incomplete spell leaves all sorts of uncontrolled and unstable forces hanging about."

She takes a long pause, letting the words sink in as her eyes slowly sweep over our faces.

I know the rule well. It's why when you're just practicing a spell, you should always skip the first few notes, so you don't create any magic that might get out of control. Playing a few measures over and over in practice is harmless, but if you start at the beginning, trigger the magic, and then don't finish it, you end up with a spoiled spell, and those can be very dangerous depending on how powerful the spell is. Even if you mess up, you have to pull it together and keep going, or let someone else jump in and finish the spell for you—which is always embarrassing.

"Often in your life," Mrs. Le Roux continues, "you will find yourself playing in situations that are distracting or unsettling. Anger, sadness, and other powerful emotions can compromise your composure, causing errors or even preventing you from completing your spell. Sometimes, you'll be with other musicians, who can close the spell if you're unable. But the leading cause of magical injury—from bruised hands to charred instruments—comes from unfinished solo spells, especially if you're dealing with Maestro-level magic."

I swallow hard, thinking suddenly of my mom.

Is that what happened to her? Did she fail to complete a spell?

Mrs. Le Roux flicks a finger, and the four class Maestros come walking solemnly onto the stage: Miss Noorani, Mr. Walters,

Miss Becker, and Mr. Pinwhistle. They stand in a row and watch us grimly. I start to feel uneasy, wondering where this is leading. It doesn't sound like we'll be peeling apples or conjuring butterflies. Mr. Pinwhistle's sour gaze sweeps over us, and lingers a second too long on me, and I could swear his nose wrinkles a little more than usual.

"Each of you will soon enter a room," Mrs. Le Roux says, "and there you will play a simple spell. Meanwhile, your Maestros will be playing another spell that you will not be able to hear. But you will see its effects. They will try to unsettle you, to make you angry, afraid, even terribly sad. Your simple task will be to control yourself and finish what you start. Play through the emotions."

As she leans in to the microphone, it's like she's staring straight into my soul.

"I cannot impress upon you the importance of this exercise, except to say that one day, your lives may depend upon it."

With that, she leaves the stage, vanishing as suddenly as she appeared.

In silent, solemn rows we file out of the auditorium and through a door that leads behind the stage. There we find a bunch of little soundproof rooms, sort of like the cubicles in the Aero classroom, except these ones aren't see-through. We're split into lines, to take our turns four at a time. I don't know which Maestro I'm paired with, but I assume it's Mr. Pinwhistle.

I end up in the back of my line. Jai's at the back of his, too, and he gives me a smile, but it's a weak one.

So we've finally found something that makes Jai Kapoor nervous.

That doesn't make me feel the least bit better.

We can't see into or hear anything coming out of the practice rooms, so I have no idea what form the exercise will take. As the kids ahead of me finish their turns and leave, they don't stick around to give the rest of us tips. Instead, most of them hurry away as fast as they can, looking like they're about to puke. A lot of them are crying. One girl sinks into the corner, hugging her viola, shaking so badly I worry she's in shock. But then Miss March appears and takes her gently away.

Jai and I exchange looks.

"Did your parents ever tell you about this?" I whisper.

He shakes his head.

It reminds me a little of the auditions, which of course sets me to panicking. Then I remember the point of this is to *not* panic, so I start panicking about panicking.

Great.

This is going to go fan-fiddle-*tastically*.

Finally, my turn comes.

Rabiah leaves the room I'm about to enter, sobbing quietly, trembling so much she can barely move her cello. I give her a questioning look, hoping she'll give me some clue what to expect, but she just shakes her head and shuffles away.

"Good luck," Jai whispers, before stepping into his little room.

Drawing a deep breath, I walk inside, shutting the door behind me.

My hands are sweating so much that I worry I'll drop my flute. I wipe them on my skirt and look around.

There's not much to see. Just padded walls and a bare linoleum floor, and a metal stand with a three-page spell on it.

Someone has written in tiny letters by the door: *It's all an illusion. Keep your cool.*

Thanks, random student.

That's *very* reassuring.

No one tells me what to do, so I figure I'm just supposed to start. First I read through the pages. It's *Rêverie,* an illusion spell by Claude Debussy for conjuring light.

I find the fingerings easily enough; it's not an easy spell, but it's not too difficult either as long as I keep my cool. I play slowly, lips pursed slightly as I blow across the embouchure.

I miss a few notes, which is to be expected since I haven't played this piece before, but the important thing is to *keep* playing, even through the mistakes. The melody that fills the little room is dreamy and haunting and a bit sad, but that's not the only reason a shiver runs through me. I'm waiting for something to happen, to try to trip me up. I wish they'd at least told us what to expect. My feet pinch, and I shift my weight to try to take pressure off them, which nearly makes me fall over.

Keep your cool, Amelia, I think. *Just keep your cool.*

Illusion is a type of elemental spell, so the magic that begins to peel away from my flute is pale blue, like shimmering sapphire dust. It twinkles and fades, and in front of me, a white orb begins to grow. At first it's faint, little more than a fleck of light, but the deeper I get into the music, the brighter it becomes. It's just like the ones Miss Noorani made when we were hunting for my echo tree.

It's beautiful.

I'm so focused on watching it and reading the music that I don't notice at first that the light around me is dimming.

The room is getting darker. And colder.

Soon the only light I have to read the music by is my glowing white orb. It hovers over the stand, while the walls, floor, and ceiling fade away into infinite blackness. It's like standing in the heart of the night, with no horizon in view. Nothing exists but the sheets of music, my flute, the ball of light, and me.

Unease stirs inside my stomach. I press it down, thinking, *It's just an illusion.*

I imagine Mr. Pinwhistle on the other side of the wall, blasting his bassoon and flooding my little room with his illusions.

But then I start to feel heat behind me. I don't turn, I don't take my eyes off the music, but I sense flames leaping up. Then they spread around me, hot and red and angry, until I'm standing in a circle of crackling fire. For an illusion, it feels incredibly real.

I begin to sweat from the heat.

Panic sparks like fireworks in my chest.

The flames are everywhere, hungry and relentless. Unlike the illusion Miss Noorani did at the Planting Ceremony, this fire actually feels *hot*. Is it real? Would they trap me in here with an actual *fire?*

Whatever your mother tried to do that night by the river, it didn't work, I hear Gran saying in the back of my mind. *And it killed her.*

I push away her words. Now is not the time to think about my mom, especially not how she died, or I'll almost definitely fall to pieces and fail this test.

Finally, the fire fades away, and something inside me unclenches as it does.

The room grows lighter, until I can see it's not the same room at all. Instead, I'm standing in the ballroom at the hotel where the auditions were held. My blue light is still hovering overhead, but it's harder to see in this bright room. There's a little acorn in a pot in front of me, and the four Maestros are seated behind it. They all stare at me with different expressions: Mr. Pinwhistle looks enraged, Mr. Walters looks bored, Miss Becker looks disgusted, and Miss Noorani looks deeply disappointed. Those looks drag at me like chains around my neck.

For a moment, I forget I'm at Mystwick.

I think I really *am* in that ballroom, failing all over again. Destroying my own dream. Risking everything for silly, stupid hope.

Nervousness and shame fill my cheeks with heat. My hands get clammy. I play and play, but the acorn doesn't so much as jiggle. It's not working. I'm going to get kicked out, I'm going to lose everything I ever wanted—

It's all an illusion.

Keep your cool.

The words come just when I need them. Though I'm trembling all over, I force my hands to stay steady.

Then the Maestros start whispering.

"You're not good enough," says Mr. Pinwhistle.

"Why don't you just give up?" asks Mr. Walters.

"Is that *chicken poop?*" Miss Becker wrinkles her nose.

Miss Noorani just shakes her head and adds, "We don't want girls like you. You don't belong here, Amelia Jones. The *real* Amelia belonged. We wanted *her,* but we got you instead."

It takes all my might not to whip my flute from my lips and yell that they're all wrong, that I *do* belong here. At least, that's what I think I'd shout, if I could.

But a part of me knows they're right.

I don't belong at Mystwick.

I'm not the real Amelia.

I was never meant to be here.

I don't know how I keep playing, but I do. Sheer stubbornness, I guess. I always did have a head like a mule, Gran would say. So out of pure spite I continue, because they can whisper all they want.

The louder I play, the harder it gets to hear them.

Then they vanish like smoke.

The room goes dark again, leaving me alone with my music and the bobbing ball of light. Except for the soft notes of my flute, there's total silence.

My heart lifts. The test must be over. Everything comes in threes, right? I passed three tests — darkness, fire, and the audition — and I'm still playing strong. I may have wobbled a bit and missed a note or two, but I didn't quit. They didn't beat me.

But I still have one page of music left to play, and the lights don't come on yet. It's just me standing in a pool of light, my glowing orb floating like a bright bubble over my head.

I feel like I've been standing here for ages. My legs are sore, my hands and arms are tired from holding up my flute, and I'm losing my breath.

Shifting slightly to give my legs a break, I feel something against my shoe.

Something like . . . water?

I chance a look down between notes and see I'm standing in an inky puddle. Or . . . not a puddle. A wide, shallow pool. And that pool is getting deeper.

In seconds, the water is to my knees.

Then my waist.

A current rises, pushing against me like I'm standing in a river that's getting stronger and stronger. Looking around, I don't see anything but dark, rising water. The light of my illusion spell ripples on the choppy surface.

The water reaches my chest. I raise my arms so it can't throw off my playing. I wonder if the Maestros use the same illusions on all the kids, and if so, how did Rabiah manage this test with her cello?

The thought comes and goes like a fly, and soon all I can focus on is keeping my flute above water. The stand with the papers somehow stays still, but the current is so strong now that I can barely stay on my feet. I brace against the flow, convinced the test *has* to end soon, or I'll be completely submerged in water.

Just an illusion! Keep your cool!

But it doesn't end.

The water reaches my chin.

Only my hands and flute and head are above the surface. The current drags at me hungrily. Despite my efforts, my fingers grow clumsy and I hit a few bad notes, and the ball of light shrinks to the size of a pea.

I'm standing chin-deep in a powerful river in almost total darkness.

I keep playing, desperate and terrified, trying to remember the last few measures of the spell since the light isn't strong enough to illuminate the pages. The notes jumble in my head, and I frantically pound the keys of my flute, but the ball of light doesn't grow again.

Then I see something: a girl standing in the corner of the room. She's so faint I can barely make her out, but something about her is familiar. Her features are blurred, like she's a water-color painting. Is she part of the illusion? She watches me silently, with eyes like gaping holes. A shiver runs over my skin.

Then she starts toward me.

I back away, fighting against the current, but the water doesn't seem to slow *her* down. She raises a hand, which is pale white and transparent.

I shake my head, still playing my flute, telling myself she isn't real, isn't real, isn't—

Losing my balance, I plunge underwater.

This isn't an illusion.

It's a *memory*.

I'm sinking, drowning, clawing for air that I cannot find. Instead of my twelve-year-old body, I feel small and weak, four years old again. I can't seem to remember how to swim. I'm totally at the river's mercy.

And it is merciless.

Opening my mouth to scream, I shut my eyes and twist this way and that, terror coursing through me. I can feel myself getting weak. Sparks dance in my eyes.

I'm drowning.

I'm drowning and I'm reaching for my mother, but she isn't there.

She *was* there, she was there beside me and so was my father, but I slipped and fell into the river, and they called my name but the current carried me swiftly away.

Out of their arms.

Into total darkness.

The lights come on, revealing the little soundproof room.

I'm curled up into a ball on the floor, sobbing for Gran. There's no water anywhere except for my salty tears and the snot running from my nose. It was an illusion after all, but my body reacted as if it were real. My flute is clutched to my chest, and the music stand has toppled over. The pages lie scattered about. The strange, ghostly girl has vanished.

"Amelia."

I shake my head, curling up tighter.

"Amelia, dear, it's over. You can get up now. You did it. You finished the spell."

Shaking, I slowly turn my head to see Miss Noorani standing over me. She bends down, softly touching my hair.

"It's all over," she says again.

It's all an illusion.

Keep your cool.

But I hadn't kept my cool at all. I feel so completely, utterly *un*cool that I start sobbing all over again.

Miss Noorani helps me up. We walk out of the room together and I try to get a grip on myself. All I want right now is Gran —her arms around me, squeezing me till I can't breathe in the way that used to always annoy me, but which I now miss more than anything. But Gran isn't here. She hasn't even responded to the emails I've sent her, though I've been sure to write at least every other day.

"Did you . . . was it you who did that to me?" I ask Miss Noorani in a trembling voice.

She gives me an apologetic smile. "You did well. Better than I'd expected, really. I thought I had you with the audition illusion."

Anger rushes through me. "And what about the river? What about my parents? Did you think you 'had me' then?"

Her brow furrows. "What? I didn't conjure your parents. Just the water."

"What about the girl?" I demand. "The girl who tried to *drown* me?"

She looks totally confused. "What girl? There was no girl. It was just an illusion."

"Just an illusion!" I'm yelling now. "Just an illusion? This, *this*, is not *just an illusion!*" I press my hand to my chest, which feels like a cage full of snakes. Angry and twisted up and crawling.

"Amelia, it's a standard exercise—"

She is cut short by a scream.

It comes from the little room on our left, despite the walls being soundproof.

I look around. "Where's Jai?"

Miss Noorani tries to grab my arm, but I pull away and throw open the door of the room.

Jai is huddled in the corner, still screaming.

A huge, salivating dog with enormous fangs is standing over him, snarling and snapping, foam dripping from its massive jaws. Weirdly, between its snarls, it speaks in a human voice that sounds eerily like Jai's dad: *"Enough! It's time to get serious! You're a disgrace!"*

Jai is trying to play his violin, but then he gives up, throwing it aside to put up his hands instead, in a feeble attempt to hold off the rabid dog.

"No!" I shout, jumping between them. "Jai, it isn't real!"

The last page of the Debussy spell is still on Jai's stand, behind the dog, while the other pages are scattered on the floor

—so he must have made it through most of the piece before the dog appeared. A faintly glowing ball of light hovers over the page, on the verge of flickering out altogether. I quickly raise my flute and play the last few lines, completing Jai's spell for him, and the light strengthens. I play so fast and so fiercely that the orb grows until it's like a small sun, blinding the dog. All the light particles that Jai's assigned Maestro assembled to create it become mine to manipulate instead. The dog doesn't stand a chance. I obliterate him totally.

I finish the spell like the good Mystwick musician I am, then lower my flute and turn to Jai. The bright light fades away.

Putting my arms around him, I hold him tight and whisper, "It's over, Jai. It was all an illusion. And it's over now."

He grips my arms so tight it hurts, but I just wince and don't let go. He's shaking like a leaf in a storm.

After a few moments, his sobs turn to sniffs, and he pulls away. Keeping his eyes averted, he mumbles, "Thanks."

I nod and pick up his violin, handing it back to him.

Hearing a grunt behind me, I turn to see Mr. Pinwhistle has joined Miss Noorani, and he's looking hard at me. I guess he was the one testing Jai.

Defiantly, I stand and snatch up my flute, then help Jai up. Together we glare right back and march out of the room.

Without a word we go past the two Maestros and head for

the door leading outside. I'm still shaking, but now it's from rage. I know interrupting Jai's test won't help me prove to the Maestros I belong here, but for once, I don't care.

"That was completely out of line, Miss Jones!" Mr. Pinwhistle says, but he's got a funny look in his eyes, like he's puzzled. "Consider yourself in last chair for the entirety of next week."

I turn and shout back, *"Worth it!"*

I let the door slam behind me on the way out.

CHAPTER THIRTEEN

Serenade with a Chance of Snowstorms

IT TAKES A FEW DAYS before the effects of the test fade away. All the seventh graders seem just as shaken as I am, and I hear girls waking up each night screaming, haunted by nightmares.

I'm no different. Three nights in a row I dream about the river ripping me from my parents. At first I hadn't believed Miss Noorani when she told me that wasn't part of her illusion spell.

Or maybe I just didn't *want* to, because that would mean admitting it was a memory. The same one that seized me in the lake after the Planting Ceremony.

If it was, I haven't a clue what it means or when it happened, though I guess it would have been before my mom died. I'm not sure how the memory ends, either. Every time I dream about it, it just ends with darkness.

Finally, Miss March, who apparently is the school nurse in addition to being the dean of students and the librarian, plays a white spell for us all on the piano in Harmony Hall, which she says will help us sleep better. It works, and the nightmares stop.

I'm mostly grateful . . . but a part of me wonders if I'll ever find out how the memory ended. I can't help but think it might be a clue about my mother's death. I almost email Gran about it, but she still hasn't replied to any of my earlier emails, and I worry she might be so angry with me she doesn't want to talk to me at all. I carry that thought around like a hard lump of ice in my belly.

But with the horrible test finally behind me, I settle into a routine at Mystwick. Thankfully, the rest of my lessons aren't nearly as bad as the illusion test—with the exception, maybe, of my biweekly tutoring with Mr. Pinwhistle. One-on-one tutoring is a required class for every student, so there's no getting out of it. At least in a class setting, I can hide among the other students, but when it's just the two of us I feel like a mouse trapped in a box with a hungry cat. Nothing I play seems to be good enough for him, and mostly he just shakes his head and grunts with disappointment.

Ensemble is by far my favorite. It's me and seven other students, including Jai. We learn group spells we could never attempt on our own, but that are less complicated than true orchestral spells. Best of all, when it's sunny, Miss Noorani takes our lessons outside.

Like today. It's been almost three weeks since I arrived at Mystwick, and though I'm still listed as last chair on Mr. Pinwhistle's chart, I feel hopeful. I'm not as far behind everyone else as I'd feared I would be, and I think I might actually be getting better.

Miss Noorani takes us to the edge of the lake, which I've learned is called Orpheus Lake, after the famous Greek god of Musicraft. It's a lazy sort of afternoon, warm for September, and the gently lapping water has a hypnotic effect.

But that isn't why I can't stop yawning.

"Pull it together, Jones," says Claudia, elbowing me.

"Sorry. I didn't sleep last night," I mutter.

"So?" Claudia scowls. "Not my problem."

I'm not so sure it isn't, and I eye her suspiciously. This time, my exhaustion has nothing to do with studying late.

Last night, someone snuck into my room at least four times and shone a light, waking me up. The third time it happened, I stayed up as long as I could, hoping to catch them in the act. Instead, I fell back asleep, only to be awakened thirty minutes later by another flash of light.

Weird thing was, every time I woke up and looked around, no one was there.

It was probably Darby, but I haven't ruled out Claudia yet. I know neither of them likes me, but still, I can't figure out *why* they'd go to the trouble of bothering me while I slept, especially since Claudia's teasing has slacked off and Darby doesn't even bother to talk to me. And neither of them look very tired.

Struggling to stay awake, I focus harder as Miss Noorani tells us to pick up our instruments.

We play a nine-instrument piece called a nonet, which has a tricky flute section. The spell is supposed to make the lake freeze over, which has Jai bouncing with excitement. He can't wait to slide across the frozen water, and even brought a pair of ice skates with him.

But every time we get close to succeeding, I bungle the flute part and the spell breaks. The ice crystals that have begun to form all crack and dissolve. We play through to the end anyway — we learned *that* lesson in the Shell — but it's too late. Not even Miss Noorani's brilliant viola playing can revive the lost magic. Everyone glares at me. Even Jai looks disappointed.

I can't help it though. I'm so exhausted I can hardly see straight. My fingers feel heavy and useless.

The fourth time this happens, Miss Noorani calls a stop to it all. "We're out of time today," she says, and everyone groans. "We'll try again on Wednesday, don't worry. Now go on to study hour."

I keep my head down as the other kids and I head up the hill toward the school.

"Nice work, Jones," says Claudia, glaring at me. "We could have been done with this thirty minutes ago and had extra free time to skate."

"Hey!" says Jai. "We all mess up sometimes. Leave her alone."

"Sorry if I offended your girlfriend," Claudia sniffs.

Jai turns beet red, and we shout at the same time:

"She's not my girlfriend!"

"I'm not his girlfriend!"

Claudia waves a hand as if to say *whatever*. George laughs at Jai's red cheeks.

"All I'm saying," Claudia adds, "is I can't understand how she even got *in* to Mystwick if she can't handle a simple piece."

My heart flips over, and I can only stare as she and George head into Harmony Hall, leaving us alone on the front steps.

"For the record," says Jai, "I saw Claudia hit five wrong notes that last time through."

"You don't have to defend me, you know," I sigh. "I *did* mess up four times, and ruined everyone's hope of skating."

He rolls his eyes. "Am I invited to your pity party, or is this a solo thing?"

"Hey!"

"Do you remember the first thing I ever said to you?"

I think back, screwing up my nose. "Um . . . something about my spider being a pyromaniac?"

"What? No, not that. I told you the Maestros like confidence."

I snort and pick at a thread on my skirt. "It's hard to be confident when your fingers turn into noodles every time you get to your part."

"Okay, that's *it!*" Jai jumps up.

"What's it?"

"You. Me. Free time. The Echo Wood. There, out of the goodness of my enormous and generous heart, I will teach you, Amelia Vanessa Jones, expert chicken charmer, how to be confident. You're always saying you're too busy to practice with me, but this time, I'm not taking no for an answer."

"I may not have enough confidence," I mutter, wishing I'd never told him about the chickens, "but you have *too* much. I think that's what they call *egotistical.*"

"Whoa, whoa." He waves his hands. "No need for that kind of language. So, we have a deal?"

"Well . . ."

"I owe it to you," he says quietly.

He means the test in the Shell, when I got between him and the dog. This is the first time he's brought it up since then, and I can tell he doesn't really want to talk about it. But if this is his way of saying thank you . . .

I sigh. "Doesn't sound like I have much choice."

"You never did," he says with a grin.

I wait for Jai deep in the Echo Wood, on a bank over a splashing stream. Our meeting place is a big mossy rock that juts over the water, shaped like a turtle's head. Jai and I found it last Sunday while we were exploring. Sundays are good for that—I usually manage to finish all my extra homework on Saturday, so I have the whole next day free. Most of the kids hit the computer lab or hang out around the lake, but the Echo Wood has become my favorite place to escape to besides the library. It reminds me of the forest back home, though of course, the sound of the Echo Wood is nothing like my old, normal trees.

I take out my flute, deciding to start with or without Jai. I have the nonet memorized, but even so, I take out the music sheet and rest it on my knees. I play the melody and don't miss a single note.

Below me, the stream crusts over with ice in response.

"Why can't I do that during class?" I moan.

Staring at the ice as it begins to melt again, I find my mind wandering back to the illusion test in the Shell, and the feeling of drowning I'd experienced. Since Miss March had played the calming spell, I haven't been dreaming about it, but every now and then, my thoughts return there anyway. And before I know it, it's like I'm sinking into the memory that's not quite a memory, groping in the dark for something — *anything* — concrete to hold on to. Panic begins to burn in my chest.

What happened that night?

Suddenly a wind picks up, blowing the sheet music from my lap. I lunge after it, nearly falling into the water, but the papers are quickly lost into the stream.

Wonderful. How will I explain that to Miss Noorani in class tomorrow?

Lying back, I shut my eyes and listen to the music of the echo trees, sighing, whispering notes so faint I can barely make them out. The air is thick and warm, making me sleepy, and I let out a long yawn. I kick off my too-tight shoes and let them clatter onto the ground, stretching my toes with relief.

Putting my flute to my lips, I start to play, half-asleep and lulled by the breeze.

I push away all the things worrying me — my pile of homework, keeping the truth of my Mystwick acceptance hidden, all those unanswered emails I've sent to Gran, the disturbing memory of the dark water.

Just like the day I got the Mystwick letter, I don't think — I just *listen* to the notes inside me trying to come out. They spark in my fingertips, guiding my hands, coiling from the flute in low, undulating scales. Mr. Pinwhistle would probably combust if he saw me lying on my back, lazily playing without a care, but I've been so stressed over getting everything perfect in class that it's nice to just let go. It's just me and the music, nothing in between, nobody to judge me, no one to impress.

I imagine myself playing so perfectly that the lake will freeze over from one end to the other, but I won't stop there. I'll make a whole *blizzard*. That will show them. *That* will make Miss Noorani believe that I belong here. We'll make snowmen and have a snowball fight and even Darby will be amazed . . .

The air turns chilly, and I shiver a bit, opening my eyes.

Blue curls of magic are rising from my flute, wrapping around my fingers and drifting through the air like feathers. They're hypnotizing. I feel trapped in my own spell, hardly thinking about what I'm doing. I close my eyes and lean into the music, letting it take control of my fingers. Last time this happened, I panicked. But now I don't fight back. I don't feel nervous or anxious. I just feel like . . . myself. Like this is me in my purest form.

The essence of Amelia.

I finish the spell with one long vibrato note that fades gently into silence.

"Amelia Jones!"

Startled, I open my eyes and sit up.

Jai is standing on the mossy stream bank, holding his violin case. He looks like he's seen a ghost.

"You're late," I say.

He says nothing, just keeps staring, until I start to squirm.

"What is it?" I pat my face, wondering if I splashed mud on myself or something when I crossed the stream. "What's wrong?"

"Amelia Jones," he says again, quieter this time. "Why didn't you tell me you could do that?"

"Do what?"

"Compose."

"I—" Surprised, I look down at my flute, then back up at him. "I wasn't Composing."

He sets down his violin and waves a hand, gesturing for me to make room. I scoot aside so he can sit on the rock beside me. His face is flushed and his eyes bright.

"That spell you played just now, what was it?"

"It . . . it wasn't anything. Just random notes. Me messing around."

"Have you *messed around* like that before?"

I shrug. "Once. Nothing really happened, though."

He jumps up and paces around the rock, fingers drumming against his case. "You have no idea, do you?"

"What are you *talking* about?"

Stopping dead, he looks me in the eye. "Amelia, you were Composing. Writing your own spell."

That makes me laugh. "No I wasn't! Composing is . . . is when you sit down with a pen and paper and work out melodies and harmonies and tempos. It's for, I don't know, old dead guys like Handel and Mozart and Schumann."

"No, it's not!" He stops walking and looks at me. "Or at least, it's more than just that. Composing is twisting raw magic into your own shape. It's *inventing* a spell on the spot, something completely new and unique. It takes an incredible amount of skill to control magic like that! It's like—like grabbing a tornado by the tail and tying it in a knot. Do you have any *idea* what this means?"

My heart is starting to pound faster. I don't understand what he's getting at, but I've never seen him so keyed up.

"It's not anything special, Jai. Anyone can make up music."

He laughs like he can't believe I said that. "Are you *serious?* Anyone can *try,* maybe, but most people would either make dud spells—music with no magic, what fun is that?—or the magic they did conjure would blow up in their faces."

"Hey! Some people like music just because it's *music,*" I say, thinking of my mom listening to the radio with her eyes shut, her hands lazily swirling to the beat. "Just because it isn't a spell doesn't mean it's not special. Or that it doesn't have its own kind of magic, the sort you *feel.*"

He waves my words away. "I'm talking about *serious* magic here. Try to focus! Do you know how rare Composers are?"

"Rare?" I laugh. "Okay, now I know you're just—"

"*Amelia. Petunia. Jones.* Listen to me!"

I frown. "*Petunia?* Really? That's your worst try yet."

He groans. "Listen to what I'm saying: there's a reason Composing without permission is against the rules at Mystwick."

"It's against the rules?" My stomach sinks. What if a Maestro had seen me?

"It's against the rules because it's incredibly dangerous! Do you know what happens when most people try to Compose?"

I shrug.

He kneels beside me. "When most people attempt Composing, *if* they produce any magic at all, they burn themselves up. Set their instruments on fire or warp the metal. Blind themselves, or char their hands. They start fires or even make explosions."

A chill goes down my spine. "I've never done any of those things."

"Because you're *actually* a Composer! Someone who can invent new spells. Amelia, this is huge. Don't you see? You're going to be rich! You could Compose spells for the best Maestros in the world! What kind do you think you'll do? Classical spells? Jazz? Rock? You can make *loads* of money doing rock spells, though my dad would say that's not *real* Musicraft. But who cares about that? You'll be famous!"

"But I didn't *do* anything. It was hardly a spell, Jai. Just music."

"Just music. *Just music!*" He stands up and points to the woods behind me. "Look what your *just music* can do."

Rolling my eyes, I turn to look—and freeze.

The woods behind me are covered in fresh snow.

It piles on the ground and on the branches of the echo trees, sparkling in the sun. Looking up, I see a small, wintry cloud formed over the canopy, but it's already dissipating.

Jai tramps into the snowdrifts and makes a snowball, then hurls it at me. I duck, but not fast enough, and it smashes my arm.

I wipe the snow from my sleeve and stare at it as it melts on my fingers, as cold and real and white as actual snow. It's no illusion spell, but elemental magic—one of the most difficult types, and this spell is far more powerful than anything I've ever done on my own before.

"I—I couldn't have done that," I say.

"*Amelia!* I watched you! I stood there and watched you create a snow cloud."

I *had* been thinking of snow when I played the music. But I shake my head, unable to believe it.

"Play it again," says Jai. "Don't you see? The Maestros will go crazy over you if they find out you can Compose!"

"I thought you said it was against the rules."

"To do it *alone*, yeah, because it's so dangerous. But if they know about it, they'll probably get you special training and everything. You'll be like a celebrity around here!"

I stare at him, my heart skipping a beat. Would Mrs. Le Roux be so impressed she'd forget about my test and just let me stay?

"Okay," I say quietly. "I'll do it again."

He nods eagerly, eyes rapt as I raise my flute to my lips.

But no matter how hard I try, I can't seem to make the spell work. I vaguely remember the tune I made up, but my fingers can't seem to replay it. I stumble and make mistakes until sparks begin bursting from my instrument instead of graceful curls of magic. The flute seems to be getting hotter and hotter.

"Amelia, stop!" Jai cries out. "You're going to make it explode!"

My fingers begin to burn.

With a shout, I drop my flute and it lands softly in the snow, which hisses as the heat turns it to steam. I bury my hands in the cold slush.

"Ow, ow, *ow* . . ." Moaning, I slump down and stare at my pink fingertips. "It's no good, Jai. I can only do it when I'm not *trying*. If I were to show the Maestros, I'd only make something terrible happen. They'd expel me in a heartbeat!"

He sighs. "Maybe you just need to practice it some more."

"No!" I yell, snatching my cooled flute from the snow. I hold out my burned hands to him. "I don't need practice, I don't need confidence, and I don't need your help! I'm hopeless, Jai. I'll never be like you and Claudia and Darby. You're all prodigies. You've had the best teachers and the best instruments and I . . . I'm just a chicken charmer, and maybe that's all I'll ever be."

"If that were true, you'd never have gotten into Mystwick in the first place. You're one of us!"

I stare at him, the truth clogging my throat for a moment. *I didn't get in! I'm not one of you!* But I don't have the guts to come clean with him and risk losing the only friend I have. So I slam my flute into its case and then jump over the stream. But I don't get a good enough start, and I just slip on the bank and land in the bottom, splashing mud and water all over myself.

Great.

I start to climb back up the bank, and a hand grabs mine and pulls me up. I collapse onto the leaves, panting.

"Thanks," I mutter, looking up.

But no one is there.

Jai is still behind me, on the other side of the creek.

A chill races over my skin.

What just happened?

Jai jumps across, landing beside me. "I'm only trying to help you, but you've got to want to help yourself."

He heads back toward the school, but I can't move. I'm still trying to figure out who—or what—grabbed my hand and helped me up the bank.

Did I imagine it? Am I going crazy?

Or am I not alone out here?

Shivering, I race to catch up to Jai. I can't get out of the woods fast enough.

CHAPTER FOURTEEN

Go Yell It on the Mountain

A WEEK LATER, MR. PINWHISTLE tells us Aeros we're going to go outside for class, and has us all bring our heaviest winter coats, even though it's still warm out.

George waves his in the air. "Are we going skiing? Or doing ice spells? Or—"

"Don't think for a minute that this will be *fun*," Mr. Pinwhistle warns. "In fact, it will be extremely dangerous."

Hooray. I need danger right now the way I need a case of pneumonia.

I suppress a yawn. My mind is foggy with exhaustion. I could curl up in my old blue jacket and go to sleep.

My nocturnal visitor was at it again last night, waking me up every few hours with the sound of rustling and a bright, glowing light. I finally told our dorm captain, Phoebe, about it, but she just said it was probably my imagination.

I know it wasn't.

I keep glancing at Darby, to see if she's yawning too. But if she's the one keeping me awake, she doesn't show any signs of exhaustion herself. She stands with a black pea coat folded primly over her arms.

Mr. Pinwhistle waits until we're quiet before saying, "For this exercise, we're going to need a little help."

He opens the door and steps back, waving someone into the classroom.

"Miss Myra," he says. "Please come in."

The old organist from the Mystwick zeppelin walks in with a crafty smile. Her sharp eyes sweep across the room, and I feel a knot of worry form in my stomach.

"Well, hello, my naive little turtles," she says. "Shall we begin?"

Five minutes later, I find myself standing on top of the tallest mountain peak for miles around. Mystwick is far, far below us, no bigger than a pea, and in every direction is a sheer cliff leading to instant death. All around us are jumbled boulders and pale clouds, with no sign of stairs or any other way down. Twenty-four other Aeros are shivering around me, eyes wide with shock. The cinnamon scent of Miss Myra's teleportation spell still lingers in the air.

Seconds ago, we were all standing in the Aero classroom, in a circle around Miss Myra as she played her organ, which Mr. Pinwhistle had rolled in himself. He told us that we were going somewhere only accessible by magic, and that we wouldn't need our instruments. So, like dummies, we left them behind.

So not only are we stranded *on top of a freezing mountain* with no way down, we don't have any magic to help us. And of course neither Mr. Pinwhistle nor Miss Myra bothered to come along for the trip. I imagine them both right now, warm and smug back in the Aero classroom, as I pull on my winter coat—that, at least, suddenly makes sense.

We're cut by a wind that's icy cold and dusty with snow. Even in our jackets, we huddle miserably like a bunch of freezing burritos.

At least I don't feel tired anymore.

"What the *heck?*" yells Claudia. "What is going on?"

"He hates us," Collin moans, looking dazed. "He hates us and he sent us up here to die."

"Oh, stop it," I say. "It's a lesson of some sort. We just have to figure it out."

Collin moans louder.

"Let's spread out," Darby says. "Look for a way down, or anything that might help."

It seems like the best plan. We take off in different directions, going slowly over the sharp rocks and slippery patches of ice. I work my way toward what looks like a path, only to find it ends at a cliff face. Shivering, I inch closer, until I'm a step away from the edge.

It's a long, long, *long* way down.

With a shudder, I back away.

Mr. Pinwhistle wouldn't just leave us here without some way to make magic. One of the only instructions he gave us was that when we were ready to come back, we should send him "a signal." Before we could ask what the heck *that* meant, Miss Myra began playing her organ, and it was so loud I could hardly hear myself think. And then—we were *here*.

Hearing a shout to my right, I climb back to the others and find them clustered around Jingfei, who's dragging something from behind a rock.

"I found it!" she yells. "I passed it three times first, though. It was pretty well hidden."

The thing is a chest, which Jingfei opens at once. We all lean over eagerly to see . . .

A stick.

Not instruments. Not a list of instructions. Not a map.

A stick.

Collin lets out a wail. *"We are going to die!"*

"Maybe it means something," I say. "Like, a riddle or a clue."

"Or maybe it's part of something else," says Claudia. "Everyone keep searching! Maybe there are more chests!"

We run in all directions, reenergized. I clamber all over the mountaintop, prying at anything that looks suspicious. The rocks are cold to the touch, and I blow on my hands to warm them.

Collin finds the next surprise: a pile of firewood at the highest point of the peak. We gather around it, stumped. With no instruments (and no matches), there's no way to light the wood.

"I bet this is what Mr. P meant by *signal*," says Jingfei.

"So how do we light it?" Claudia looks ready to snap. Her hair is frizzed by the wind and her eyes look reddened. But is that because of the cold — or was she possibly up all night, snooping in our room? I watch her a little more closely, waiting for a yawn or some other sign that she's my nighttime pest.

"I guess we keep searching," Jingfei sighs.

Groaning, the others disperse. But all we turn up is rocks, rocks, rocks. I don't know how long we've been out here, but it has to have been an hour already. Is there a time limit to this thing? If we're up here *too* long, will Mr. Pinwhistle have Miss Myra teleport us back? After all, we still have more classes to attend, and dinner, and study hall . . .

Surely he wouldn't leave us up here in the dark.

Right?

But another hour passes, and there's no sign that Mr. Pinwhistle even remembers we exist. We give up searching for more chests because there simply *aren't* any. We've moved every rock we can, scoured each inch of the peak, but finally we're forced to admit that the stick is our only hope.

Claudia does find a sort of cave, which is barely big enough for all of us to escape the wind. We huddle together, miserable, freezing, and now starving.

"Maybe if we beat the stick against a rock?" Collin suggests sadly. "Like, make some sort of rhythm?"

At least he's still trying.

But even if that were the answer, none of us are percussionists. And anyway, creating magic with nothing more than a beat is really hard, which is why Percussos usually use something like a xylophone or a glockenspiel when they're doing individual spellwork. So I don't see how a simple stick would help anyway.

George sniffs. "You know, guys, this is just the sort of place where the Necromuse would slip up behind you."

"Oh, for the love of Bach, shut up," snaps Claudia.

He shrugs and adjusts his glasses. "Just saying, watch your back."

"The Necromuse isn't real."

"Careful. That's exactly the sort of thing someone says . . . before he *strangles* them."

Claudia huffs and turns her back to George. But I scoot closer.

"So who is he, anyway?" I've always loved scary stories, and it's not like we're doing anything else right now.

"They say he's the devil's right-hand guy," says George, who, I have to admit, has a pretty fantastic scary-story voice. "He was banned from Musicraft a few years ago for playing black spells. He even has the Bars to prove it."

I know what the Bars are—metal staples clamped onto the ears of musicians who use magic for evil purposes. If they try to play a spell, or even get too close to someone else who is playing one, the Bars will set off a high-pitched tone in their ears that is *really* painful, enough to make them faint or claw their ears until they bleed. I've seen it in movies, and it's awful.

"The Necromuse is the bane of the Musicraft world," says George. "He raises the dead and binds them to his will—"

"How?" I ask. "If he's Barred, how can he even play spells?"

He gives me an annoyed look. "He plays *through* the pain. That's, like, his signature. You can tell who he is because his ears are always bleeding. Now as I was saying, before I was rudely interrupted, he raises the dead and—"

"Why?" I ask.

George blinks. "Why? Well . . . because he's evil, that's why."

"Yeah, but he still must have a *reason* to raise the dead. What does he want?"

"Want? He's a bad guy. Bad guys just like doing bad stuff. You know, for the heck of it."

I sigh. "I'd hoped this would be a better story."

George puts out his hands like he's a zombie and goes after Jingfei, pretending that he's trying to eat her head. Jingfei slaps his arm, not in the mood for dumb games.

"Stupid, stupid, stupid," says Claudia. "I can't believe I'm stuck up here with nothing but a bunch of idiots and a *stick*."

"It's not a stick," says Darby.

"Of course it's a stick. Don't be a—"

"It's a baton," says Darby. "For Conducting."

Everyone blinks.

"Oh," says Jingfei. "Really?"

"Why didn't you tell us that an *hour* ago?" Claudia asks.

Darby shrugs, twirling the baton. "What use is a baton without musicians to Conduct? We have no instruments."

"You still could have *told* us!"

For once, I agree with Claudia.

The others have given up, clearly. A couple of kids have curled up like they're going to sleep. No one talks. I guess now the plan is to wait until Mr. Pinwhistle swoops in to take us home.

Well, the others may be content to fail, but I'm not. The problem is, I don't know the first thing about Conducting.

But I know someone who does.

I go sit beside Darby, and as usual, she pretends I don't exist. But this time, I'm not going to give her what she wants by *also* pretending I don't exist.

"It was meant for you, wasn't it?" I say quietly. She's still holding the baton, and I point to it. "You knew it was. That's why you've had it all this time."

Her fingers tighten around it. "I'm not a Conductor."

"But I saw you, in that video with the other Amelia."

She sucks in a breath, shaking her head. "That was just for fun. We were . . . being silly."

"Well, we could really use some of that silly right about now. Darby, the baton wasn't put here by accident. It was meant for *you*. You have to get us off this mountain."

"How?" she demands, so loudly that the sleeping kids wake up. "*How*, Amelia? Even if I could Conduct, *who* would I Conduct?"

She turns away, hugging the baton to her stomach and hunching her shoulders.

With a sigh, I lean against the cave wall, staring out into the darkening sky. The wind is picking up, colder than ever. I pull my arms inside my shirt to keep them warm, but even so, I'm shivering so hard that my teeth clatter.

Then I see her.

A girl, standing just outside the cave.

"Hey!" I shout. "There's someone out there!"

Everyone jumps up. "Where? Who?"

"I don't see anyone," says Claudia.

I peer into the gloom, but the girl seems to have vanished.

"Jones's brain must have frozen," Collin gasps. "How long before *all* our brains freeze?"

Rolling my eyes, I take a quick count. All the Aeros are accounted for, so whoever I saw, it wasn't one of us. But I *know* someone was there.

"I'm going to look," I say.

"You're crazy!" Claudia shouts. "Come back here!"

"Let her go," says Darby, but not in a helpful sort of way —more of a hopeful, maybe-she'll-fall-off-a-cliff sort of way. My roomie really knows how to warm the heart.

Ignoring them all, I step into the icy wind and call out, "Hello?"

It's darker than I thought. I can barely see where I'm stepping, and the wind pushes at me so hard that I have to lean into it. The snow has turned to ice, which pelts me like bits of glass.

"Hello? Who's there?"

"Amelia . . ."

I whirl around, but can't tell which direction the voice came from.

Moving faster, clambering dangerously over the cold rocks, I search everywhere, until I lose sight of the cave and everyone inside. I force myself to slow down a little or else I really will fall off a cliff.

Then I spot her again.

She's standing . . . *in midair.*

And then I realize I've seen her before.

During my test in the Shell.

She tried to drown me in Miss Noorani's illusion river.

I can't make out anything except her vague form, like she's made of light, not flesh and blood, just like she was the last time I saw her. Is she some sort of illusion? A spell? If so, that means there's someone around here with an instrument. Someone with a way off this horrible mountain. But I don't hear any music.

"Hello?" I whisper. "Are . . . are you real? Why are you following me?"

I edge closer to the girl, holding out a hand, feeling for where the rock drops away.

Then she lunges at me.

With a scream, I fall backwards, my whole body going cold as she swoops *through* me. I hit the rocks hard, knocking the breath from my lungs. When I turn, I see no sign of the girl.

"Where are you?" I shout hoarsely, clutching my ribs. I stumble upright, raising a hand to block the sleet from stinging my eyes. But I'm completely alone again.

And suddenly, I know what the girl is.

The word is right there in front of me, but I'm almost too scared to think it.

Ghost.

CHAPTER FIFTEEN

Music Is There for Those Who Listen

THAT'S WHAT SHE LOOKED LIKE. That's what she *felt* like. But that's impossible, right? I mean, ghosts aren't *real*. It had to be an illusion—or, like Collin said, my brain's too frozen to think straight.

What am I *doing* up here?

How did I end up on a frozen mountain peak, thousands of miles from home, and now with a *ghost* following me?

At that moment, despair washes over me.

Maybe I *don't* belong here. Maybe I'm fighting for something I can never have.

It was easy enough to say I could do it when I had my flute in my hands, but right now, I have nothing. I came here to get answers about my mom—who was she? Am I anything like her? But instead, all I get is a possible, honest-to-Bach ghost. And she's not the only thing haunting me. I can still hear the squeaky A note from my audition, howling with the wind, reminding me every second that I'm not good enough.

Wait a minute.

That note isn't my imagination.

It's coming from above me.

I turn and look up, squinting in the gloomy light, until I see it: a hole in a rock, as neat and round as if it had been cut out with a pair of scissors. The wind is howling through it, creating an almost perfect A note.

Weird.

I stand up and walk closer, only to trip over another jutting rock. I reach out to pull myself up, and find another hole.

Then I see them *everywhere*.

All across the mountaintop, there are rocks with holes in them. You'd miss them completely if you weren't looking for them, because they're impossible to see without eyeing them straight on. That's probably why we didn't see them earlier. When I get closer, I can hear the wind howling through them at different pitches.

And then it all makes sense.

It's just like the school motto: *Music is there for those who listen.*

I run back to the cave as quickly as I can, shouting for the others. Because of the wind, they don't hear me until I'm just steps away. I skid to a halt, breathless, and gasp out, "I know what to do! I know what to do!"

A few people look up curiously, but Claudia scowls. "Let me guess. You saw an entire freaking *elephant* this time?"

185

Ignoring her, I walk to Darby. "You said if we had instruments, you could Conduct us."

She looks up. "That's not exactly what I—"

"I found instruments."

Now everyone jumps up, looking interested. Even Claudia folds her arms, waiting for me to explain.

Skipping the part about the ghost, or illusion, or whatever she was, I tell them about the holes in the rocks, and how the wind makes different pitches as it whistles through them. At first they look doubtful, but then they follow me out to have a look themselves.

"Listen!" shouts Collin. He puts a hand over one of the holes, blocking the wind and stopping the sound it makes. Then he removes his hand and the note sounds again.

"This is it," says Claudia. "The *mountain* is our instrument!"

"The holes are spread out," I say. "But there are twenty-five of them. We each take one and put our hands over the holes, then remove them to play the spell. It's sort of like handbells, where we all are in charge of different notes. This is how we light the signal fire!"

"But there are only twenty-five holes," says Claudia. "And there are twenty-six of us."

I nod. "That's because Darby has a different job." I turn to look at my roommate, who stands silently with the baton at her side. "Every orchestra needs a Conductor. She has to be in charge of the spell, making sure we play together."

Darby looks down at the baton, then up at me, her eyes wide. "I—I can't."

"Yes, you can," I say. "Or is someone else here trained to Conduct?"

No one volunteers.

"Well, that's settled then," Claudia says. "Darby's Conducting, and each of us takes a wind-hole thing. Anyone have an idea for a spell to light the firewood?"

"The Itsy-Bitsy Spider," I say at once.

She rolls her eyes. "That's a *drying* spell, Jones."

"So speed up the tempo. Trust me. It will work."

She looks doubtful, but shrugs.

It takes a few minutes to get everyone organized, and then we have to figure out which holes make which notes. We arrange ourselves in a scale, after discovering that all together, the holes cover four octaves. It takes a bit of arguing before we settle on an arrangement that uses all the notes. As I point out, it's going to take each of us playing to generate a powerful enough spell to light the cold, wet firewood. Finally, though, we get it worked out and move into our places. Some of the holes are difficult to reach, and a few students have to lie on their stomachs or stand on tiptoe.

Darby reluctantly takes up position where we can all see her, though we can't all see each other. She somehow has to remember which of us has which notes, and get us all to play them at the right time. Meanwhile, we each have to focus on the pile of firewood, which we can see above us on the highest rock, behind Darby.

"Ready?" Darby shouts over the wind.

I nod, my hand clamped over the hole in my rock. Claudia's on my left, and Collin on the right.

The first time we try to play the spell, it goes terribly. Darby mixes up the notes, and we don't even produce a single wisp of magic.

Frustrated, she has us start over. Her baton bobs to keep the tempo, but more importantly, she points at whoever's turn it is to play. The second time, Collin misses her direction and doesn't release his note in time, and the spell bungles again.

"Hey, Collin!" shouts George. "Pay closer attention to your A hole!"

George laughs so hard at his own stupid joke that we have to wait a whole minute before starting again. Three more times we fail, but on the fifth try, we finally manage to get a bit of smoke off the firewood.

It's still not enough.

"We have to play faster!" I say.

"This spell isn't working!" Claudia argues. "We should try Haydn's Fifty-Ninth Symphony."

"Claudia." I give her a flat look. "We're playing with *rocks*. We can't exactly grind out a symphony here."

"The problem isn't the spell!" shouts Darby. "It's me! I keep messing up."

"You're doing great!" I call back.

"No, I'm *not!*"

"Just try one more time!"

Her eyes are glittering with tears, but she raises her baton. I draw a deep breath, then focus myself once more. This *has* to work.

This time, we succeed—sort of. As our notes sound— hollow, breathy tones that remind me of a pan flute—streams of blue magic curl from the rocks, looking ghostly in the twilight. I've never seen magic done like this before, and it makes my skin break out in goose bumps that have nothing to do with the cold. This isn't just any spell.

This is *big magic*.

This is what I came to Mystwick to learn.

I watch the flickering magic as it coils through the air, hoping it will reach the wood, that the signal will light, that we'll *finally* get off this mountain.

But instead of the firewood catching flame, Darby's baton does.

She yelps and drops it, the slim rod crackling with fire at one end.

"Don't let it go out!" I yell, leaving my rock to sprint toward her. I grab the baton and cup my hand around the flame. "We can still make it!"

Darby stares at the flaming baton. "I messed it up," she whispers. "I was concentrating on the baton, making sure I kept the tempo, instead of —"

"Forget it!" I say, and I take off, jumping from rock to rock, making my way toward the pile of wood. The flame on the baton starts shrinking.

"Hang in there," I mutter. "C'mon, c'mon . . ."

I reach the wood just in time, managing to stick the baton into the smaller kindling at the bottom. The twigs catch fire and I desperately blow on them, for once grateful that Gran made me join Girl Scouts in her quest to persuade me to give up Musicraft. In moments, a steady blaze has spread across the wood. With a sigh of relief, I hold out my hands, relishing the warmth.

The rest of the class gathers around, looking just as relieved, but we're all too tired and cold to cheer. Darby hangs back, sitting on a rock with her back to us.

Cautiously, I approach her. "Darby? Are you okay?"

"Leave me alone, Jones."

"You did it. You got us to create fire."

"Not the right way. *You're* the one who lit the signal. I couldn't even focus long enough to finish one stupid spell." Now she

turns a bit, but doesn't look me in the eye. "I'm an oboist, Jones. And I'm a really good one. But I'm not a Conductor. Not anymore. That was . . . that was something I only did with *my* Amelia. She got me into it. And ever since she died . . ." She turns away again. "Just leave me alone, will you?"

Sighing, I go back to the fire and sit.

A few minutes later, a rock beside the bonfire jiggles, and Jingfei—who'd been sitting on it—jumps aside with a shout. The rock slides away, and from beneath it pops Mr. Pinwhistle.

We all stare at the Maestro, and he glares back.

The rock was covering the way down the whole time—a deep, square hole with a ladder inside.

"Took you long enough. Now what are you waiting for?" he growls. "I'm freezing my butt off! Let's go!"

It's a long climb down the ladder to a tunnel in the heart of the mountain. My cold fingers make it hard to grip the rungs, but at least I'm not the only one. We're all stiff and slow.

Once on level ground, we follow Mr. Pinwhistle closely through the dark tunnel, since he's the only one with a flashlight. The walls are rough stone, the floor mud, and eerie dripping sounds echo around us. I wonder how deep this cave system goes, and hope I never have to find out. Who knows what other kind of demented tests Mr. Pinwhistle has up his sleeves?

And yet, for all the pain this little "exercise" was, I can't help but feel proud of my part in solving it. Maybe now the others will take me more seriously.

After what feels like hours of walking, the tunnel ends in the Echo Wood, just behind Harmony Hall. The dark trees are almost welcoming after the mountain. They're still tonight, no wind to stir their magic. In silent single file, we leave the woods and make for the hall, but before he lets us go inside, Mr. Pinwhistle stops us.

"Well?" he grunts. "What did you learn?"

There's a moment of silence. Jingfei coughs.

Finally, Collin bravely raises a hand. "Um . . . to always bring a jacket to class? Just in case?"

Mr. Pinwhistle sighs long and deep, his hand dragging across his face. "Anyone else?"

"Music is there for those who listen," I whisper.

"Eh?" Mr. Pinwhistle cups a hand around his ear. "What did you say?"

I swallow, then say louder, "Music is there for those who listen?"

He lowers his hand, giving me a thoughtful look. "Well. Now, that *is* an important lesson, isn't it? Also, for those of you who care, remember that you should never rely too much on traditional instruments. A little imagination can come in handy when you're in a tight spot, and there's more than one way to make music. Anyway, go inside and get your dinner. I suspect it's cold by now. And don't forget, we have a transposing test tomorrow."

An hour later, I'm finally lying in my bed, full after a meal of tomato soup and grilled cheese—which, contrary to Mr. Pinwhistle's prediction, the cafeteria had kept warm for us. Phoebe even brought us hot chocolate, with a knowing look on her face that tells me the mountaintop test must be a yearly thing.

Darby is a silent bundle of blankets across the room, probably already asleep. We haven't spoken again since Mr. Pinwhistle appeared to take us back, and I realize it was too much to hope things between us might have changed. She still seems determined to ignore me and everyone else.

But right now, it's hard to be upset about that. I've never been so happy to be so warm.

Then I remember the girl on the mountain.

The see-through girl who hovered in midair and attacked me as if she was trying to *make* me fall off the cliff.

My mind spins like a hamster wheel.

The wind that messed up my apple-peeling test. The person shining lights in my room all night long. The girl who tried to drown me during my test in the Shell.

Somehow, I just *know* they're all connected, and the girl I saw on the mountain is the cause.

Maybe it's time to finally admit the truth I've been too afraid to face:

Someone at Mystwick *is* trying to sabotage me.

And that someone is a ghost.

CHAPTER SIXTEEN

Nothing but Treble

"THE SECRET OF COMPOSING," intones a deep, dramatic voice from behind the library shelves, "has nothing to do with the notes written or the key chosen; rather, a spell's purpose is directly linked to the emotional desires of its Composer."

"Jai," I groan, "I told you to leave it alone."

It's been several days since the mountaintop test. I'm trying to find a book on memory spells—maybe there's something here that can help me recall the drowning memory I still haven't been able to remember—but he's been following me around for the past twenty minutes, reading from a Composing book, trying to get me interested. I pull out an index of white spells and Jai's face appears in the gap left behind.

"Hey," he says defensively. "I said I was going to help you, and that's what I'm doing."

"By getting me kicked out? Composing is against the rules. And where did you even find that book?"

He waves the copy of *Composing: Basics for Beginners*. "Snagged it from behind the librarian's desk when she was helping Collin find a spell to cure his pimples. There are all kinds of books back there they don't want us to know about. I heard my dorm captain talking about them—apparently only teachers have access to that shelf."

I roll my eyes and slide the index back into its place, having found nothing useful in it, but Jai comes around the corner, the book open in his hands.

"According to this, whether a spell is green, blue, white, or yellow has nothing to do with the notes themselves, which is why two spells can sound very similar but *do* totally different types of magic. It's all about the Composer, and what they were *thinking* when they wrote the spell for the first time. So when you Composed that snow spell—"

"I was thinking about snow," I murmur.

He nods, his eyes bright. "See? It's not complicated at all. You just have to focus really hard on what you want the magic to do when you Compose the melody. According to this book, it's all about maintaining something called *purity of focus*." His eyes scan the page. "Some people think every spell has a piece of its Composer's *soul* trapped inside of it."

"That's ridiculous," I say, even as my scalp tingles at the thought. "Seriously, Jai. I can't think about Composing right now. I have bigger problems."

Now that I've realized I'm being haunted, I've started seeing evidence of my ghost everywhere.

A few days ago, in Orchestra, Mr. Pinwhistle had us play a concerto that should have made us all levitate an inch off the ground. He told us that if we wanted, we could experiment with harmonies, improvising a little to add to the spell's strength, like a lot of students did during the Planting Ceremony. I decided to follow the written notes, figuring it's better to nail the melody than to try something fancy and end up ruining the spell for everyone.

Except that when I'd tried, I'd lost control of my flute.

The keys started pressing in weird combinations with a mind of their own. I stared in shock, my own hands frozen as my instrument went completely bananas. I stopped blowing, but the keys kept clicking, pressed by invisible fingers.

It was then that I'd realized I was not alone.

It was *her*, trying to mess me up.

"No!" I'd shouted. "Just leave me alone!"

Everyone turned to look at me, a few students falling out of tempo and missing notes, but they recovered quickly. Because, after all, *they* weren't being targeted by some maniac from beyond the grave.

My face had been on fire. I couldn't exactly explain to them that I was yelling at a sabotaging ghost, could I? I raised my flute, hoping I could still salvage the situation, but then Mr. Pinwhistle marched up to me and took it right out of my hands.

"Miss Jones," he growled, "if you wish to act like a child, you ought to use a child's instrument."

I had to play a plastic kazoo for the rest of the class, like a five-year-old.

Things just got worse after that.

The next day, in Theory of Musicraft, my report on traditional Egyptian healing magic flew off my desk like there was a strong wind. But we were indoors, and it didn't happen to anyone else. Even Miss Noorani looked irritated with me. Jingfei —whose presentation on Chinese navigational spells was interrupted by me chasing down sheets of paper—"accidentally" spilled her apple juice on me at dinner as payback.

In my one-on-one session with Mr. Pinwhistle later that day, I'd stared in horror as behind his back, the magnetic music notes on the whiteboard began to move, rearranging themselves to spell a word, R-E-S-O-P- At first I didn't get it, but then I realized the ghost was spelling backwards—the word POSER. I rushed to the board and scrambled them before Mr. Pinwhistle could see, my heart racing.

He'd stared at me like I'd gone insane.

But what could I say? That a ghost was trying to get me expelled by telling him I'm a poser, a fake? It's not like he doesn't already think it every time he looks at me. The other students might not know I'm here by accident, but the Maestros do, and everything the ghost does to trip me up only makes me look worse in their eyes.

The more it's happened, the more convinced I've become that it's not just my imagination.

The ghost is real, and she's determined to get me expelled.

Looking at Jai now, his nose glued to the book on Composing, I almost tell him everything—about me taking the other Amelia's place, my upcoming test to prove I belong at Mystwick, the ghost . . .

But if he believes me, he'll probably just try to fix that too. I can't get him on the ghost's bad side with me, not after everything he's done to try to help me. And if he *doesn't* believe me, he'll think I'm nuts and probably stop hanging out with me at all. Or worse, he'll realize I don't belong here, that I'm not the musician he thought I was, and he'll know I've been lying to him this whole time. He's my only real friend here. If I lose him, I think I might lose hope altogether.

"Thanks," I say to Jai. "Really. But even if I *might* be able to Compose, I can't risk it. I can barely play normal, not-against-the-rules spells—I'd definitely blow something up trying to invent my own music."

"Look," Jai says, shutting the book. "We're friends, right?"

"Um, I guess so."

"You *guess* so? That's your problem right there!"

"Huh?"

"Confidence, Amelia Polly Jones! We *are* friends. You *are* a good musician. Why can't you just believe that instead of always feeling sorry for yourself? Your magic is only as strong as—"

"—*my belief.* I know, I know!" I throw my hands up. "You keep saying that!"

He sighs. "And yet it never seems to stick. If you could just *try* Composing again—"

"Will you stop pushing me? I told you a million times, it's not going to work!" I turn and walk away before he can start reading from that stupid book again. He'll get in who-knows-how-much trouble if Miss March catches him with it, anyway.

"Hey!" he shouts, getting a loud shushing from everyone else on that floor.

Ignoring him, I mumble something about needing to practice and hurry away.

But instead, I go back to the dorm, having come to one terrible and final conclusion: I have to fix this myself. And before I can do that, I need to know *why* this is happening to me.

It's time to have a chat with the ghost.

I plan my ambush for Friday night. Even though I'm so tired I could collapse, I sit up on my bed after Darby nods off. I'm prepared—I snuck some ice cubes from dinner in my pocket.

They're mostly melted now, and my clothes are soaked, but there's enough left of them to hold in my hands, put down my shirt, anything to keep me awake.

By midnight, though, they've all melted, and I have nothing but wet pajamas to show for it.

Leaning against the wall, I squint hard into the dark, waiting to see if my nightly visitor will appear. This time, she's not getting away with it. This time, I'm prepared.

As long as I don't lose my nerve. It's not like I've ever dealt with a ghost before.

I borrowed a camera from Jingfei, telling her I wanted to take pictures of the campus to send to my gran. But in truth, I'm going to try to get a picture of the ghost. The camera's in my hand, turned on and ready to go at a moment's notice. My flute is in my other hand. I'm not sure what I'll need it for, but it's best to be prepared.

Just got to stay awake.

Just got to keep my eyes open.

Just got to . . .

I wake with a start, panicking.

Darby's clock beams that it's almost three in the morning. In the dim glow, her form hunches under her covers, black hair spread across the pillow.

After I fell asleep, I must have slumped over onto the sheets.

There's a wet patch of drool under my face, and it comes away in a gross string as I sit up.

I snatch up the camera and turn it back on, thinking *something* must have woken me up.

And that's when I get the chill.

It starts in my scalp and creeps down my body like a ring of ice. I have goose bumps straight down to my toes. It's like I jumped into the cold lake. When I exhale in surprise, my breath forms a little white cloud over my face.

Then I *feel* it: a presence in the room, right behind me.

I whirl around toward the door, raising the camera. The shutter clicks, flooding the room with light and momentarily blinding me. Darby bolts up with a yelp.

"What the—"

Then she stops, because she sees it too:

The ghost.

It's a girl, all right. Or something *like* a girl. Long dress, long hair, her back to us, every bit of her silver-white and transparent. Her feet hover above the ground and her hair floats around her shoulders. But as soon as we set eyes on her, she turns, too fast for me to see much more than a flash of startled eyes.

Then she's gone, vanishing all at once.

"Find her!" Darby shouts, falling out of bed and fumbling for the knob.

I gape at her. *"What?"*

She doesn't wait for me, but yanks open the door and bursts into the hallway. Gritting my teeth, I drop the camera and run after her, my heart pounding and my whole body cold. I've never been so scared in my life, but I can't let Darby get murdered by a ghost in the middle of the night.

Or can I?

As I run after her, I do, for a minute, reconsider.

But in the dark hallway, I don't see that Darby has stopped dead. I smack into her, and we both crash to the floor.

All down the hallways, lights flicker on. Doors open and heads poke out.

Darby and I untangle ourselves. She's pale and breathing hard, looking . . . well, like she's seen a ghost.

"Gross," she says. "Why are you all *wet?*"

"It's not what you think!" I say quickly.

"*What* is going on?" Our captain, Phoebe, storms down the hallway, clearly not impressed with us for waking everyone up.

I start to say "Gho—"

But Darby throws her elbow into my ribs. *Hard.*

"She means, we were *going* to the bathroom," Darby says. Then she glares at me.

"Well," says Claudia, snickering at me, "looks like you were too late."

"It's *ice!*" My face flushes with heat. "Ice melted on my PJs!"

"Everyone back to bed!" Phoebe orders. "If you have to pee, go now, because I don't want to hear a single peep for the rest of the night!"

Darby and I head back to our room, enduring a lot of glaring eyes on the way. She walks rigidly, sticking close to me like she's worried I'll break and tell everyone what we saw. I don't know what she's playing at, but clearly she wants to keep this between us.

Once we're back in our room, she shuts the door and whirls to face me.

"Don't. Tell. *Anyone.*"

"Why?" I pace the narrow floor between our beds, my hands digging through my hair. "Darby. That was a *ghost.* There was a *ghost* in our *room.*"

I remember the camera and grab it off the bed. I pull up the screen and click through a million selfies of Jingfei before I finally find it: the photo I took just before the ghost ran away.

Darby looks over my shoulder.

We both suck in our breaths.

There she is, vague and filmy, looking like nothing more than a blurry wisp of smoke. I can't show this to anyone, at least, not as the proof I need. They'll just say it's a weird glare or something.

But I know better. And so does Darby.

"She's real," I whisper.

Darby meets my gaze. She looks not terrified, but excited.

As if finding a ghost in our room at three in the morning is a *good* thing.

"Oh, she's real," she says. "And I know who she is."

"You . . . do?"

I swallow as Darby leans toward me, grinning like a jack-o'-lantern.

"It's her," she says. "It's *Amelia Jones*."

CHAPTER SEVENTEEN

Dead Girls Tarantella No Tales

"Darby! Darby, this is crazy!" I have to jog to keep up with her. It's pouring rain, and we have to practically swim from breakfast to the library. In addition to the downpour, it's getting colder each day as fall marches toward winter. I've got my sweater buttoned over my flute case, as extra protection against the water. Darby's wearing a huge poncho that makes her look like a ghost herself, albeit a shockingly yellow one. I'm pretty sure that poncho would be visible from space, it's so bright.

"If that's all you're going to say," Darby says, "then leave. I don't need your help anyway."

"Shouldn't we at least *tell* someone? Miss Noorani, maybe?" With Darby to back me up, maybe that's all the proof the Maestros will need.

But Darby doesn't even bother replying.

After shoving down breakfast, she took off at a sprint, and I couldn't let her do any investigating without me. I hurry behind, yawning with exhaustion. We didn't sleep a wink the rest of the night, but stayed up talking. I told her about all the weird stuff that had been happening to me, and how I thought I was being sabotaged by the ghost.

"Why?" Darby had asked.

"Huh?"

"*Why* is she trying to sabotage you?"

I'd been caught off guard, able to only stammer a weak lie: "Because . . . she must be jealous, you know, that I'm hanging out with her old best friend."

But she'd seemed unconvinced.

We reach the library doors and slip inside, shaking rain off our clothes and shoes. I wince at the puddle we leave on the carpet, but we're not the only ones. Everyone inside is soaked through, even Miss March, who's shelving books on our left with her pan flute, her spell sending each one back to its spot on dusty golden streams of magic.

"Don't drip on the books!" orders Miss March. Then she mutters, "Strange weather. Strange weather, indeed . . ."

I glance past her at the phone on the library counter, where kids are lined up to call their parents, and remember it's been a while since I tried to call Gran. But my guilt turns into anger—if she really wanted to talk to me, she'd answer one of the dozens of emails I've sent. Anyway, even if I did call, what would I say? *Hey, Gran, don't worry about me, everything's fine and class is great and oh, by the way, I'm being haunted by the ghost of the girl whose spot I stole, no big deal, gotta run now! Bye!*

Yeah, right.

Darby heads upstairs, with me close behind, unable to get two words in. On the third floor, she goes straight to the computers and sits hard in an empty chair. Her fingers fly on the keys, pulling up the digital card catalog. Every spell in the library is logged here for easy lookup.

Dragging a chair from the next desk, I sit and watch over her shoulder as she types in: SPELL FOR CONTACTING GHOST.

She pounds the Enter key, and a little loading symbol pops up — a tiny metronome clicking, clicking, clicking . . .

Then the screen goes black.

A little message appears in red letters: ERROR. REQUEST DENIED.

"That's weird," Darby mutters. "What—"

Another message pops up: BLACK SPELLS ARE FORBIDDEN AT THE MYSTWICK SCHOOL OF MUSICRAFT.

We stare at the screen. Darby looks like she's about to punch through the glass. My heart pounds in my chest like a furious tarantella, notes galloping and tumbling through me.

I frown. "Here's what I don't get. If black spells aren't real, then why are they against the rules? That's like saying it's against the rules to ride a unicorn in Harmony Hall. Or summon a fairy to do your homework for you."

Darby slams her fists on the keyboard, rattling the whole table and all the computers on it. The other kids sitting there look up, startled.

"What's the use of a school of Musicraft," she growls, "if they won't teach you the most important spells?"

"Um . . . okay, well, I'd never filed ghost communication under *most important* before, but—" When she turns her glare on me, I quickly add, "But I can see why you're upset."

She lets her face fall into her hands. "We just need a plan."

"Right. So, I was thinking . . . maybe it's time to tell the Maestros."

"No!"

Her shout is so loud everyone on the third floor says *"Shh!"* at the same time.

Darby leans close, her eyes blazing. She's like an entirely different person right now.

"This isn't the only place at Mystwick where we can get spells," she says.

"Look, if you want to talk to the ghost so badly, just wait around a bit. She'll show up sooner or later—probably *sooner* —trying to yank my flute away or something."

"And you're just going to *let* her?" Darby gives me a disgusted look. "You really are nothing like my Amelia. She wouldn't let some dead girl push her around. She'd take action. *She'd—*"

"Fine, fine!" I throw my hands up. "You win. Just please stop telling me what the *other* Amelia would do, all right?" I do enough of that myself.

"Come on, then, and no more wimping out."

She stands up and charges back to the stairs. Sighing, I run after her. Whatever she's up to next, I don't know if I should leave her alone to do it. I've never seen her like this. She's all fired up, ready to snap.

I nearly bowl over Jai when I go running down the stairs after Darby.

"Whoa!" he says, rubbing his ribs where we'd collided. "Is this how you just are, naturally? Like a walking tornado?"

"Sorry."

He's blocking the way down, his arms wrapped around a book — the Composing book, I realize.

"I managed to get a slot in the best practice room, after dinner," he says. "It's far away from any other rooms, so we could, I don't know . . . maybe try to get you to conjure up another snowstorm?"

"Jai! Shh!" Looking down, I see Darby's almost at the first floor. "I told you, I can't do that again. It's too risky."

"I've been reading up," he says, tapping the book. "There's some good stuff in here that might help—"

"*Jai.* I'm in the middle of something with Darby right now."

"What? You two are, like, friends now?" He presses his

hands to his head in mock terror. "Is this some kind of alternate universe? Have I woken up in the right reality?"

"Oh, shut up and come on!" I grab him by the backpack and pull him along. He yelps, but falls into step beside me, shoving the book back into his bag.

"What's going on? Hey, wait! My umbrella's back there!"

He grabs it and opens it, shielding his violin case. Then we burst through the front doors and into the rain. Darby is a short distance ahead, making for the Shell, her oboe case jutting under her poncho like a third arm. She doesn't even look back to see if I'm still following.

"Last night, Darby and I saw a ghost in our room," I explain.

Jai stops dead. "Okay. Either I *did* wake up in an alternate universe, or you're making fun of me."

Sighing, I turn to face him. "Look, someone's been trying to sabotage me and I think it's the ghost and Darby thinks so too. She thinks . . ." I draw a deep breath, then finish, "She thinks it's the ghost of Amelia Jones. The *other* Amelia Jones."

He blinks at me, then slowly backs away, pointing his umbrella at me like a defensive sword. "Okay . . . Clearly you two have been playing one too many mental spells—"

"She's telling the truth," says a voice.

We turn to see Darby standing a short distance away, the rain plastering her hair to her face.

She glares at me. "Why did you tell him? I thought I said *no* telling *anyone!*"

"He can help us!" And maybe help *me* keep Darby under control. She's in a wild mood that makes me almost as nervous as the ghost of Other Amelia herself.

"I can?" Jai echoes.

"He's a great violinist," I say. "Whatever spell you're looking for, he can help us play it."

"I *can?*"

"If it's a black spell, we'll need all the help we can get," I add.

"A *what* spell?" Jai waves his hands. "Whoa, whoa, whoa. Let's just back up a few—"

"Ugh!" Darby growls, and she turns away, chewing her lip. Then she whirls back to us. "Fine! But if you tell even one more person, ghosts will be the *last* thing you need to worry about!"

"Fine!" I shout.

"Fine!"

"Uh . . . ladies," says Jai, raising his hands. "I don't remember agreeing to—"

"Come *on,*" Darby snaps, and she drags him along by his umbrella.

"So, what are we waiting for, exactly?" Jai asks.

He's trapped between Darby and me. We're crouched behind a statue of Beethoven next to the Shell, watching a little side door into the concert hall. The rain is coming down sideways, but we're all so drenched by now that we barely notice. Our instruments are sheltered under Jai's umbrella; like the musicians we are, we're far more worried about keeping them dry than ourselves.

When we tried the door, it was locked. I suggested we wait until it stops raining and then try an unlocking spell with our room key whistles; Darby pointed out it wouldn't work, since every door only opens to a unique set of notes, and it could take years to figure out the melody to open this particular one.

"Someone will come soon," she says. "They'll unlock the door, and we'll slip in behind."

"Or we could try the front doors," Jai replies. "They're always open."

She shakes her head. "There's no access to the basement from inside. This is the only way in."

"How do you even know that?" he grumbles, half to himself.

"What's in the basement, Darby?" I ask.

"Someone who can help us."

"Someone who'll skin us alive," Jai adds. "Rebel Clef meets down there."

"Rebel who?" I ask.

"The school rock club. Which happens to include some of Mystwick's biggest and meanest."

I swallow hard, starting to feel bad for dragging him into this. "I guess you can leave if you want."

"No he can't," Darby says quickly. "He knows too much. He stays."

Jai gulps.

So we wait. At least the rain slacks off a bit, but thunder begins booming over the mountains. *Another* storm moving in. It seems there are more and more of them every day.

Strange weather, indeed, Miss March had said to herself.

If we don't get inside quickly, we'll be stuck in a monsoon.

Darby might be convinced someone will come by before long, but I'm starting to doubt it. It's a good thing it's Saturday, or we'd have missed two classes already. Jai's stomach growls. He takes a bag of peanuts from his backpack.

"So, how do you know it's the other Amelia?" he asks. "Not that I believe there's a ghost, but say I did, for like, five minutes. Why her?"

"Because," Darby says, "Amelia Jones was the only person I ever knew who actually pulled off a black spell."

I stare at her. She hadn't told me that before.

Jai freezes, a peanut halfway to his mouth. Then, slowly, he lowers it. "Say *what* now?"

Darby looks away, her eyes distant. "A year ago, Amelia told me she had found a spell. A *black* spell."

"You didn't actually see her do it?" I ask.

She shakes her head. "But she wouldn't lie to me. We're—we *were*—best friends."

"So what was the spell?" asks Jai.

"Her dog got hit by a car, and Amelia said she used the spell to bring it back to life."

His jaw drops open. "A resurrection spell?"

Darby nods.

"But that's impossible!" Jai looks angry. "Resurrection spells are just stories. Like the Necromuse, raising up evil zombie servants. If resurrection spells are real, why didn't my dad use one when my grandpa died last year?"

"Black spells are the most powerful of all," Darby says, and for once, her tone is actually gentle. She looks at Jai with pity. "But they're also the hardest to play. Like, really, *really* hard. The best Maestros in the world can't play them. Or if they try, and they mess them up, things go very bad, very fast. Amelia told me that the spell she used had been used before, by another musician who tried to resurrect his dead sister. But he messed it up, and the sister came back . . . *wrong*. It was like her body had come back without her soul. She burned down their house with both of them inside."

"That's not true," scoffs Jai. "It would have been all over the news, and we'd have heard about it."

"Why do you think we didn't?" she snaps. "Grownups don't want to admit that black spells are real. They wouldn't publish that kind of story. Because if everyone knew they existed, they'd be trying to bring back the dead all over the place, or other stuff that would have terrible consequences. They're forbidden because they mess with laws that shouldn't be bent — things like life and death."

"You seem willing to bend them," I point out.

Darby shrugs. "I never said I was perfect. Anyway, I don't see *you* running in the other direction either."

She's got me there. This is the only way for her to talk to her dead friend, and I want to stop her dead friend from destroying my life. I guess neither of us has much choice.

Shaking my head, I ask, "But *how* would Amelia come back as a ghost? It's not like she could have played a black spell while she was dead."

"Maybe someone else summoned her," says Jai, who is apparently now a believer. "And let's think . . . who around here would *want* to summon Dead Girl?"

He eyes Darby.

"Hey!" Darby snarls. "First of all, her name isn't *Dead Girl!* And believe me, I wish I *had* summoned her. But I didn't."

"Why is she bothering our Amelia anyway?" asks Jai.

Hastily, before either can give that too much thought, I cut in. "Maybe we're going about this all wrong. What if we just try to talk to her? You know, ask politely? No magic necessary?"

Darby shakes her head. "You saw her run when we spotted

her. She's probably worried we'll try to banish her back to the realm of the dead."

"And . . . we *aren't* going to do exactly that?" Jai asks. "She's trying to get Amelia—*this* Amelia—expelled!"

Darby shrugs. "I don't see a problem."

I groan. How did she get to be in charge of this mission anyway? I don't remember voting to make her leader. And clearly she has no issue getting me kicked out.

"There," Darby says, pointing. "Told you."

A student is hurrying over from the cafeteria, carrying a guitar case on his back. He looks like a senior. When he reaches the locked door, he plays a quick tune on an ocarina he takes from his pocket—too soft for us to hear—and the door opens.

"Now!" Darby hisses. She yanks on a string wrapped around her finger; it stretches all the way to the door and around a rock by the wall. When she pulls on it, the rock shifts and slips to jam the door open, just slightly. The kid who went in doesn't even notice.

Darby grins. "Open sesame."

"Not bad," Jai says, impressed.

"You go in first," Darby says. "Tell us when the coast is clear."

"*Me?*"

Before he can argue further, Darby gives him a firm push through the door. "Signal when he's out of sight!"

"Fine, fine," Jai grumbles. "But I'd like to have it formally noted that I *strongly object to this plan.*"

"Move that skinny butt, Kapoor," growls Darby.

Jai makes a face at her, then creeps into the dark hallway. I start to step in behind him, but Darby grabs my shoulder and shoves me into the wall. I gasp, surprised at how strong she is.

"Darby! What are you—"

"We need to talk."

"Now?"

"It was no coincidence, was it?" she whispers, her eyes piercing mine. "You being here, being my roommate. Another Amelia Jones."

My heart begins to sink. I only stare at her, speechless.

She looks like she's about to shake me, as if that could rattle the truth out of me. "You were never supposed to get into Mystwick, were you? You're obviously behind everyone else, always messing us up in the orchestra and ensembles. You've been last chair in Aeros since the first week of class. So I have to ask myself, *how* does a musician as terrible as you get into a place like this? And why would *my* best friend return from the grave just to haunt *you?*"

My mouth is so dry I can't even answer her.

"I don't know how it happened," she breathes through her teeth, "but you *stole* her place."

"It was an accident," I whisper, going limp. "I got your

Amelia's acceptance letter. It was a mix-up. But the Maestros are giving me a chance to prove I have what it takes. Please, *please* don't tell anyone. Not even Jai."

Even as her eyes burn with anger, she blinks away a tear. She finally releases me, just as Jai calls out that the hallway is clear.

"I know what you are now, Amelia Jones," Darby says. "But I want to talk to my friend. So we do this *my* way. Or I'll make sure you're kicked so hard out of Mystwick, your *grandkids* won't have a shot at getting in."

CHAPTER EIGHTEEN

Between Rock and a Hard Place

"WE ARE SO DEAD," Jai moans. "I mean, I'm an adventurous soul, don't get me wrong. But messing with *these* guys? We are so, so, *so* dead."

"Oh, you're about to be dead, all right," Darby mutters, "if you don't shut up already."

"I'm just saying, if your plan to find Dead Gir—" He coughs, glancing at Darby. "I mean, if your plan to find *Other Amelia* involves us dying and meeting up with her in the afterlife, then this is a super-duper, A-plus, stellar plan. That's all I'm saying."

"Whatever happened to *confidence?*" I ask, voice wobbling as I stare into the darkness ahead of us, as if I'm one to talk. I'm still rattled by Darby's words, and can barely even look at her without feeling the urge to cry. "Seriously, Jai. Because I could use some right now."

"There's a difference between confident and *stupid,* Amelia Cranberry Jones."

"*Cranberry?* Seriously?"

"I'm a little stressed right now, okay?"

"Shut *up*," Darby growls.

The basement of the Shell feels like a dungeon. The walls are thick concrete, moldy and damp, and the ceiling is so low it feels like we're in a tunnel. No windows or lights brighten the space. There's just a long dark hallway, and occasional rooms stuffed with dusty furniture. Darby holds a little flashlight, which she bounces off the junk piled there.

The light passes across a skeleton, and I yelp.

"They're just drama club props," Darby says, rolling her eyes.

"Why are we down here, again?" I whisper. "Can't we find this person in the dorms or the cafeteria or something?"

"And have half the student body see us? Do you *want* people to know we're hunting a black spell?"

"Well, this place gives me the creeps."

"You think the *place* is bad," Jai mutters, "wait till you meet the *people*. These are the kids who put a charm on Collin Brunnings last week just because he sat at their lunch table. They made him think he was a hippo. The Maestros found him hours later, sitting in the lake trying to eat a *raw fish*." He moans. "We are *so* gonna get hippo'd."

"Quiet!" hisses Darby.

At the end of the hallway is a door, and on the door is a black pirate flag with the words TURN BACK OR BE DISEMBOWELED.

"So dead," Jai whispers.

"I know what I'm doing," Darby growls, raising a hand to knock.

But before she can, the door flings open with a blast of rock music. Every hair on my body stands on end, as the sound hits me like a bolt of lightning, and I clap my hands over my ears.

A jumble of noise erupts from the room—screeching electric guitar, clashing drums, wailing voices, all amplified by the small space so it smacks into us like a tidal wave. The tempo is furious, while the bass is so low and loud it makes my teeth vibrate. It's like each instrument is competing to drown out the others. Mixed into all the chaos is a voice yelling words I can't even understand.

We yell and stumble backwards, running into each other, and I bolt for the exit.

Then a light appears in the hallway ahead, blocking the way. It pulses orange in time with the chaotic noise behind us, then stretches and forms into a giant glowing tiger. Yellow eyes glint at us, and fangs flash white as it snarls. I grab hold of both Darby and Jai, wincing as the rock music grows even louder and angrier. The electric guitar sounds like someone's cutting it in half with a chainsaw.

Ahead of us, the tiger crouches low, eyes fixed on us.

"Oh, no," Jai whispers. "No, no, *no*—"

All at once the tiger charges.

Even though I know it's just an illusion, I still turn and run—

Straight into the room where the band is playing their ear-splitting spell.

Darby and Jai are right on my heels, screaming. Together we spill into the room and crash to the floor, as the tiger pounces over our heads and skids on its claws.

Not real, not real! I think, but I still shriek when its jaws clamp on my head—only to feel nothing.

Instead, the tiger bursts into a glittering cloud of sparks. The band finishes their spell with a crashing drum solo, and I slap my hands over my ears until they're done.

Motes of blue light fade around us, as the last echo of sound seeps into silence.

Then I look up at the band members, who are all staring at us with expressions of disgust.

"*Gross,*" says the lead guitarist, who must have been the one yelling into the mic. "Guppies." He's the kid we followed in here. The others—two girls with guitars and a guy on drums—watch us with slitted eyes.

"How did you get in?" says one of the girls, sneering through her purple lipstick. "Man, you guys are so dead."

Jai moans.

The room is decked out in posters of rock bands, and there's a disco ball hanging from the ceiling. In the center is the band, standing in a mess of cords and amps, and all around them are beanbag chairs, a threadbare couch, piles of spells, and half-finished bags of snack food. Broken equipment is stacked in haphazard piles, from old amps to kick-drum pedals to snapped drumsticks. It's like the room hasn't been cleaned in *decades*. The whole place smells like ranch chips and that smoky, used-fireworks smell that means illusion magic has been recently played here.

All I can think of to say is, "I didn't even know we *had* a band."

"It's high schoolers only," says the kid. "Rock spells are way too dangerous for kids."

"Man, you guys get *all* the fun." Apparently over his fear now, Jai walks to the drum set like he's going to touch it, and the drummer smacks his hand with a stick.

"No touching, zit face!" the drummer hisses.

"You have more zits than me," Jai points out, and even though it's true, the drummer jabs him in the stomach with his stick.

"We're here to see Rosa," Darby says, lifting her chin.

The kid puts down his guitar. "Nobody sees Rosa unless she calls for them. You guys aren't even supposed to be down here. This place is band members only!"

He grabs Darby's sleeve, but she chops down on his arm so fast I almost miss it. With a screech, he backs away, holding his elbow and staring at her like she bit him.

Darby shrugs. "Self-defense classes. My dad said they'd build grip strength and improve my oboe skills." She stares thoughtfully at her clenched fist. "He wasn't wrong."

The guitarist's face turns red as the other seniors laugh.

"Ohhh, watch it, Jason, or the little girl might break your kneecaps," snickers Purple Lipstick.

"Just let them see Rosa," says the drummer. "They'll regret it soon enough."

The guitarist turns back to Darby. "Whatever. Look, you can try to talk to her, but if she tells me to kick you out, I'm kicking you out."

Darby holds up a finger and gives him a smile. "You can *try* to kick me out."

He scowls. "This way. *Hey!* No touching!"

Jai yanks his hand away from the electric guitar he was about to poke, looking sheepish.

The others sneer at us as the kid leads us to a doorway covered with a curtain of colored beads. They form a picture of a grinning skull, ready to swallow up anyone stupid enough to enter.

"Don't come running to me when she kicks your butts," the kid growls, as we push through the beads. They clatter behind us like bones.

The small room within is dimly lit by an ornate chandelier hung from the ceiling, draped with strings of crystals. A girl reclines on a red leather couch against the back wall, her black combat boots propped up, metallic pink headphones clamped over her ears and her foot bobbing to the music she's listening to. She's idly polishing a saxophone, but glances up when we enter and narrows her eyes, then removes the headphones.

Rosa Guerrera, Darby told me this morning, is the daughter of Fernando Guerrera, the mogul who owns Spellstones—the largest chain of spell stores in the world. Making Rosa one of the richest girls at school, if not *the* richest. With that in mind, I'd expected a prissy heiress, but the girl in front of us is more rebel than princess.

Rosa's hair is dyed pink at the ends. Over her Mystwick uniform she wears a black leather vest, and instead of the usual white socks the rest of us girls wear, she has on dark tights with tiny silver stars all over them. Her lipstick is apple red, and when she looks up at us, I see little music-note tattoos curling up her neck.

Slowly, Rosa sets down her saxophone and lowers her boots, then leans forward on the sofa.

"*What,*" she says in a low voice, "are three *rats* doing in my sanctum?"

Jai starts backing away, but Darby grabs his shirt and holds him in place.

I decide I better explain, since this did all start with me. And Darby's likely to say the wrong thing and get us *all* charmed into thinking we're hippos. Looking at Rosa now, I can fully believe the story about Collin.

"We need a spell," I say.

Rosa studies me for a long minute, then leans back, clicking her dark nails together.

"Try the library. Any library. Preferably one *far* away from here, before I settle on how to punish you for breaking into band territory."

Though a huge part of me wants to do just that, I shake my head. "The spell we need isn't *in* the library."

Rosa tilts her head, revealing more of the music-note tattoos. "Oh? Well, well. That *is* interesting. You've bought yourself two minutes of my time, guppy. Use them wisely."

I look at Darby. Darby looks at me.

The she bursts out, "We need to trap a ghost."

Now Rosa *really* looks surprised.

She stands up, crossing her arms. Her nails are long enough to double as guitar picks. Then I realize they probably do. "This keeps getting better. Still. You're practically in diapers. I couldn't give you such a powerful spell. You'll only get yourselves killed."

"Killed?" Jai whispers.

Rosa grins. "Black spells aren't outlawed for no reason, peabrain. People *die* trying to play them. And catching ghosts isn't like rounding up humfrogs. Look, I'm only trying to save your lives."

She shrugs and sits back down, picking up her saxophone. "Leave now, and I won't have the band rewire your nervous systems." Grinning, she adds, "You'll feel like you have spiders crawling under your skin for a *week*. It's a spell the ancient Mayans used to drive their enemies insane. I have the only copy in the world."

Darby steps forward, her eyes on fire. "I'm not leaving here empty-handed. If you can't give me what I need, I'll tell the Maestros you're peddling black spells, and they'll expel all of you."

"Are you sure about that?" Rosa smirks and rises to her feet. Even though she's a senior, she's pretty short, while Darby is tall for her age. They're almost eye to eye. "My dad gives an *awful* lot of money to this place. They practically paper the walls with it. And if you think I'm dumb enough to leave my merchandise where the Maestros can find it, then you don't know me at all. And trust me, I'm just *waiting* for an excuse to show you what I'm *really* like."

Hastily, I slip between them and put on my best smile. "Maybe we could make a deal?"

Rosa looks down at me like I'm a fly she could squash with her thumb. "What?"

"There must be something we could offer you in exchange."

Rosa rolls her eyes. "What could you possibly have that I need? I've got enough money to buy this *school* if I wanted. No . . ." She regards us thoughtfully, one black nail digging into her lower lip. "But there *is* something you might *fetch* for me."

We all three nod eagerly.

"Anything!" Darby throws in. "What do you want?"

Rosa smiles sweetly and says, "I want a cat."

The three of us blink at each other, then her.

Then I echo, "A . . . *cat.*"

"Not just any cat," Rosa replies. "I want Euphonia Le Roux's musicat."

"Whoa, whoa, whoa!" I hold up my hands. "That isn't an option. We're not stealing the headmaestro's cat."

"I'm not going to hurt it," Rosa says. "I just need it for five minutes."

"Deal," Darby says.

"*No* deal!" I glare at them both. "I want to know why Rosa wants the musicat."

"Because it's cute." She grins. "I want to cuddle it."

"Baloney."

Rosa laughs. "Fine, then. If you must know, that cat knows a spell—a spell that's never been written down. In fact, it's the strongest spell you'll ever see in your boring little lives. If the cat hums it for me, I can copy it, then let it go. It'll run back to Mrs. Le Roux, who'll never even know it was gone. As long as *you* don't mess this up, anyway. And if you do, and you even *look* in my direction, I will make dead sure you're *all* ghosts by the end of the week. Got it?"

"Deal," Darby says again. This time, she grabs Jai and me and drags us toward the door, through the curtain of beads.

"Wait!" I shout. "How do we even know you *have* a spell that will help us? How can *we* get the musicat? We're just seventh graders!"

Rosa only smiles. "And therefore expendable. *Adios!*"

She lets the curtain of beads sweep shut.

The other band members push us out into the hallway, then slam the door. We hear it lock from the inside, and one shouts, "Scram! Or you get the spiders!"

We stare at each other in the dim hallway.

"Darby, you had no right to make that deal! We should have discussed it first."

She scowls. "We both want to talk to Amelia. This is the only way that happens."

"But kidnapping a cat?"

"I think you mean catnapping," Jai points out.

Darby looks me squarely in the eye. "We do this *my* way, remember? Or else—"

"Fine!" I clench my hands into fists as she gives me a smirk and then walks away, leaving the threat of blackmail hanging over me. I have no choice but to give in, and she knows it, or she'll tell the whole school how I *really* got into Mystwick.

"You're *okay* with this?" Jai asks me, his eyes wide.

"If we don't help her, she'll just do it alone. At least this way we can keep her under control."

"Is that a joke? Your roommate's almost as scary as those seniors back there! She nearly made that guy cry when she chopped his arm!"

"Just . . . *come on.*"

Grinding my teeth, I run to catch up to Darby.

Behind me, Jai groans, "Definitely, absolutely, so, so, *so* dead."

CHAPTER NINETEEN

Croak, Croak, Croak Your Boat

I**T'S NOT A VERY GOOD PLAN.**

But it's the only plan we've got, and Darby insists we try it as soon as possible.

And that's how I find myself hiding in a bush with Jai on the edge of Orpheus Lake two days later. We'd have launched the plan earlier, but we had to wait for the rain to let up. It's been storming and raining nonstop for three days now, and the lake is so full the dock is almost completely underwater, but finally we get the clear sky we need.

And not a moment too soon. Yesterday, the ghost of Amelia Jones visited me in the middle of lunch—when I was surrounded by hundreds of other students. One minute, everything was normal, and the next, I looked down to see someone had formed my mashed potatoes into a tiny snowman.

Darby was the only person who noticed, and her eyes went wide. I just shook my head at her; there was no way I could tell her Amelia was reminding me of my little snow incident in the

Echo Wood. Is that her game? To alert the Maestros to my Composing? It's probably the fastest route to my getting expelled, so I don't doubt it for a second. Putting up with my terrible performances in class is one thing; if they find out I broke such a big rule, they'll probably skip the zeppelin ride and teleport me straight back into Gran's kitchen.

Our plan to kidnap Wynk, the musicat, takes place during the transition period when everyone's going from late classes to the cafeteria for dinner. In the confusion of people running around, no one will miss us. And hopefully, they won't be able to hear us either.

"Anything?" Jai asks, clutching his violin.

I push aside some leaves to peek at Darby, who sits on the front steps of Harmony Hall, like she's waiting for a friend. Totally casual. Nothing suspicious here, no sir.

The idea is to get Mrs. Le Roux out of her office so Darby can run in and grab Wynk. Which means we have to create a big enough distraction outside that the headmaestro is forced to deal with it herself.

I shake my head and zip up my jacket. It's been getting colder every day, and the dropping temperatures are just a reminder that my test is getting closer. Only a month until my fate is decided once and for all.

"What's she waiting for?" Jai growls. "We've been sitting here for hours!"

"More like ten minutes," I point out. But my nerves are on edge, about to snap. The longer we wait, the closer I get to chickening out altogether.

Settling back on my heels, I polish a spot on my flute with the hem of my skirt. The bush we're in is big enough that we could be standing upright if we wanted, but we're trying to keep the rustling branches to a minimum. Being discovered in a bush with Jai Kapoor isn't exactly the sort of distraction I want to cause—and there's no good way to explain ourselves if we *were* caught. I think we'd both just die of humiliation on the spot.

Sighing, I watch Jai methodically rub rosin over his bow.

"You know," I say, "one day we'll be high schoolers too. And Rebel Clef will need new members."

Jai glances at me sidelong. "Really having trouble picturing you shredding a guitar, Jones."

"I'm not talking about *me*, dummy. *You*."

He presses his lips together and plucks the E string on his violin. "I told you, my dad would never—"

"Oh, come on! I saw you checking out Rebel Clef's guitars. I know that's what you listen to when you pretend it's just Bach and Beethoven in your ears. Are you really going to let your dad stop you?"

"You don't understand," he mumbles.

"My gran hates Musicraft," I say. "She did everything she could to stop me from coming here. But here I am." I spread my hands. "All I'm saying is, one day you're going to have to tell him how you really feel. Release the inner rock star!" I wave my hand in the air, my index finger, pinky, and thumb spread wide.

Jai cocks an eyebrow. "What is that?"

I waggle my hand. "You know! The rocker symbol."

"That's sign language for *I love you*. You gotta put the thumb down."

I snatch my hand out of the air, face suddenly hot. "Oh."

He rolls his eyes. "Look, maybe your dad's all touchy-feely, but mine's about as huggable as a homicidal porcupine."

I drop my gaze, my stomach shriveling into a hard knot. "I wouldn't know. Haven't seen mine since my mom died. I don't even remember what he looks like."

It's mostly true; I can remember his voice, his laugh, and even what his footsteps sounded like when he came through the front door. But his face is a blur in my memory.

"Do you know his name?"

I hesitate, then say in a tight voice, "Eric. Eric Neal."

Jai's eyes widen. "Well, did he go to Mystwick?"

"For a while, but he dropped out." That seems to be his thing, dropping out. Out of school, out of responsibility, out of my *life*.

"Then he must be in the records," Jai says, "or maybe in a yearbook. We could look and—"

"No."

He gives me a startled look, and I realize I sounded harsher than I'd intended.

"I don't care, okay?" I say. "Look, if he wanted to be around, he would be. But I'm not going to waste time finding someone who doesn't want to be found. I don't care if I *never* meet him, and that's the truth."

Jai nods and doesn't say anything else about it, for which I'm grateful. My face is burning as it is, and like always when I think about my dad, anger ignites in my chest until it feels like I can't even breathe.

To distract myself, I look up at Darby.

She's standing up, furiously tapping her nose, like she's been doing it a while.

The signal! Oops.

"Go, Jai!" I hiss, and then I stand and raise my flute, beginning to play "Row, Row, Row Your Boat." It's the most basic of hovering spells, so it isn't very strong. Usually it can lift something an inch or two. Jai joins in, his back against mine in the small space, branches poking us from every side. There's barely enough room for him to move his bow, but he makes it work.

The melody is light and quick, and Jai and I play overlapping one another, a continuous stream of notes pouring out in pale-yellow wisps. I focus hard on the water, glinting just steps away.

We're far enough from the buildings that no one should hear us.

But the humfrogs do.

And the result is so instantaneous I almost swallow my tongue.

Dozens—no, *hundreds*—of frogs rise out of the lake, looking startled. From the water, the banks, even the bushes around me, the little creatures lift off and float through the air, webbed feet kicking like they're trying to swim. The sound of surprised croaking breaks out, loud enough that some of the students shout out, pointing toward the lake.

Jai and I exchange looks. He's grinning ear to ear. I can't smile back without breaking off playing, so I raise my eyebrows instead.

This is going perfectly. Hopefully the sight of a couple hundred floating frogs will be enough to lure Mrs. Le Roux from her office. Everything is going according to plan.

Then, of course, the plan goes haywire.

See, no one told us that humfrogs repeat melodies they hear. And that like musicats, they're one of the few animal species with the peculiar ability to create magic with their voices.

Because that's what they begin to do now.

All across the lake, the flying amphibians' croaking starts to blend together in a scratchy, noisy, froggy symphony. And hearing a couple hundred frogs hum "Row, Row, Row Your Boat" in unison is easily one of the most terrifying things I have ever heard. Worse, while the spell may be weak when just a few people play it, as the Fourth Rule of Musicraft promises, the more individuals who join in, the stronger it gets.

The result here is like Jai and I tried to light a campfire—and caused a wildfire instead.

Frogs. Go. *Everywhere.*

I soon realize I don't have to keep playing, because the frogs are drowning me out anyway. They don't even sound like normal frogs—their voices are deep but agile, almost human. It sounds like they're really singing "Row, row, row!" And the more they sing the hovering spell, the higher and higher they float—and the more they spread out, like a cloud unrolling across the school.

I jump out of the bush, horrified. There's nothing I can do to stop it. Swarms of frogs float through the air. Now everyone up the hill can see what's going on, and students start wandering down to take a closer look. They're so focused on the floating frog choir that they don't notice Jai and me tumbling out of the bushes, pulling our instruments with us.

"Jai! Jai, what do we do?"

He turns to me, eyes wide. "Um . . ."

"Do we finish the spell?" I ask.

"It's not *our* spell to finish anymore." He waves a hand at the clouds of frogs thickening the air. I can barely even hear him for the thunderous croaking.

I see what he means. "Row Your Boat" is a perpetual canon, meaning its magic can go on and on and on until the musicians playing it decide to stop. One of my favorite stories when I was little was about how the orchestra on the *Titanic* played it nonstop for days after the ship hit an iceberg, floating the entire thing safely to land.

But unlike me, Jai, and the *Titanic's* orchestra, frogs have no way of deciding when to end a spell. They'll probably keep croaking it until they all . . . well, *croak*.

"Did you know this would happen?" This part of the plan had been Darby's idea. Actually, the *entire* plan had been Darby's idea.

"Of course not." His eyes grow wide. "Amelia, watch out!"

A frog, spinning a bit wildly through the air, smacks me in the face. I yelp and duck as more of them go soaring overhead. In their alarm at finding themselves suddenly airborne, the frogs seem to have sped up the tempo of the spell, singing at an increasingly frenzied pace. This, I realize, only serves to make them fly *faster,* and their frantic flopping sends them into crazy spins.

"We could try to transpose the key!" Jai says. "Reverse the spell!"

We raise our instruments and try it, sloppily; Jai gets it right before I do, but soon so many frogs are smacking into us that we're forced to lower our instruments and cover our faces, our pitiful attempt quickly drowned out by the roar of croaks.

Turns out, it's impossible to play *any* kind of music when you're being pelted by panicked, flying frogs.

I even try singing the notes in minor key, hoping the frogs will repeat that instead, but all I get is a slimy, wet frog smacked on my mouth. Spitting and gagging in disgust, I wrap myself around my flute to protect it and give up.

"Jai! We have to get inside!"

He just shakes his head at me, and I realize he can't hear me.

Then I feel a strange sensation, like someone is pulling at my legs. My whole body starts to feel lighter and lighter.

Because I'm lifting off the ground.

With a scream, I grab hold of the bush, anchoring myself to the earth as the frogs' spell starts to take hold of *me*. Beside me, Jai is doing the same thing, and this time I can hear him yelling even over the croaking frogs.

"Don't let go!" I shout. But I hardly need to tell him; he's clinging to the bush like . . . well, like he's a balloon and it's the only thing holding him down.

My legs are now pointed to the sky. Completely upside down, I have a weird view of the lake, where I see more things popping from the water—fish and turtles are starting to fly too. The frogs' spell is so strong it's even reaching the *bottom of the lake.*

And if someone doesn't fix this mess fast, all those poor fish will be belly-up in minutes.

Twisting my neck, I manage to look up the hill to see it's worse than I thought. All the students who came out to watch the frogs have gotten caught in the spell as well.

Students cling to the grass, to bushes and posts, to each other. One girl is gripping a statue of Bach with one hand, while holding on to another girl with the other. That girl, in turn, is holding on to the feet of a screaming boy. All around them frogs are spinning, floating, soaring.

Even the rocks and twigs and other loose stuff on the ground are starting to drift away. Backpacks and instruments cases, loose papers and books and pens and someone's shoe . . .

Then the branch Jai's holding on to snaps.

He screams as he begins rising into the air with nothing to grab ahold of.

"Jai!" I yell, and I let go, trying to swim through the air to him.

We collide and go into a wild spin, frogs pinging off us.

"That was bloody stupid!" Jai shouts in my ear. "Now we're *both* dead!"

Immediately I see he's right, that jumping after him was about the dumbest thing I've ever done in my life. We hold hands to keep from being pulled apart, but that just means we're rising higher and higher together, borne on a spell that's

showing no signs of weakening. And now, I don't *want* it to stop.

If it does, we're going to have one nasty fall.

Jai looks at me.

I look at him.

And together, we both start screaming.

The kids on the ground get smaller and smaller. We're almost higher than Harmony Hall now. I scream until my throat burns and I choke on my own voice.

We're not the only ones drifting up into the sky: I see other students—dozens of them—who lost their grips too, slowly tumbling through the air, screaming, crying—except for one, who I recognize as the drummer from Rebel Clef. That maniac is *laughing*.

Then Jai points frantically, so I look down and see the most amazing, wonderful, *beautiful* thing I've ever seen in my life:

Mrs. Le Roux.

She drifts out of Harmony Hall, carrying a cello, looking completely calm. Like floating through a sky full of singing hum-frogs with half the student body is just another day at the office.

After she's a few feet off the ground—really, how does she manage to make even flying look so graceful?—she props her cello on one foot, raises her bow, and then starts to play.

"It's no use!" I shout to Jai. "We already tried—"

"No, look!" he replies.

I gasp.

Of course!

The humfrogs repeat the melodies they hear. And unlike me and Jai, Mrs. Le Roux doesn't panic, even as frogs bounce off her.

At first, Mrs. Le Roux's music doesn't seem to make a difference, but then the frogs drifting right next to her start to change their tune. They sing *her* spell instead, and as they do, they begin to descend. The spell spreads from there, as more and more frogs switch to the new spell.

In minutes, the sky fills with the sound of Brahms's "Lullaby," and the frogs, fish, turtles, students, and other random objects all start drifting back to the ground. The animals return to the water as soon as they land, as if they can't wait to disappear into the murky depths and possibly never resurface. I wouldn't blame them. Once they vanish beneath the water, they fall silent.

The spell Mrs. Le Roux chose is gentle, and nobody goes crashing to their death. Instead, we touch down lightly, soft as feathers, amid the soothing notes—as soothing as a thousand frogs can possibly sound, anyway. I'm not sure this is what Brahms had in mind when he wrote his famous lullaby. But at least it's working.

I've never been so happy to feel solid ground.

Dropping to my knees, I hug the grass.

"Oh, earth!" Jai says beside me. "I'm never taking you for granted again!"

All around us, students cry out in relief as they're returned to the ground. Mrs. Le Roux is the last one to touch down, settling onto the grass without missing a single note. She plays a few more measures, finishing the spell. Now all the frogs are silent, and the only sound is Mrs. Le Roux's sonorous cello. The last note draws out, deep and melodious, and then it fades away.

Everyone breaks into applause.

Mrs. Le Roux slowly lowers her bow, then raises furious eyes.

The applause cuts short. Silence falls at last.

Mrs. Le Roux looks around, her lips tight. "I don't suppose anyone is going to take responsibility for this?"

No one speaks.

She studies every face. When her gaze finds me, I train my features to absolute stillness. But all my insides turn to water and for a moment, I'm *sure* she's seen how guilty I am.

But then she moves on.

I let out a slow, relieved breath as everyone starts shuffling away. Jai and I turn to each other and exchange amazed looks —amazed that we somehow got away with this.

Then a hand pounds my back, and I whirl with dread, thinking it's Mrs. Le Roux.

But it's Darby, her face flushed and eyes shining.

"That went perfectly," she says.

Jai looks like he's about to pop an eyeball. "Perfectly? *Perfectly?*"

"You knew," I whisper, feeling sick. "You knew the frogs would repeat the spell, and that it would all get out of control."

A little smile curls at the corner of her lips. "Look, Mrs. Le Roux would never have come outside on account of a few floating frogs. A bunch of floating *students,* on the other hand?"

I gape at her. "Jai and I could have been killed!"

She shrugs. "But you weren't. Anyway, I bet you got a nice view of the campus. I'm almost jealous."

I'm furious. I could happily watch *her* float into outer space right now. Was this some kind of revenge scheme, her way of getting back at me for taking her Amelia's place? "How dare you—"

"Jones," she says. "Look."

She takes off her backpack, glancing around to be sure no one's watching, then unzips it slightly.

Two yellow eyes glow inside, then a clawed paw darts out, nearly scratching my nose. I shout and step back as Darby quickly zips it shut.

"Like I said." She smirks. "Perfectly."

She carefully slings the backpack over her shoulder, then takes off in the direction of the girls' dorm, where she and I are supposed to meet Rosa for the trade, according to the note Darby found in our room this morning, slipped under the door in the night and signed unmistakably with a kiss of apple-red lipstick.

"She's nuts," I tell Jai. "She's completely, totally insane."

He nods. "Yeah. But . . . the view up there *was* pretty great."

He yelps when I punch him in the shoulder.

CHAPTER TWENTY

The Sound of Musicats

THE NEXT FEW DAYS, all anyone can talk about is the Great Humfrog Float, which is what they're apparently calling it now. And soon, the story—much like the spell it started with—has gotten completely out of control.

"There's a rumor that a kid is missing," whispers George in the computer lab on Thursday. "They say it's a tenth grader. Floated right up into space."

"That's not true," I say.

"Oh, it's totally true," Jai puts in. "I was there, saw the whole thing. See, what happened was—"

He launches into a long, complicated version of the story that is about 90 percent total lies. I just sigh and poke at the keyboard, working on yet another email to Gran that she won't reply to. I've tried to keep a low profile during these conversations, in case anyone starts to get suspicious about my involvement in the disaster.

No one's been charged with the crime. Yet. But I swear I'm

getting more and more sideways looks from the Maestros. Jai says it's just my imagination, but I'm not so sure. Still, we got the black spell from Rosa, and that was the important thing. She even let Darby and me watch while she recorded Wynk's humming spell, and let us set the musicat free outside when she was done. What the spell was for, I have no idea — and I'm not sure I want to know.

Dear Gran, Nothing new to report, except that I learned how to set a table using magic! No need to add that every dish I'd moved with my spell ended up shattering on the floor without ever actually touching the table — thanks to a ghostly arm knocking them out of the air. To everyone else, it had looked like I'd flubbed yet another lesson, and they'd just rolled their eyes and said, "Typical Amelia." Even Miss Noorani had just sighed and handed me a C–.

How long will you stay mad at me? Are you never going to talk to me again?

Biting my lip, I erase the last two lines and hit Send, forgetting to add my usual *Love, Amelia.*

By Friday, the Great Humfrog Float story has died down, as everyone starts talking about musical zombies instead, which seems to be some kind of annual school-wide game played in the woods.

"That's when you'll have to play the spell," Rosa had told

Darby and me. "Rebel Clef will be playing during the game, and trust me, over the sound we'll make, *nobody* will notice."

To hear some of them, you'd think it was the most important day of the year. Kids break off into groups to whisper strategies. The seniors scope out the woods where the game will be played. And on Friday night, the girls' dorm hums with activity late into the night, despite curfew. I can hear girls running back and forth from each other's rooms, shrieking and laughing. Since it's the weekend—and the dorm captains are as much into the pregame excitement as the rest of us—nobody says much about it.

But Darby and I are too anxious to even think about the game.

Or at least, *I'm* anxious. I don't think anything could make Darby nervous, but she does sit on her bed for hours, studying the black spell and practicing the fingerings on her oboe. The spell is written for piano, and Darby has spent the last few days painstakingly rearranging it for a flute, oboe, and violin trio instead.

"Strange," she mutters. "This spell is clearly rare and old. I've never heard of it. But it doesn't have the usual markings that tell you what class and type it is."

"Why would it?" I ask. I've been trying to French braid my hair, the way Gran would do it for special occasions, but I keep ending up with a tangled mess. Finally I just rake my brush through my hair and give up. "If I were selling black spells, I wouldn't go around advertising what they were."

"Yeah . . ." She tugs thoughtfully at her lip, then pulls a pencil from behind her ear to make a small change to the arrangement.

It's weird. It's almost like ever since Darby and I saw the ghost in our room, we've been on the same team. Not really *friends*—ever since she found out my secret, she's gone from being moody and withdrawn to outright mean, and even said she'd volunteer to be part of the orchestra that rips out my echo tree—but at least we're allies. We both need to talk to Other Amelia, and we need each other to do it.

"What will you say to her?" I ask softly.

I'm not sure she's going to answer. She's quiet for a long time, staring hard at the sheets of music.

But then she says, "I don't know. I hadn't really thought about it. I just want to say something. Anything. Goodbye, I guess. Tell her about my crappy roommate who took her place."

I sigh. "Apparently she already knows all about me."

Darby looks up then, her eyes hard. "Yeah. Funny, isn't it? How she comes back from the grave to haunt you, but not to talk to me."

"Huh?" I've got a pillow in my lap, and I hug it tighter.

"I mean, it *is* a total Amelia move," she adds. "Revenge was always her thing. But she could have at least said hi to me. Or not disappeared when I tried to talk to her."

"Like you said, she was probably just scared."

"And where has she been since then?" She glares at me like it's *my* fault Other Amelia is avoiding her.

But what can I do? I'd be more than happy if the ghost shifted her attention to Darby. She struck three more times this week, blowing away my sheet music, moving my flute while I was playing it, even spilling my bowl of tomato soup at lunch. Everyone at the table had laughed so hard that Claudia choked on her bread and had to be given the Heimlich maneuver by Miss Becker. At least that distracted everyone from the fact that the ghost was busy dragging her invisible fingers through the spilled soup, spelling out a message just for me: WATCH OUT—

I'd dashed my hand through the soup before anyone could see, and before Other Amelia could complete her threat.

But I don't tell Darby about any of that. Even though besides Jai, she's the only person who would believe me. The more I talk about Other Amelia sabotaging me, the angrier Darby gets, and I need her as much on my side as possible. Because what if she decides to team up with Other Amelia in getting me expelled? I can't last against both of them.

"We better get some sleep," Darby says at last, putting away the black spell. She keeps it hidden in a folder under her mattress. "Tomorrow's the big day."

I nod and slide under the blankets.

In the hallway, a girl yells, "You are going *down* tomorrow, guppies! Hahaha! Get ready to be *zombie-fied!*"

I shiver and don't fall asleep for hours.

CHAPTER TWENTY-ONE

Catch Us If You Canon

AT DUSK ON SATURDAY, everyone gathers on the edge of the Echo Wood, dressed in dark clothing and toting their instruments—all except us guppies, who weren't allowed to bring anything.

Musical zombies is kind of like capture the flag, only instead of flags, you're supposed to capture seventh graders using charm spells. The students are divided into the four Mystwick classes: Aeros, Percussos, Chordos, and Labrosos. Whichever of the four teams has the most of us guppies locked up in their "camp" at the end wins the game, and gets to claim the other classes' desserts at every meal until Christmas.

"You mean we don't even get to *play?*" Jai groans. "What's the point if you're just going to be bait?"

"Are you kidding?" says an eleventh grader. "The fact that we get to round up guppies is the *best part!*"

I wave to Jai as he's led away with the rest of the Chordos. I hope he doesn't get charmed, because I don't know if Darby and I can play the ghost trap spell on our own.

"Got the sheet music?" I whisper to her.

She nods and pats her pocket. Our instruments, wrapped in protective plastic bags, are hidden deeper in the wood, where we stashed them earlier in the day.

We follow the senior Aeros into the woods, walking in silent single file. It's dark under the trees, and the seniors shush anyone who tries to talk. They don't want to give away the location of our camp. Above, the branches of the echo trees look like bony fingers, most of the leaves fallen by now. But even so, the sound of Canon in D, the great summoning spell that protects the school, still echoes faintly in the branches.

Then we hear a sudden roll of frantic drumbeats, and someone says, "It's Rebel Clef!"

Rosa was right about her band: the minute they start playing, the whole Echo Wood fills with their music. The rock spell is dark and tense, the bass echoing in my bones, while the screeching guitar riffs wash over me like a swarm of spiders. Balls of fiery light drift through the trees, making the whole place a huge playground of shadows and light. The fireballs prowl around like they're looking for someone to devour, pulsing in time with the beat of the booming bass drum. Even though I know they're not real fire, just illusions, I still duck when one swoops overhead.

Accompanied by the pounding tempo of Rebel Clef's spell, we reach Camp Aero, a square clearing with torches burning at each corner and a sort of pen in the middle. That's where the older Aeros will put the seventh graders they catch from Percusso, Chordo, and Labroso.

Darby and I are "branded" with the other Aero guppies: the eighth graders solemnly paint red stripes on our faces that indicate we're bait. I shiver, even dressed in my Mystwick sweatsuit and jacket. The sky is cloudy and the wind restless, like it's going to storm later. The echo trees shudder and creak overhead. The place might be peaceful and beautiful in the daylight, but at night, with Rebel Clef's fireballs stalking the woods, it's like a nightmare. Us guppies are all wide-eyed and scared, but the older students are obviously loving every minute.

"Man, I'm glad I'm not in your shoes," says the eighth grader painting my face.

"Thanks," I mutter.

"Listen up, guppies!" yells Phoebe, our self-appointed Aero commander. She's got instruments hanging all over her — a piccolo in her hand, a flute case on her back, her belt holding a harmonica, a pan flute, and an ocarina. "Your job is simple: run and don't get caught. And you're on your own out there. It's against the rules for us seniors to stay too close to you. So if you hear a charm spell, go in the opposite direction. If they get too close, and you get charmed, you'll spend the rest of the night as a zombie. And you'll be in charge of washing *our* dirty gym clothes the rest of term!"

"This is a stupid game," Darby mutters.

"But if, at the end of the night, you're still charm-free," Phoebe adds, "you'll get full honors: access to the senior break room for the rest of the year!"

We all perk up at that. The senior break room is way better than ours—rumor has it they have free arcade games and Ping-Pong tables.

Then I remember Darby and I have more important business.

Off through the trees, the Rebel Clef drummer starts a long drumroll.

"Almost time!" Phoebe yells. "Loosen up, guppies!"

Around me, the other seventh-grade Aeros start panicking. George looks like he's about to pass out. Claudia is pale and frozen in place.

But Darby looks fierce and focused. She meets my eyes and gives me a small, secret nod. I return it, my heart pounding as fast as the Rebel Clef drum.

When the band launches into a loud, furious guitar solo, the older kids start shoving us toward the trees, screaming "Run! Run! Run!"

Darby finds me, grabs my hand, and pulls me into the woods.

"We have to reach the rendezvous spot before any other teams find us!" she says. "Or we'll get charmed and lose our chance at pulling this off. And that chatty boyfriend of yours better not get himself caught."

"He's not my—"

But she's already sprinting away, and I have to race to catch up.

We run through the woods, dodging the flaming balls and sticking to shadow, aiming for the place where Jai found me Composing a few weeks ago, and where our instruments are hidden. He should be running from the Chordo camp now to meet us there.

Suddenly I skid to a halt, grabbing Darby's hand.

She pulls away. "What are you—"

"Shh! Listen!"

I can hear a Percusso playing a glockenspiel ahead, and I think they must be pretty committed to be this far out in the woods with such a big instrument.

"Charm spell," Darby whispers.

I nod. "And they're right between us and our instruments."

"Out of the way, guppies!" calls a voice behind us.

We turn and nearly get bowled over by Phoebe, who's sprinting toward the hidden Percusso. I wonder how she can run at all, carrying enough instruments to equip a small orchestra. She whips up her piccolo and blasts a freezing spell, blue lights zinging from the opening of her instrument to speed through the trees, and we hear a startled shout ahead as the Percusso's spell cuts short.

Phoebe lowers her piccolo and glares at us. "Seriously? Two minutes in and you're already almost getting caught?"

"Geez," Darby mutters. "It's only a game."

We dart past Phoebe, as she splutters about how we're stupid kids who don't know the difference between a trumpet and a trombone.

A short distance ahead, we pass the Percusso, who's frozen in place by Phoebe's spell. She has a small glockenspiel in front of her, supported by a neck strap, but her fingers are locked on the keys, barely able to even twitch. Behind her is an unlucky Chordo seventh grader, his eyes wide and vacant in his trance state. I'll bet he was the first one caught tonight. He reminds me of Rooter when I charmed her out from under the coop.

"You won't get far!" the Percusso shouts at us, her voice strained as she struggles to move her frozen lips. "This is our territory!"

"These guys take this *way* too seriously," Darby says.

"Maybe it's more fun when you're not the bait," I reply.

She laughs, and I think that's the first time I've ever heard her do that.

We charge on through the trees, stopping every now and then to get our bearings. Wherever we go, we can hear Rebel

Clef's music like a distant heartbeat, pumping through the Echo Wood. The trees faintly resonate along, but this far out from the band, the spell sounds slightly warped. And there's a funny tune mixed in, a high, eerie tone . . .

Darby and I slow to a stop.

An angel steps out from behind a tree ahead of us, playing a deep, haunting melody on her viola.

Her long, dark hair shimmers around her shoulders. Her spell floats around her, airy, white curls of magic that make her shine. The melody is entrancing, velvet notes pouring into my mind and filling it with soft, warm light, light that obliterates all thought. A feeling of peace suffuses me, and I feel all my muscles relax. My worries release, carried away by that smooth current of magic.

The violist's dark eyes seem to glow as she approaches us. Closer and closer she gets, until she's standing between us, smiling over her viola. Darby stares too, eyes wide, mouth open.

When the Chordo girl walks on, Darby and I follow.

Slowly, she leads us through the trees, her spell unending, her magic delicate and bright. White, wispy lights caress my face and wind in my hair, drawing me along. My head is full of pleasant, fuzzy warmth, and all I want is to keep feeling the way I'm feeling right now. *Forever*. I've never been so free of pain and struggle and worry.

Dimly, I remember that I was supposed to be going

somewhere. To do something important. But I can't recall what it was, and now it seems so small and silly.

Someone ahead of us shouts. A boy, waving us over. He seems happy to see us. I don't really care.

"In here!" says the boy. "Hurry, hurry! That's two at once, Riya! Amazing!"

The girl leads us into a fenced area surrounded by torches. In the firelight, she's even more beautiful. I want to lie at her feet and profess my undying loyalty.

Then she lowers her viola and the spell breaks.

"Ugh!" she moans. "My fingers feel raw!"

Darby and I blink at each other blearily. My head clears as the last of the charm fades away, and a feeling of horror sweeps over me as I realize the position we're now in.

"*Nooooo . . .*" Darby groans, rubbing her head. "This can't be happening!"

"Oh, it's happening," says the Chordo girl cheerfully. "You two were easy pickings."

"My turn," says the boy. He looks at his teammate. "Watch these two while I go hunt."

She nods and perches on the fence. The boy closes the gate and heads into the woods, lifting a guitar and starting to strum the most beautiful tune . . .

"Snap out of it, Jones!" Darby yells.

I blink, startled, and then clap my hands over my ears. Is this how Rooter felt every time I charmed her out from under a coop or down from the branches of a tree? Like her mind had been stolen and played with like putty in someone else's hands?

I've got a lot of apologizing to do to that chicken.

The Chordo girl, Riya, laughs. "You might as well get comfortable. It's going to be a long night."

Miserably, I sit in the corner. Darby paces in front of me, looking furious.

"We could sneak out," I whisper.

She shakes her head. "She'll just charm us before we can go three steps."

Groaning, I lie back on the loamy forest floor and stare up as a Rebel Clef fireball passes overhead. Is it my imagination, or does that thing have a *face?* It looks like a fiery, grinning skull. I wouldn't put it past Rosa, going the extra mile to scare us all. The fireball passes over and straight through a tree outside the fence.

I glance at Riya, just to see if she might be looking the other way so we can sneak off, but she's looking right at me. She smiles and blows me a kiss.

And I sit up straight, stomach turning over. "Riya! Riya, behind you!"

But Riya only rolls her eyes. "Nice try, guppy."

"No, *really!* The tree! The tree is on fire!"

Darby looks up and gasps.

I'd thought the fireballs were just illusions, but where it hit the tree, flames are now spreading. The leaves are going up in smoke, and burning branches crash to the ground.

Riya must sense the light, because she finally turns, and then falls off the fence with a yelp.

"Fire!" she screams. *"Fire!"*

She turns and runs in the other direction as the fire jumps from one tree to the next, forming a massive curtain of flames. I stare at it, taking one step forward and sniffing the air.

Huh. *Vanilla.*

"Are you crazy?" Darby yells. "Come on! It'll be here in seconds!"

She pulls on my sleeve, but I push her away and grin. "This way!"

While she gapes, I run toward the fire—and straight through it.

"It's an illusion!" I shout. It's just like the fire from the Planting Ceremony, which everyone had thought was real. There's no heat coming from these flames at all.

I see Darby hesitate on the other side of the fire, but then she must make up her mind, because she sprints toward me. Even so, she gives a little shriek when she passes through the flames.

"Told you," I say. "Listen."

Someone is playing a violin ahead, and I have a good idea who it is.

"Jai!" I shout when he walks out of the trees.

He grins as he wraps up the spell, then takes a low bow. Behind us, his fire flickers out, and the trees—which had looked charred and smoldering—are back to their normal state.

"I got to the meeting spot and you guys weren't there," he says. "Figured you got yourselves zombie-fied. So, you're welcome."

Darby grunts. I think she's embarrassed, since she'd been so sure *he* would be the one to get charmed.

"Come on," she says, "we've lost too much time already."

I high-five Jai as we follow her into the trees. "That was amazing! You should have seen that girl take off."

He shudders. "This game sucks! Those seniors are maniacs! We're going to need *therapy* after—"

"Let's *go!*" Darby growls.

CHAPTER TWENTY-TWO

The Chords of Binding

AFTER RETRIEVING MY FLUTE and Darby's oboe, we head deeper into the woods, trying to get as far from the other students as we can. Pinning my case under my arm, I rub my hands together, trying to warm them. The night's getting colder and colder; my breath starts appearing as a misty puff in front of me.

We walk until we can't see any light from the fireballs or hear Rebel Clef's spells. This deep into the woods, many of the trees aren't even echo trees, just regular aspens and pines. We must be at the very edge of the school property. Beyond, the mountains rise up and block out the sky.

"Okay," I say, after ten minutes of hiking. "Think this will do it?"

Darby drops her case and clicks it open, taking out her oboe. "We'll need light to read the spell."

"On it," says Jai, striking a quick rendition of "This Little Light of Mine." A soft blue ball of light flickers into existence over our heads. It's just enough to illuminate the spell sheets Darby made for us, transposed from the original spell.

"This isn't too hard," Jai says, eyeing the pages as he lowers his violin. The blue light flickers, and we don't have much time before it fades altogether.

"I'll take the melody," Darby says. "Jai, you pick up here, and Amelia can come in here." She points at different sections on the sheet, the notes all precisely drawn in her neat hand.

"Ready?" I say, looking at each of their faces. Their features seem to jump in the flickering blue light, looking eerie with the paint striped across them, red for Darby and blue for Jai.

They both nod.

"Wait a sec, Jones," says Darby. "We need to settle something. If this works, I get to talk to her first."

"Fine. But remember, you agreed to ask her to leave me alone."

She shrugs, looking aside.

"*Darby.* That was the deal!"

"Yeah, whatever," she says, scowling. "I remember."

"Hurry up," Jai urges. "This place is giving my *goose bumps* goose bumps."

Darby rolls her eyes and puts her oboe to her lips.

"Ready?" she says around the reed.

Jai and I both nod.

The spell is called *Dies Irae.* I've never heard of it before, and neither have the other two, which makes sense since it's a black spell. All we have to go on that it'll work is Rosa's word. But just as I put my flute to my lips, a voice in the back of my head wonders if she can be trusted.

But it's too late to chicken out now.

The melody is stately and grand, a solemn procession of notes. It reminds me of the old cathedrals I saw in London, when we picked up Jai on the zeppelin—somber and ancient and regal. We play at an even tempo, thankfully, since I don't think my cold fingers could manage anything faster. It's a fairly simple tune, though I notice Darby gave me the easiest arrangement, while she and Jai thread in more complicated bits.

The sound of our three instruments blends together, and soon, streamers of light flow from each of us to twine in the air, a slowly revolving knot of light. We all stare, and I see the other two are as confused as I am.

"Yellow?" Jai says.

Since Darby and I can't talk and play at the same time, we just shrug.

Maybe that's how black spells are. It's not like we've ever seen one before.

But Darby's face is hard, her eyes suspicious. I wonder if she thinks this was all a dupe.

Still, I've never seen a spell work like this. The streamers whirl overhead and grow, until we stand beneath a spinning ring of golden light. It bounces off the trees around us, a bright-yellow lasso tethered to our three instruments. I can't look long, because I'm struggling to follow the notes on the spell sheet lying between us.

A minute later, we finish the spell. The last notes fade into the trees, and the yellow magic dissipates.

"Did it work?" whispers Jai.

We stand very still, listening.

The trees sway slightly. Crickets chirp from the leaves. Over-head, the sky rumbles in the distance, warning of a storm on its way. My breath fogs the air and then fades.

I peer into the dark forest, turning a full circle to check every direction. Jai and Darby do the same.

Then we all look at each other.

"Maybe I arranged it wrong," Darby says. "And the more you rearrange a melody, the weaker it gets."

Jai rolls his eyes. "Or . . . maybe there's just no such thing as gho—"

He cuts off in a scream as a shadow grabs his ankle and he slams into the ground.

"Jai!" I shout. "What—"

Something grabs me by the waist.

Then it drags me backwards, like an arm around my middle, and I yelp and drop my flute onto the leaves. The thing holding me tightens until I can barely breathe. Loud creaks and rustles sound all around. It's like the whole forest has come alive. I scream until I can't breathe.

In front of me, Darby yells as something seizes her too. In the pale glow of Jai's spell light, I see what grabbed us.

It's the *trees*.

With a gasp, I find myself pinned against the trunk of a tall aspen that's holding me in place with two strong branches. Jai is locked against a pine, and Darby is in the clutches of another. Its needles block her face until she reaches up and rips them away.

"What happened?" she groans.

We look around at each other, bewildered. There's no sign of the ghost of Other Amelia. Our instruments are scattered on the ground. My heart misses a beat, hoping my flute's okay.

"Rosa," I croak out. "She tricked us!"

"It was a trapping spell, all right," says Jai. "But not for a ghost. For *us*."

"Why? Why would she do that?"

Darby growls. "She was just using us to get the musicat!"

"We are *so dead*," moans Jai.

"Let's just use our heads," I say, trying to keep calm. "It's not like we'll be stuck here forever. Someone will come looking."

I try furiously to think of a way out of this, but even if I could reach my flute, I can't think of any spell that will free us from the trees, not without possibly hurting ourselves in the process.

I hear a sniffle and realize Darby is crying. She came here thinking she'd talk to her dead friend, but instead, it was all a trick. I know how much she wanted this, how badly she needed to see the other Amelia. What if I'd been given the chance to see my mom again, only to have it ripped away?

"We'll get out of this," I say. "And then we'll find Rosa and get the *real* spell."

"Don't talk to me about what's *real*," she snarls.

I stare at her. "Darby, no. Don't—"

"She's a fake, Jai," she spits out. "She's not even supposed to be here."

I just stare at her, my heart sinking.

"She's only here by accident," Darby says. "She's not good enough for Mystwick, and never will be. She failed her audition, so she *stole* my Amelia's place. While the rest of us worked our butts off, practicing for years and years to get here, sacrificing everything to come, *she* tricked and lied her way in!"

"I didn't!" I shout. "It was an accident! A mix-up!"

"You're not good enough for Mystwick. You don't belong here. You never did. You're just a big, awful joke."

Jai looks at me, his eyes round, and my heart sinks. He stares like he's seeing me for the first time, and I just *know* he's going to be mad at me for never telling him the truth. Maybe even mad enough that he'll never talk to me again. After all, why would he want to be known as the kid who hangs out with the school joke?

But then he turns back to Darby. "So? Who cares? She's here now, and she's one of us. I don't care if she turns out to be a googly-eyed, tentacle-waving slime alien from Neptune, she's still my friend!"

My heart lifts. I give him a small, grateful smile, and wonder how I could ever have doubted him. I was so ashamed of admitting the truth, I couldn't see what a good friend he really is.

"Just for the record," I say, "I *am* from planet Earth."

Darby glares at me in the fading light of Jai's spell. "The *real* Amelia was a great musician, and my friend. She was a hundred times better than you'll ever be!"

I want to shout back, to tell her it's not true, but I realize she's right. I've seen the videos of Other Amelia. And she *is* a hundred times better than me. I *am* just an accident. Even the one thing that could make me special—my Composing—only happens when I'm not trying to make it happen. Another accident.

Overhead, the sky rumbles with thunder, and lightning flashes in the distance, veins of white behind a bank of dark clouds. I shiver as the wind picks up. The trees sway around, sounding like bones clacking together.

Please, please don't let it rain, I think, staring mournfully at my flute, exposed on the ground.

The temperature drops until my teeth start to chatter. I buck and twist, but nothing will free me from the tree's grasp.

Giving up, I slump forward. It's hard to breathe with the tree squeezing my lungs. I sag over the branch, hopeless. At least it's still dry.

Then Jai screams.

I look up at once and spot her: in the trees, barely visible in the gloom.

A ghostly blue girl, half-transparent in the darkness.

The three of us gape as she watches us, as if she's curious why we're stuck out here in the middle of a storm.

"Amelia!" Darby shouts. "Amelia, it's me!"

The girl looks at her, but it's hard to read her expression when I can barely even make out her face.

Did the spell work after all?

But then the ghost turns and glides away, and soon vanishes.

Then Jai's light winks out, and we're plunged into darkness.

Jai and Darby say nothing. When lightning flashes again, I catch a glimpse of my roommate crying, and Jai looking totally spooked. He's actually speechless for once. His eyes meet mine, and I realize this might be the first time he's really believed the ghost existed.

Other Amelia doesn't appear again.

"That was a ghost!" Jai gasps. "A GHOST!"

"Yes," I sigh. "We know."

His eyes are practically falling out of his head. "But did you *see* it? She was there, then she wasn't. There, not there. There . . . *not there.* WHY ARE YOU GUYS NOT FREAKING OUT RIGHT NOW?"

"Shut up, Jai!" Darby says.

"This is not normal! This is not how the world works! Ghosts are supposed to be like zombies and the Necromuse and an A in History of Musicraft. *Not. REAL.*"

Darby scowls. "Keep blabbering and I'll get that hippo spell from Rosa and make sure you both spend the rest of the year flopping around in the lake!"

Jai moans and pulls his head down like a turtle trying to hide in its shell.

As I shiver against the tree, partly from the cold, partly from my own raw nerves, I wonder if musical zombies got canceled because of the lightning. If so, will they realize three kids are still missing? Will they even bother looking in this weather?

The lightning storm seems to last for hours. My body aches from being pinned so long. And Darby's words keep pounding in my head.

You're only here by accident.

I'm not good enough.

I'll never be good enough.

My name is Amelia Jones, I think. I work hard and I don't give up easily. My mom was a Maestro and if I just try hard enough, if I just *want* it badly enough, I can be one too.

This is where I'm supposed to be.

This is what I was *born* to do.

But deep inside, I realize I'm not sure I believe that anymore.

Deep inside, I can feel myself starting to give up.

CHAPTER TWENTY-THREE

Time to Face the Music

M<small>RS.</small> L<small>E</small> R<small>OUX'S</small> <small>MAUVE NAILS</small> glint as she slides the ghost trap spell across her desk.

"I am . . . dismayed," she says in a low voice. "And deeply disappointed in you three."

It's early morning. The sky is still strawberry pink, and through the windows of the headmaestro's office I can see the peak where Mr. Pinwhistle teleported my Aero class, what feels like *ages* ago. Clouds lump behind the mountains, dark and threatening, bringing yet more storms. I'm still shivering from last night's adventure.

Me, Darby, and Jai all slump in our chairs. I can feel Mr. Pinwhistle and Miss Noorani looming behind us, and on the floor beneath the desk, Wynk is asleep, humming to herself.

It took the Maestros until dawn to find us. Apparently we'd hiked farther than we'd thought. And spending an entire night pinned against a tree during a storm makes every minute feel like an hour, even without Jai yelping at every flash of lightning and Darby glaring at me like she was trying to melt my bones.

I was sure we would all die out there.

The Maestros were furious when they found us, partly because we'd sneaked away to perform a dangerous spell, and partly because they'd had to search for us in such terrible weather. They hadn't realized we were still in the woods until almost midnight, after all the kids had been sorted and sent to bed in the aftermath of musical zombies. They'd cut the game short at half past ten, when the storm had begun.

At least they gave us hot cocoa to warm us up. I clutch my half-empty mug like it'll be snatched away from me at any moment. My flute is safely in its case by my feet.

Only one good thing came out of the whole disaster: we're in a fraction of the trouble we could have been in, because the spell we played turned out to be no black spell at all—just an ordinary yellow one. Mr. Pinwhistle had recognized it and known a counterspell that would free us.

So Rosa *had* duped us. Though in this case, it was for the best. If it had been a black spell we'd been caught with, I know we'd all three be on our way home right now. We might even be getting metal rods stapled to our ears, barring us from all music for good, the ultimate punishment.

"We were only trying to win the game," Jai says with a cheery smile.

I don't know how he manages to look so perky after the night we just had, but I'm glad the three of us agreed to make him the spokesperson. Well, Darby and I agreed to make him the spokesperson—the only thing we were able *to* agree on after the spell turned on us. Jai wasn't so enthused, but I guess he realized he had the best shot at getting us out of this in as little trouble as possible. Darby's too blunt and I'm already on the thinnest of ice with the Maestros. But Jai has the sort of charm that makes him every teacher's pet, and now he turns it on full blast.

"We thought we could trap the older students," adds Jai. "Then we could free the zombie-fied kids and surprise everyone —seventh graders winning musical zombies! Who'd have seen it coming? In retrospect, of course, I can see how that might have been bending the rules too far. We're very sorry, and we promise to never do anything like it ever, ever again."

He gives a sheepish grin, then sucks down his hot chocolate. I hide a smirk, impressed with how convincing he's made the whole thing sound.

"I knew we should have discontinued that ridiculous game years ago," Mr. Pinwhistle grumbles.

"You went outside the game boundaries," says Miss Noorani. "You were supposed to stay within hearing of the band."

"We got lost," Jai says, looking for all the world like a scolded puppy. "There was this crazy Percusso after us, so we ran. It was so dark, and there were fireballs everywhere . . . I guess we just sort of freaked out."

At least the Maestros seem to buy our story.

But now the headmaestro is eyeing *me*. "You three wouldn't happen to know anything about the humfrog incident last week, would you?"

"Humfrogs?" Jai echoes. "Humfrogs . . . oh! You mean the Great Humfrog Float? Haha! Nope. Don't know anything about that."

He grins again, scratching the back of his head, but there's sweat on his forehead.

Okay, so maybe he's not as great of a liar as I'd thought.

But I guess since the Maestros can't *prove* we were behind the humfrog incident, they let it drop. Actually, they all seem sort of distracted. Miss Noorani and Miss Becker are whispering heatedly in the back corner of the room, talking about last night's storm like we're not even there.

I wonder why the weather's got them so on edge. Maybe they're worried some buildings will flood.

In the end, we get sentenced to two weeks of detention. We lose all computer, snack, and break room privileges, and earn extra transposing homework, which is of course the most tedious kind there is. I can't even email Gran to tell her my usual pack of lies about how awesome my classes are and how happy and totally unhaunted I am. I almost call her on the phone in the library, where Darby calls her parents from, but I know I couldn't possibly talk to Gran without her hearing the truth in my voice. And if she found out how bad things really were, she'd drag me home in a minute, saying "told you so" all the way.

Days later, trapped in a small classroom with Jai and Darby, hearing only the tick of the clock and the scratching of their pencils as they complete the work twice as quickly as I can, I find myself zoning out altogether and thinking about other things.

Like how everyone seems to whisper when I walk by them now, and how Claudia even called me "the fake Amelia" in Ensemble, when Miss Noorani wasn't listening. Darby must have told the whole school about how I actually got into Mystwick. My classmates had been annoyed with me before because of my constantly messing up spells. But now it's like *I'm* a ghost, because no one will even talk to me anymore. All I get is weird looks and whispers behind my back. Only Jai will sit with me at meals. In homeroom, Claudia asks Darby if she can move into my bed after I'm expelled, knowing very well that I can hear them talking. Not even Darby ignoring her remark made me feel better.

But I have an even bigger problem to worry about now: my test is in three weeks, and I'm nowhere near ready.

Everyone at school is in a bad mood thanks to musical zombies getting cut short, and also thanks to the rain and storms, which seem endless. It may have stayed dry the night we were stuck in the woods, but that ended the next day, when a down-pour started . . . and didn't stop.

Two weeks go by without a single day of sunshine.

One of the boys' dorms floods, and they have to move all the sixth- and seventh-grade boys into the high school building. Jai complains about having to sleep on the floor by a senior who farts all night long. The ceiling of the Shell springs a leak during one of the junior's recitals, and the stage has to be shut down during repairs. Being trapped inside for days on end has us all cagey and mean. At least, I think spitefully, they're all stuck inside too while I'm in detention. I'm not missing out on much.

One day, when I'm headed back to my dorm after a late night practicing in Harmony Hall, I hear the Maestros talking in the next room, which is some kind of teachers' lounge.

"I contacted the weather service," Miss Noorani is saying. "And they confirmed it: these storms are concentrated over Mystwick. No one else is experiencing this kind of weather."

"Is it a spell, you think?" Mr. Pinwhistle asks.

I walk a little more quietly, leaning toward the door to hear.

"It's certainly magic of some sort. And until we know the source, there isn't much we can do about it."

"Our attempts to clear the clouds with elemental magic only bring an hour or so of relief," says Miss Becker. "When normally, they'd result in a full day of clear skies. This is definitely magic, and it's getting stronger."

"What do you mean?" asks Mr. Walters.

"I mean, the storms are growing more frequent. The lake is nearly twice its usual depth, and at this rate, the other dorms will flood too. I fear the bad weather isn't the spell itself — but the side effects of the spell."

"If you're right," says Miss Noorani, "then this is all leading somewhere. Something is about to happen, and we have no idea what it is. Nor do we know whether it's an accident, or something intentional, someone *targeting* Mystwick. Without knowing the source, how can we defend the students?"

"We might have to start thinking about evacuation."

"We haven't had to do that in over twenty years," Mr. Pinwhistle says. "We've dealt with all manner of strange magic. We can deal with this too."

"Yes, but usually we know what the problem is and can make a plan to fix it. This time is different. This is something we've never seen, and our contacts in the other Musicraft schools are as baffled as we are. All we can do is wait and see what happens."

"What do we do in the meantime?"

"We continue as usual." That's Mrs. Le Roux. I didn't know she was in the room too. Her deep voice cuts in like the calming, steadying note of her cello. "We stay watchful and wary, but we do our jobs: instructing and protecting our students."

The others murmur agreement. I turn and tiptoe quickly away, wondering what it all means.

Something is about to happen.

I glance up at the high window above, where rain runs down the glass in thick streams. Beyond it, lightning bursts in a sky dark with clouds.

For some reason, I think of spilled tomato soup, the color of blood, and an invisible finger writing *Watch out.*

Why can't I shake the feeling that this weather, and the Maestros' fears, are somehow linked to the ghost of Amelia Jones?

CHAPTER TWENTY-FOUR

Desperate Measures

O**N THE LAST DAY** of our detention, I get official notice: my test is set for a Friday evening two weeks from now —Halloween.

I guess when Mrs. Le Roux said things would continue as usual, she meant it. The Maestros might be worried about the weather, but it was too much to hope that might be enough to make them forget about my test.

I have no idea what it will involve, but I know I'm nowhere *near* ready.

I'm falling even further behind in my classes. None of the Maestros even try to give me solos anymore. Instead, they ask me to sit out when the class attempts more difficult spells. "Watch and learn," they tell me, as if I'm going to get better that way. But I think what's really happening is they've given up on me.

And I can't figure out if I've given up on myself.

I still practice as much as I can. I do all my homework, take lots of notes, and let Jai tutor me whenever he offers. Why he's still hanging out with me, I don't know. All I do is get him in trouble.

"You need to relax," he says. "Anybody would make mistakes playing that tense."

But that's easy for him to say. He's already better than a lot of the high schoolers.

Me? I'm just lucky to be here. But my luck is running out.

Darby and I don't talk again after the night in the woods. Every morning, I wait until she's dressed and gone before I get out of bed, and at night, she's already asleep when I get back from my late practice sessions. Even when we get stuck together one day under the cafeteria awning, a storm raging all around us, she waits for the rain to end in silence and totally ignores me.

And the ghost is definitely still around.

Even when she's not doing anything to mess me up, I can still feel Other Amelia hovering around me like a shadow. I never really feel alone, and sometimes, my skin breaks out in goose bumps for no reason. I wonder if it's because she brushed against me.

The night before my test, it pours harder than it has all month; rain runs down the windows and the path from the dorms to Harmony Hall is under an inch of water. I tie plastic bags over my shoes and slog through it, my flute case double-wrapped in ponchos, which Miss March has been handing out like breath mints.

I shut myself in a practice room and play the same piece of music, over and over and over. It's a calming spell, but it doesn't seem to be working, even though the air around me is full of bright white magic, like glowing feathers drifting in the air.

I finally take a break, stretching my kinked-up muscles — and that's when I see an outline in the wisps of magic, an empty spot where no glowing lights appear. Something is there the same way the mountains are there at night — visible only by the hole it creates.

"Amelia?" I whisper, freezing. "Amelia Jones, is that you?"

The emptiness moves, and feathers of light flutter around her, and then I'm *sure* she's there.

My whole body turns into one big goose bump. It feels like ice slips down my back.

"Why are you doing this?" I ask. "Why can't you just leave me alone? I know I took your place, I know this isn't fair. But . . . I just want a chance. And it's not like getting me kicked out will help *you* any." I glance around, having lost sight of her. "Amelia? Hello?"

A loud thump sounds right beside me, and despite myself, I let out a shriek.

Then I realize it was just someone knocking on the door.

"Come in," I say weakly.

Jai pokes his head in. "Well, *somebody's* jumpier than a jitter-bug today."

"You surprised me," I grumble. "And what the heck's a jitterbug?"

"Here's a hint: if you ever see your dog mysteriously start tap dancing, it's probably infested with singing jitterbugs. They're like fleas, but . . . *musical.*" He slips into the room, holding his violin. "I had a free period, and thought I'd see if you wanted to practice together."

"Don't bother. I'm a lost cause."

"I can help you."

"I'm beyond help."

"Oh, stop being so mopey. The Maestros like—"

"Don't!" I slam my flute against my palm, glaring at him. "Don't tell me the Maestros like confidence, or that if I just relax I'll magically get better!"

"If you'd just let me help you," he presses, "you might figure out how to Compose again and show them you *do* belong here! There's no *way* they can kick you out of Mystwick if they know you're a Composer! Or if you want, I could just tell them that I saw you make that snow spell—"

"Then I'd *definitely* get expelled! Just stop with the helping me, will you? You're always pushing me, like you have any right to do that, when *you're* too much of a coward to even tell your dad you want to play rock spells!"

As soon as I say the words, I kick myself. What am I doing? Jai is my only friend here, the only person who has stood by me no matter what. He's given up so much of his own practice time to help me, never asking for anything in return. And I just burned all that to the ground in a fit of anger and fear.

But the words are out, spilled like garbage juice. There's no taking them back.

Jai's eyes darken. "If that's what you think, then maybe you *deserve* to be expelled."

He steps out and slams the door.

"Jai! I'm sorry! Wait—" I run after him, but by the time I reach the hallway, he's gone. I sink to the floor in the corner of the soundproof little room, clutching my flute and staring at my shoes.

Finally, I take the photo of my mom from my case and stare at it.

"I made it," I whisper. "I made it to Mystwick, just like you did. Just like I thought I was *supposed* to. This is what I've always wanted, but now . . . I'm about to lose everything."

I can't help feeling that if I lose this place, I'll lose her too, all over again.

What if Jai is right?

If only there *were* a way to prove to the Maestros, beyond all doubt, that I belong here . . .

Shutting my eyes, I imagine them watching, shocked, as I conjure snow from thin air, with a spell all of my own making.

Maybe that *would* show them. Maybe they'd be so impressed they wouldn't even care that I was breaking the rules.

I lick my dry lips and raise my flute.

Just like that day in the Echo Wood, I try to let my fingers take over, allowing my mind to relax so music can flow through me. My fingers press keys at random, feeling out a melody, searching for guidance from my subconscious. If I could just control this deep, strange part of myself, if I could only figure out how to unlock that power—

Sparks burst on my flute and fall to the floor, catching the crumpled music sheets on fire. In moments, I'm surrounded by leaping flames. I scream and press myself against the wall, my body going cold with terror.

Then the sprinklers overhead click on, and me, the papers, and the whole room get doused with a sudden freezing spray. I quickly cover my flute with my shirt, protecting it, but there's no hope for my collection of spells. The drizzle lasts a full minute, long after the fire is out, and the whole time I stand there in shock, water dribbling down my face.

When the sprinklers finally shut off, I find my flute covered in scorch marks. They'll wash off — the fire wasn't that hot, and it'd take a lot more heat than that to permanently damage the instrument — and the more delicate parts of the instrument, like the flute pads, are still intact and unharmed, thank goodness.

One of the perks of playing flute, instead of something wooden like violin or piano. But still, that was a close call. *Too* close.

The hall monitor who watches over the practice rooms runs up, looking pretty angry that I've just made his job a whole lot harder. He'll have to mop up the mess and scrub the scorch marks off the floor.

"You okay?" he growls. "Need to see the nurse?"

"I'm fine." I slip away, flute in one hand, case in the other. I wonder if he'll report this to Mrs. Le Roux.

My last hope is gone. There's no way I can Compose for the Maestros. Mr. Pinwhistle had been mad enough when I made his mustache grow. I don't even want to imagine his reaction if I set it on *fire*.

My test is tomorrow. I should go to dinner, but even the thought of food makes me sick. So instead, I go to my room and start packing.

CHAPTER TWENTY-FIVE

In the Key of Perfection

I MEET THE MAESTROS on the steps of Harmony Hall. They're all there—along with Mrs. Le Roux—dressed in coats and hats, since the night is cold. At least the rain has stopped for now, though the ground squelches and puddles lie everywhere. Students are scattered across the grounds, many in costume. I can hear the boom of Rebel Clef's drums in the gym, where the Halloween party is taking place. Instead of their usual rock spells, they're playing a version of one of my favorite blue spells, *In the Hall of the Mountain King,* by Edvard Grieg. The eerie, suspenseful melody drifts over the school grounds, and a few loose illusions slip free of the gym, shadowy specters conjured by the band members. Looking like ghosts draped in black shrouds, they float through the air, then vanish when they stray too far.

But the sky is as dark as midnight, even though it's only just after dinner. Black clouds knot and bunch over the mountains. The air feels tense, like one wrong move will make the whole sky break loose. A cold wind prowls the school, ruffling the skeletal trees and the peacock feathers on Mrs. Le Roux's broad-brimmed hat.

"Good evening, Miss Jones," the headmaestro says. The others just nod at me. Not even Miss Noorani has a smile for me now.

I fidget with my flute case, unsure what to do, then fall behind them when they start walking, limping a little. My too-small uniform shoes are pinching more than usual today.

I'd expected us to go inside, but it seems this test will take place outdoors, behind Harmony Hall, in the Echo Wood.

Or at the edge of it, I discover, when the Maestros all stop and circle around a waist-high tree.

My tree, of course.

It's still bent like an elbow, its leaves fallen, leaving it even more scraggly. Looking at it, I think, *One day it will be perfect to hang a swing on.*

If I can save it from being uprooted, that is.

"What do you want me to do?" I ask.

Mrs. Le Roux gestures at my tree. "This is your opportunity to show us what you've learned."

For a moment I wait, to see if she's going to add anything

more. But it seems these are all the instructions I'm going to get.

But it's pretty clear what she means: This is my chance to redo my first audition. My chance to get it right.

I'm surprised.

I'd expected something much harder—a grueling, hours-long exam demanding me to play spell after spell, throwing obscure magic theory questions at me.

But this?

This is . . . *easy*. In fact, I couldn't have hoped for a simpler test.

Then I realize: Maybe this is just a formality. So they can say I earned my way here, instead of landing here by accident. Maybe they were never going to kick me out at all.

My heart starts to beat faster. I can *do* this. I know I can.

As long as Other Amelia doesn't interfere. Now would be the perfect time for her to strike, if she wants to get me kicked out for good.

Please, I think. *If you're here,* please *just give me this. I'm begging you.*

Since it's clear the Maestros want to see which spell I'll choose, I go with "Papageno's Aria," a quick green spell from my favorite opera, *The Magic Flute,* which is based on my favorite book. And probably my mother's favorite book—so that has to be lucky, right? It's an intermediate spell, not as high-level as some of my classmates might be capable of, but impressive enough. At least, I hope so.

It's a light tune, notes bouncing happily along, and I have the whole thing memorized.

And as I play, the magic spirals from my flute and wraps around the little tree, straightening its limbs, pushing the trunk upward. It even puts out fresh new leaves, which unfurl like tiny petals of silk. The tree creaks and sways, glowing with green light. I don't look at the Maestros once. I learned *that* lesson. Instead I focus wholly on the tree. The perfect musician. Everything I've learned in my classes I pour into my flute, even remembering to keep my posture just right.

I don't miss a note.

I don't think even Other Amelia could have played better, and she doesn't so much as pull my ponytail as I play.

As I hold the final note, the little tree's leaves shiver, sending a shower of sparkling magic dust shimmering to the ground. And then it's done.

Breathing hard, I lower my flute and can't help the smile that spreads over my face.

My echo tree is straight. Strong. *Perfect.* Just like all the other echo trees in the Echo Wood. Before, it looked out of place, crooked and strange. An accident.

Now it belongs.

Now you could walk right past it without ever knowing it was different.

I look up at the Maestros. They exchange looks that I can't read.

Miss Noorani then glances at me and raises a finger. "Wait a moment, Miss Jones."

She and the other Maestros move a few feet away, where they whisper among themselves. Urgently. Like they can't agree.

Uh-oh.

Not good.

My heart starts to sink again. What did I mess up? I hit every note, I fixed my tree. Was it my spell choice? Did they expect something more advanced?

While I watch them, I pass my flute from hand to hand, sweat starting to slide down my temples despite the cold. Overhead, the echo trees groan with their orchestra sound, dissonant notes that usually seem beautiful, but tonight they have an eerie, flat tone. Like a warning.

The wind is rising, stronger and stronger. Looking up, I see the clouds are lower than they were, and they're moving around, swirling and swelling. A burst of lightning cracks inside them, lighting them up from the inside, searching for a way out. The air tightens up more. If the wind were a violin string, it would snap at the first touch of the bow.

The Maestros are still arguing. They don't seem to notice the storm that's about to break loose. Mr. Pinwhistle is smashing his fist into his palm, his mustache fluttering in the wind.

Oh, no. Please, *please* don't let it come down to Mr. Pinwhistle convincing the others to expel me. I don't get why he *hates* me so much. I've never complained once about the extra homework he assigns to me. And it's not like the mustache growth was permanent. So what's his problem?

I can't watch them anymore. It's just making me feel sick.

Instead, I pack away my flute and then grip the case with both hands, staring hard at the ground. My echo tree, which shone with magic just minutes ago, now sits dark and dull. But as the wind strengthens, its leaves rustle, then clatter like chimes.

"Miss Jones."

Looking up, I see Mrs. Le Roux and the others watching me.

I swallow hard. "If there's a problem, I can do it again. I can play a harder spell, I know I can. If —"

"Miss Jones, you played very well."

Then why does she look like she's about to deliver bad news?

"However," she adds, "we feel that . . ."

I don't hear the rest, because it's plain on her face what she's saying:

I failed.

They're sending me away.

A roar fills my ears that has nothing to do with the weather. I sway on my feet, my stomach dropping to the ground. My flute feels like it weighs a hundred pounds, and my hands begin to sweat as I cling to the case.

". . . and in the end," Mrs. Le Roux finishes, "the vote was four to one."

The Maestros all look at me apologetically, except for Mr. Pinwhistle, who's already storming back toward Harmony Hall. I glare at his back, knowing he's the one responsible for getting me expelled. He must have swayed them to his side. But who was the one who voted for me? I search their faces, and settle on Miss Noorani. She gives me a small, sad smile.

At least one of them saw something in me.

Half of me wants to rise up and fight, to demand answers. *Why?* What did I do wrong? What could I have done differently? Wasn't I perfect? Wasn't I everything they wanted me to be?

But the other half of me has given up. It's tired of fighting, of reaching for the impossible.

Face the facts, Amelia Jones. You're not your mother. You're more like your dad—a loser. A wash-up. You're not good enough.

You never were.

I go back to my room and change into my old clothes. I fold my Mystwick outfits carefully and store them in the closet. All my things are packed, and I leave tomorrow after breakfast on one of the zeppelins.

That's when I lose it.

I curl up on the bed and bawl like a baby.

I'm not proud of it, but it's the truth.

Outside, I can hear the students shouting. Rebel Clef's spells crash against the window, just dull thumps and vague lyrics from this distance. There will be candy and cake and punch in the cafeteria, but I don't have the heart to go get it. And I don't want anyone to see me like this. They'll ask why I was crying, and then I'll have to tell them . . .

It's better if I just sneak out. No goodbyes. Amelia Jones, gone in the night. They'll find out I flunked out, of course, but at least I won't have to see their faces when they do.

The only regret I have is Jai.

I hate leaving with things between us like they are. I hope he's not too mad at me.

I hear footsteps in the hallway outside, and then three familiar notes from a whistle-key. Sitting up, I wipe my face furiously, but when Darby walks in, she must see right away that I was crying.

She blinks, then looks away.

"You're back early," I say, my voice scratchy.

She shrugs. "Didn't feel like partying."

She takes off her jacket and hangs it up, then glances over her shoulder at me. "You failed your test."

It's not a question.

I sigh, then nod. "I don't . . . I don't know what happened. I played perfectly. It still wasn't good enough. I guess you were right all along. I don't belong here. I'm not like your Amelia, and I never will be."

Darby stands in front of her small desk mirror and brushes her hair. It's grown out a bit since school began, now hanging below her shoulders. Still razor-straight and black as ink.

"Nobody could be my Amelia," she says softly. "She was fire and vinegar, my mom used to say. A girl who knew what she wanted, and did whatever it took to get it."

I wish I could be like that. I thought I was, before coming to Mystwick.

"You'll be glad to have the room to yourself," I say. "At least until they find someone to take my place."

Darby snorts. She sets down her hairbrush and throws herself across her bed.

For a minute, I think she'll say something almost halfway nice. Like, that she'll miss my awful flute playing. Or that her new roommate will be even worse than me. Some insult you have to dig through in order to find the compliment, Darby-style.

But she just flops over on her side, her back to me.

So I guess that's it.

Goodbye to you too, roomie.

Angrily, I jump up and walk to the window. It's not even eight o'clock yet, and our curfew is extended for the holiday. Maybe I *will* go to the party, if only to stuff my pockets with candy for the ride home. If I slip in the back door of the gym, no one will even notice me.

But when I reach the window, all thoughts of candy vanish from my head.

I blink.

And blink again.

"Darby."

"I don't want to talk."

"DARBY."

She sits up, frowning. *"What?"*

I shake my head. "It's . . . It's . . ." But my voice sinks into my stomach, and my stomach sinks to the floor. My body goes cold from head to toe, as I try to make sense of the *thing* outside our window.

Darby shoves me aside to look. Her eyes grow wide, and she presses her hands to the glass.

"Is that . . . a *tornado?*" she whispers.

CHAPTER TWENTY-SIX

Crescendo

"OH MY GOSH," I whisper. "Oh. My. *GOSH*. That can't be real."

Lightning flashes in the sky, and the windows rattle when the thunder claps. What I'd mistaken for Rebel Clef's drums was really the storm. And now the clouds over Orpheus Lake are bulging downward, while the water is rising up, forming a dark funnel, half cloud, half water.

It's a tornado, all right, spinning over the water. The sky is black, darker than midnight. The trees around the school whip wildly around. As I watch, an oak by the lake cracks with a sound like a gunshot and crashes into the water. Tiles peel away from the roof of the boys' dorm and are sucked into the dark vortex.

It looks like a scene from a movie, not real life.

This must be the thing the Maestros were worried about. But I wonder if even they could have anticipated something so huge and terrible. Is it magic? Some sort of black spell?

Either way, at this rate, the school will be *destroyed*.

I spot a group of people at the lake's edge, illuminated by a familiar blue light, little more than silhouettes holding instruments.

"It's the Maestros," says Darby. "Hey! Where are you going?"

Flute in hand, I yank open the door. "To see if they need help."

"Help? It's a freaking *tornado!* You can't *help!*"

But she follows me out, her oboe under her arm.

We race down the hallway and down the stairs and out the doors, then across the grass toward the lake. Other students are gathering there too, still in costumes, most with their instruments out. I see superheroes and cats, zombies and witches, and a group of older kids too cool to dress up, but now looking as terrified as the rest of us.

"What's going on?" I yell to Claudia, who's holding her clarinet like she might use it to bash the tornado. She's dressed up as a pop star. George is with her, in a Beethoven costume, and a bunch of other seventh graders are gathering around us.

Claudia turns, her face pale. "They say it's a spell gone out of control."

An adult—Mr. Ahmed, the history teacher—is moving through the clustered students, shouting, "Back inside, all of you! Now! Go to your dorms and wait in the halls! You know the drill!"

Students are starting to disperse, some running back to the buildings, but some resist, trying to watch.

George yelps as his Beethoven wig flies right off his head. "Someone said it's a black spell!"

"The strongest spell they've ever seen," adds Claudia.

My skin turns cold. That's not the first time I've heard a spell described that way in the past month. I look at Darby, and Darby looks at me.

"Are you thinking what I'm thinking?" I ask.

She shakes her head. "Rosa would never—"

But I'm already off, dodging Mr. Ahmed and running toward the Maestros. They're lined up on the bank, instruments ready, but no one is playing. They seem to be arguing about what spell to perform.

"No one could work a black spell on school grounds!" Miss Noorani is shouting. "We would know the moment they began, thanks to our wards."

"It's elemental," insists Mr. Walters. "It must be. If we try *Concertina B*—"

"That's only going to make it worse!" Mr. Pinwhistle shouts. "You idiot, are you trying to destroy the school?"

"Look at that thing! Mystwick is going to get destroyed either way!"

But weirdly, the twisting cyclone isn't moving like a tornado would. It's just twisting over the lake, clouds and water wrapped together. The roar of it is deafening. Spray thrown by the funnel lashes my face.

"Miss Noorani!" I shout. "I think I know—"

"Amelia!" She waves me away. "Go inside, now! It isn't safe!"

Frustrated, I look around, until I spot her—Rosa Guerrera. She's standing with the other members of Rebel Clef, watching the tornado with her mouth hanging open. She's dressed up in her usual black leather, pink hair dye, and crazy tights, but for Halloween, she's taken it up a notch, adding a black cape with red feathers on the collar, and black lipstick.

I sprint toward her, leaning into the wind that roars off the lake.

"Did you do this?" I pant.

She looks down at me, her lips twisting. "Excuse me?"

"The musicat, the spell you wrote down, was it this?"

She blinks. "What? That was just one of the spells that maintain the school wards, sort of like the password to get in. I needed it so my boyfriend could sneak onto campus and bring me some real food. That cafeteria slop is only fit for guppies and animals."

"That's all?" I blink. "But . . . that's so . . ."

"Boring?" she asks. "Yeah, well, I have a reputation to uphold, you know. And the fact that you think *I* did *this*"—she waves at the tornado—"means it's working." She smirks, but her eyes still look uneasy.

"But if it wasn't you, then who?"

"Someone with a lot of power," says another voice, from behind me. "Someone dangerous."

I turn around and see someone covered in face paint and wearing an enormous, frizzy wig. Judging by the inflatable electric guitar they're holding, they're supposed to be some kind of rock star, but with the black paint around their eyes smudged down their cheeks, they look more like a crazed racoon.

I stare. *"Jai?"*

He blinks, almost looking like he's about to reply. But then he must remember our fight, because his jaw clamps shut and he looks away.

George holds up a hand. "Whoa, did you two finally break up?"

Suddenly the sky seems to crack, and we all duck, even Rosa. But it's just a clap of thunder, so loud and close I can feel it vibrating in my rib cage.

"All right," Rosa says. "Come on, guppies. It's time to go inside."

"I'm not going anywhere," says Jai. "I want to see—*Hey!*"

One of the Rebel Clef players grabs him and hoists him over his shoulder. It doesn't take much effort; Jai is a skinny kid and the senior has arms like tubas. He starts up the hill, while Rosa grabs my hand and pulls me along.

"I may be mean," she says, "but I'm not leave-a-kid-to-get-struck-by-lightning mean."

I go, because I know I'm pretty much useless out here anyway. The Maestros will handle . . . whatever it is out there. But looking back, they seem so small against the storm and the strange, stationary tornado.

It's odd.

As I stare at the funnel, there's also something about it that seems familiar to me. The way it's twisting, the pattern of the water, the smell of burned matches—

CRRRRAAAACCKKKKKK!

The sound hits us with physical force. Me, Rosa, Jai, and the guy holding him are all thrown flat to the ground. The wind is pressed from my lungs.

"What happened?" groans Rosa.

Gasping for breath, I roll over and look down at the lake —and feel my heart shrink to the size of a walnut.

"Whoa."

Inside the tornado, it looks like someone hacked at the sky with a giant pair of rusty scissors. What's left is a jagged dark crack, through which there swirls a murky, infinite darkness. Wind rushes from the opening, pushing at the grass and the people and the trees in the distance.

The Maestros are all climbing to their feet, struggling to stand in that terrible wind.

And then, from the hole inside the tornado, *things* start to emerge.

I almost miss them at first, they're so faint. But then more and more swarm out of the void beyond and there's no mistaking the ghostly silver forms. They flicker through the air, circling like vultures, fluttering like strips of airy white cloth.

"*Dios mío,*" gasps Rosa.

"Watch out!" someone screams.

I turn, then duck just in time—one of the silvery forms is diving straight at us. Just as I hit the ground, it swoops overhead and soars away, aiming for Mr. Ahmed.

"Ghosts," I say in horror. "They're all *ghosts.*"

Mr. Ahmed doesn't dodge fast enough. The thing passes right through him, and Mr. Ahmed seizes up—then topples to the ground.

I'm up and sprinting toward him before I half realize what I'm doing. All I can think is that we *have* to help. Rosa and Jai are right behind me.

"He's alive," Rosa says, pressing her fingers to his neck.

"Agh!" Jai shouts, stumbling back when Mr. Ahmed's eyes flicker to him. The man can't move, but his eyes still flit around. He looks terrified.

"He's paralyzed," says Darby. "And look—he's not the only one."

The silvery creatures are chasing down all the adults,

paralyzing the Maestros one by one. Something about their touch is enough to lay a person flat. Before our horrified eyes, they get Mr. Walters and Miss Noorani, then Miss Becker. Mr. Pinwhistle and Mrs. Le Roux stand back to back, playing a furious duet, him on his clarinet and her with her cello, but it's not enough.

Two of the creatures swoop at them, and Mr. Pinwhistle drops like a stone. Mrs. Le Roux tries to fight them both off, yellow magic blossoming from her cello. But pinned between the pair of them, she falls quickly.

Everyone looks stunned. I don't think any of us expected the Maestros would actually fail to get control of the chaos. We trusted they could protect us from anything.

"What do we do?" Jai whispers.

We all look at Rosa, because she seems to be the most likely one to take charge now that all the adults are lying paralyzed on the ground. She is wide-eyed, her face pale, looking nothing like her usual, tough self.

"I . . . I think we should go inside," she says. "Maybe the Maestros—"

"Look out!" yells Darby.

A silver ghost is swooping toward us again. This one is clearly a girl, because she's wearing a skirt that flutters around her. Her long hair sways over her shoulders. She seems a little more solid than the others, all silvery white lines. While the others scream and start running, I stand transfixed, watching her get closer, because I know this ghost.

It's Amelia Jones.

And she's coming straight for me.

CHAPTER TWENTY-SEVEN

The Ghost of Dissonance Past

I RUN.

Not toward Harmony Hall with the others, but to the left, trying to draw Other Amelia in the opposite direction of my friends. This is between us, just her and me. The two Amelias.

But that doesn't mean I *want* to face her.

I tear across the grass, clutching my flute. Lightning streaks overhead, as if pointing the way, and a few drops of rain land on my skin. I pull my jacket over the flute and run faster. My heart pounds in my ears, screaming at me to go back. But I don't dare stop. If the ghosts can paralyze the Maestros, there's no telling what Other Amelia will try to do to me.

Is *she* behind all this?

Has she been waiting all this time, just toying with me, while planning her real attack? She'd seemed mostly harmless before—annoying, infuriating, and scary—but not *deadly*.

Now, I think she might be fully capable of throwing me off a cliff or drowning me in the lake.

She knows what she wants, Darby had said. And she knows how to get it.

Apparently, getting revenge on the girl who took her place was enough to make her break through the wall between life and death. And she brought all her ghost friends with her.

I round Harmony Hall and break for the woods. After all, didn't Mrs. Le Roux tell me the trees are there to guard the school? Maybe they can guard me now.

The trunks of the echo trees fly past as I dash deeper into the forest. Looking back, I see Ghost Amelia flickering behind me, still pursuing, but losing ground. Feeling surer of my path now, I charge onward.

But no matter how fast I go, Ghost Amelia is always behind me, a faint silver light in the trees. I can still hear the roar of the tornado, but it's distant now, and mostly I just hear my own panting.

My strength starts to flag. My legs grow weaker and my feet scream inside my too-small shoes. It feels like I swallowed fire, my lungs are burning so badly. Every breath is a painful gasp.

"Please," I find myself saying, "please leave me alone. I'm sorry! I never meant to take your place!"

If she hears me, she doesn't care.

The woods around me are unfamiliar. I realize I've circled the school, getting lost in my panic. Instead of going deeper into the Echo Wood, I turned right at some point and kept going, and now

I'm completely confused. But when I try to stop and get my bearings, I feel Other Amelia's cold fingers brush the back of my neck.

Chills slide down my spine.

I've felt that touch before, the day Jai found me Composing in the woods. I fell into the stream and a strange hand pulled me out.

Why did she help me then? What made that day different?

When the ground beneath my feet starts to crunch with rocks and not leaves, I realize I took the wrong direction completely.

I'm running toward the cliffs below the school.

With a yelp, I slide to a halt, but not fast enough. The edge of the cliff lunges out of the darkness, and suddenly I'm tipping over it. I drop my flute in an effort to regain my balance.

Even so, my feet slide right off the edge, and then, so suddenly I can't even scream—

I fall.

Everything is silent

frozen in slow motion

as my stomach rises into my throat and the world drops away beneath me—

And then a chilly hand grabs mine.

I slam against the cliff's face, but I'm not falling anymore.

With a groan, I reach up, and another cold hand reaches down to help. Scrabbling at the rock with my shoes, I do my best to climb, while the person on top of the cliff drags me up and over.

Finally, after what seems an eternity, I land on solid ground and sob in relief. I've never felt so happy to lie so still.

"*What,*" says a voice, "are you *doing?*"

I freeze, then slowly, slowly look up.

The ghost kneels over me, her face a picture of shock.

"You almost killed yourself!" she says.

With a groan, I roll onto my back, then sit up. My whole body is aching.

"You're . . ." I look her over, really seeing her for the first time. For some reason, she's clearer and more solid tonight than she's ever been before.

She looks only a little older than me. Her hair is long and curlier than I'd realized. And she's wearing a Mystwick uniform, of all things, beneath a black graduation gown. Not a ghostly shroud after all.

"You're . . . not Amelia Jones," I finish.

"Darling." She gives me a sympathetic look. "*You're* Amelia Jones."

"I know I am! Who are you?"

"You still don't know?"

She smiles.

And

time

stands

still.

Every single hair on my body rises up.

Because at that moment, I *do* know.

I know, because that face is the face I've been holding in my memories all my life.

A face I've been *dreaming* of.

An impossible face.

"No," I whisper. I stumble to my feet and walk a few steps away. "No, no, this isn't real."

"Amelia . . ."

"I must have hit my head or something. This is a dream. I'm unconscious."

Tears squeeze from my eyes. I don't dare look at her. I can't. It's too much. I'll bust open.

"*Amelia,* look at me."

Shaking, I slowly turn around.

And there she is.

Mom.

I make myself look at her, to let it sink in. She doesn't look as old as she was in the photos Gran has of her and me when I was a baby. She looks younger, maybe Rosa's age, and of course there's the uniform . . . I realize then that this is the version of Mom I know best, because this is what she looks like in the photo in my flute case.

Mom on her Mystwick graduation day.

Everything inside me breaks at that moment. I run to her,

half expecting to run right *through* her. Instead, I feel her arms wrap around me. I crush myself against her, feeling like I swallowed the tornado, storm and all. I don't even mind that she's a bit cold; it's like hugging a snowman.

She holds me tight, just the way I remember her doing when I was little. My face burrows into her shoulder and my hands meet behind her back. I squeeze her the way Gran squeezes me, like I'll never let go. Like I can pin her to the world of the living by sheer force of will.

My heart explodes in my chest. My throat twists into a knot. I breathe so hard and fast that a sob slips from my lips and tears squeeze from my eyes to run down my face. My body isn't big enough to contain this moment. The *world* isn't big enough to hold it all.

The feeling expanding inside me is the strongest magic I have ever felt in my entire life.

My mom is here.

My mom is holding me.

I press myself into her, trying to make myself believe this is real. Wondering that she doesn't seem like a stranger. My memories of her are so fuzzy, sometimes I can't even picture her face, and yet . . .

I *know* her.

She presses one hand into my hair and kisses my temple.

"How?" I murmur. "How is this possible?"

"Sweetheart, *you* made it possible."

Reluctantly, I pull back, but I take both her hands. "Me?"

She nods, then starts to whistle.

The tune is familiar, something I've heard before . . . No, something I've *played* before.

In my treehouse.

After my horrible audition.

When I was so upset and lost that I didn't half know *what* I was doing. I just grabbed my flute—*Mom's* flute—and played the notes that were spinning around inside of me. I'd thought it was some sort of summoning spell, the way all the leaves and twigs were swirling around.

"My spell," I whisper. "That day in the woods . . ."

Mom nods. "It was a black spell, Amelia. A very powerful one, to open the path to death itself."

"A black spell? But . . . it was like a rainbow of color."

"They're called that not for their color, but because they're forbidden. Make no mistake of what that spell was—or that *you* Composed it."

I stare at her. "*I* brought you back. Like that day I made it snow in the Echo Wood. I was thinking of snow while I was Composing, only I didn't *know* I was Composing. And when I made all the leaves fly around, I was actually thinking about *you*. About how I'd give anything to just talk to you, even for a moment."

318

I remember it with perfect clarity—how I'd imagined my mom then exactly as I see her now: in her graduation gown, with her Maestro's pin. And somehow I summoned her exactly as I'd pictured her.

She nods. "You pulled me right through the veil between life and death. I tried to talk to you then. Oh, how I tried to hold you! But I was too weak, too thin. It was all I could do just to watch you, while you had no idea I was there."

I look down at her ghostly pale hands in mine. They're still a bit see-through. My fingers are visible through hers. "But why like this? Why couldn't I bring you back . . . you know, *all* the way?"

Her hands tighten on mine. "Amelia, you must never try that. Not *ever*, do you hear me?"

"But why?" My heart leaps around, singing with a hope I never even dared imagine possible. "Mom, if I could *really* bring you back—"

"Amelia, *no!*" She sounds like Gran when she says it. "Summoning the ghost of the dead is one thing. Bringing them back to life is another. It's beyond dangerous. It's *twisted*. And it always has terrible consequences."

"But you don't *know* that! If I could summon you here, I could do anything! Mom, I have to try. I have to—"

"I *do* know, Amelia. I do." She sinks down to the ground, her form flickering. I drop with her, refusing to let go of her hands.

We face one another on our knees, Mom's eyes squeezing shut. "I know better than anyone the cost of such magic."

"Mom? What do you mean?"

Her eyes open, then slowly lift to meet mine.

"Because, Amelia," she sighs. "I brought *you* back. And I paid for it with my life."

Something opens inside of me.

A big, black hole. It swirls with dark clouds, flashes with understanding.

At the bottom, a memory.

Black water. Strong current. Dark river.

My breath, gone. All light, gone. My parents, gone.

Me, *gone.*

The memory has been with me all along, lurking deep in my mind. It darted out from hiding the day Phoebe threw me in the lake, and again in the little practice room when Miss Noorani tested me with illusions. So much has happened since then I'd almost forgotten about it.

Somehow, I *knew,* but I just couldn't believe.

"Amelia, listen to me very carefully," Mom says, and it's like she's talking from a great distance away. "When you were little, we would go camping, you and me and your father. We had a favorite spot, by a river. But that night, it rained. It rained so hard the river rose. Our tent flooded. Your father and I were packing everything into the car, so we could drive home. And then . . . you were gone. You toddled off to the water, and it just . . . snatched you up."

Her voice shakes. Her hands tremble in mine.

"We found you downriver, but it was too late. You were . . ." She stops, her eyes closing, tears like ghostly pearls running down her cheeks. "Your father ran to get help, but I couldn't give up yet. I still had my flute."

She lets go of my hands to pick up the instrument, which still lies in the dirt where I dropped it. She holds it in her palms lovingly.

"I was a Composer too, Amelia."

I press my hands to my lips, murmuring, "You brought me back."

She nods, raising the flute to her chest, fingers knotted around it. "I Composed a resurrection spell, and right before my eyes, you sucked in a breath and your eyes opened. But magic like that is *very* hard to control. The spell went wild, until I was no longer playing it—*it* was playing *me*. That's what can happen when you Compose something too big. Composing is driven by weaving your willpower into your notes, which means you have to concentrate fully and completely on the thing you want your magic to do. You must want it with your whole being, with a perfect purity of focus. But if your focus wavers even a little—because of fear or doubt or anger—then the magic takes control of you, and it consumes you. Do you hear? When I Composed that spell by the river, I had just a seed of doubt in my heart, just enough fear that it wouldn't work, and that's why it backfired on me, even as it saved you."

Her words frighten me. The magic she's talking about, it's so big, so powerful, so beyond anything I can understand . . . So I nod, and her face relaxes. She pulls me into another hug.

"I missed you," I whisper. "I can't lose you again."

"Oh, Amelia." She kisses my hair, over and over. "You never lost me. I've always been with you, tucked between the notes you played, hidden behind your measures and scales and arpeggios. That is how you remember me, and that is how I remain a part of you. But I can't stay with you like this. I don't belong to this world anymore, and even if I tried, for as long as I remain here, *other* things can get in too."

"Other things? Do you mean those other ghosts?"

"Just so, my love. When you opened that doorway three months ago, it was just big enough for me to slip through— a door opened. But by leaving your spell unfinished, you also left a powerful amount of magic uncontrolled—a door that continued to open, wider and wider. And that loose magic has been tethered to you all this time, following you wherever you went, getting more unstable." She pulls back, raising her hands to frame my face. Her eyes are silvery as the moon. "That's what I've been trying to warn you about. I knew it was only a matter of time before the veil between life and death broke altogether, and the others would escape through the spell you created. I'd hoped you could stop it before it went this far."

I suck in a breath as understanding floods through me. "I thought you were someone else, someone trying to sabotage me. But you were trying to *talk* to me."

"I needed you to embrace the part of you that is most powerful, the part of you driven by your instinct and your belief."

"My Composing," I whisper. Thinking back to all the times she blew away my music sheets or interfered with my playing, it now makes sense. She was trying to tell me I didn't need the music, that I could make my own. She was trying to get me to stop following the notes on the page, so I could listen to the notes *inside*. "That day you wrote on the whiteboard," I say, "you spelled *poser*."

"*Com*poser," she replies. "If you had let me finish, anyway."

"And the message in the soup, telling me to watch out—"

"It was supposed to say, *Watch out, there are a bunch of ghosts coming*. Or something like that." She pauses, wincing. "I ran out of soup."

"You were trying to help me, all along."

"It wasn't easy. I was so weak, and every time I tried to reach you, I only got weaker. But tonight's Halloween, the night when the wall between the living and the dead is at its thinnest. That's why I'm able to talk to you now, when I couldn't for all those months. It's why I can hold you. But it's also the perfect time for those *others* to break through. Those ghosts, Amelia, they're the worst of the worst. They're the spirits of people who have scores to settle in this world, who want to seek out revenge on people they once knew and wreak havoc on countless lives for no other reason than that it makes them feel a little bit alive again, and they'll do anything to stay in this world—even if it means destroying the school and everyone in it so you can't send them back. They know that a musician powerful enough to release them is also powerful enough to banish them again."

My stomach lurches. "We have to stop them."

"*You* have to stop them," she replies. "It's *your* spell, Amelia —you decide what it does. Do you remember the Second Rule of Musicraft?"

Lest you be doomed by your own art, always finish what you start.

"I have to finish the spell," I whisper. In my treehouse that day, I'd broken off playing because I'd been so surprised by the magic I'd created. Which means all this time—just like Mrs. Le Roux had warned—that magic has been hanging around, getting more and more unstable. My mom knew, and she was trying to tell me. "And I have to focus on what I want that spell to be. That's how Composing works—like you said, and like Jai tried to tell me. Weaving my willpower into music." What had they called it?

Purity of focus.

Mom nods. "You must not only finish it, but decide *how* will you finish it. Close the spell. Tie up all that loose magic."

A bubble of hope rises inside me — then bursts.

"But I can't Compose whenever I want. I'm not like you. I can only do it by accident." Groaning, I let my face sink into my hands. "I screwed up the biggest audition of my life. I fail even when I play every note exactly right! I'm not like the other kids here, or the other Amelia. She was the real musician. I'm not even like *you!*"

But Mom smiles.

"*Exactly.* Because you're *you,* Amelia, someone special and unique and powerful. But your magic will only ever be as strong as your belief in *yourself.* That is the only way you can save your friends and your school and make things right."

She holds the flute toward me.

"It's time for you to decide: who is the *real* Amelia Jones?"

I stare at the flute. It seems to glow in the ghostly light she casts. Ever since she was taken from me, I've longed to talk to her and ask her what I should do. And now she's telling me.

But the strength to do this has to come from me, not her.

My magic is only as strong as my belief.

My hands shake. My heart beats like a drum.

All I've wanted was a chance to prove I could do it. To her. To Gran. To the Maestros and all the students.

But now I realize, the only person I ever needed to prove myself to was *me*.

Drawing a deep breath, I look my mother in the eye and give her a nod.

I reach out and take back the flute.

CHAPTER TWENTY-EIGHT

The Music Inside

W̲HEN MOM AND I reach the lake just minutes later, I let out a gasp of horror.

More ghosts have poured through the rip in the middle of the tornado—where there had been a dozen, now there are too many to count. They fly in thick flocks, like enormous dark crows, screeching and hammering at windows and doors. Their faces are horrible, twisted masks, with hollow eyes and wide, empty mouths, as if years of raging against their fates has erased their old identities completely, transforming them into monsters. Only Mom seems human still, and she watches the other ghosts with sad eyes.

I see shimmers of magic and realize the students inside the buildings must be playing repelling spells to keep the ghosts from getting in. The Maestros are still lying on the ground, paralyzed. And it's starting to rain harder. I wrap my flute in my coat to protect it, which leaves me shivering.

Hearing a shatter of glass to my left, I turn to see a ghost has broken through a window in the boys' dorm. A dozen of the silvery figures swoop inside, and screams sound within. I guess someone must have hit the wrong note in their repelling spell.

"There are too many!" I shout over the tornado's roar.

Mom grabs my hand.

"Only you can stop them!" she shouts back. "You have to complete the spell."

I stop and shake my head, pulling away. "I need one thing first!"

Running back down the hill, I grab Mrs. Le Roux by the hand. I wonder if she even knows what's going on.

"I'm sorry," I say to her, even though she gives no indication she can hear me. "This is all my fault. I can fix it, I think, but I need to borrow this."

I pull something from her pocket, then sprint back up the hill to Harmony Hall, stumbling on the wet grass, and pound on the front door. Mom watches my back, keeping away any ghosts who might decide to take a dive at me.

"Let me in!" I yell. "It's me, Amelia!"

The door cracks open and Rosa peers through. When she sees my mom, she snarls and starts to slam the door shut.

"No!" I shout. "She's with me!"

"She's a *ghost!*"

Suddenly Darby is there, yanking the door open. "Amelia?" she says, eyes wide. "*My* Amelia, is that you?"

My mom leans close and whispers, "I'll wait outside. Just remember: listen to the music *inside* of you, Amelia."

I nod and squeeze her hand before she drifts away, hoping it's not the last chance I'll have to speak with her.

I'm trying very hard not to think about the fact that by saving the school, I'll have to lose her again. I worry if I think about it too much, I'll change my mind.

I love my mom with all my heart, but she's not mine to save. The school and all its students and teachers, however, just might be.

The rest of the Rebel Clef band stands in the great foyer, with Jai and a bunch of other seventh graders. The other students must be holed up in the dorms and gym. Most are holding instruments at the ready, looking unsure whether they should play something. The few seniors are playing a repelling spell, stationed at the windows. There aren't any adults in sight.

I see Darby watching me with burning eyes.

"That was the ghost who chased you," she whispers.

I nod.

"She's not Amelia."

"I'm sorry, Darby. It was . . . my mom. I'm sorry it wasn't your friend. But I need your help now. I know the spell that will stop the ghosts, but I can't play it alone."

I turn to the others, raising my voice. "My flute won't be

enough—the sound of the tornado will drown me out. We need an orchestra. As many students as we can gather. Then we have to go outside and finish this."

"If the Maestros couldn't stop this, how could we?" Jai asks.

I draw a deep breath, then say, "Because the spell that let those ghosts into the school? It's *mine*. I Composed it."

Claudia shoulders through the others. "*You're* a Composer? That's ridiculous! You're delusional. The *real* Amelia—"

"I *am* the real Amelia!"

I don't realize how loudly I shouted it until I see all the students in the room are staring at me.

For a moment, I want to run away and hide from all those stares. An hour ago, I was ready to do just that. I was ready to give up.

But not anymore.

Because I *am* the real Amelia Jones.

I always was. Somewhere along the way—even before coming to Mystwick—I lost myself. I tried too hard to become someone I wasn't, the perfect, model musician. I tried to be the *other* Amelia, or my mom, when instead, I should have done what my mom has been trying to tell me to do all along: listen to the music *inside*. Because that's my strength.

That's what makes me real.

And it just might be what saves Mystwick.

"Darby," I say, letting out a long breath. "I'm sorry your

friend died. It wasn't fair. She should be here. But that doesn't mean I *shouldn't*. I'm here now, and I'm asking for your help."

She's glaring at me, her eyes wet with unshed tears. "You want my *help?*"

I nod. "I need you to Conduct."

I hand her the baton I plucked from Mrs. Le Roux's pocket. She stares at it like it's a snake.

"Please?" I wrap her hand around the baton. "I need you, Darby. Only you can lead us through this spell. I know the notes, but I need someone to weave them together."

Every moment we waste arguing, more ghosts escape the tear. If we wait much longer, they might be too strong and too many for us to repel.

Darby glares back at me. I can see her at war with herself, and I'm not at all sure she's going to help. But I have to ask. Because it's true — I need her. I need *all* of them.

Finally, Darby looks down at the baton, her face crumpling. "I . . . I don't know. The last time I tried . . . You remember. I totally failed."

"You're the most fearless person I know," I say. "But your magic is only as strong as your belief. Well, *I* believe in you, Darby Bradshaw. Do you?"

Her fist tightens around the baton.

"Well?" I ask. *"Do you?"*

She looks up, a spark igniting in her eyes.

"I'll do it," she whispers.

I wrap my hand around hers. "What's that? I can't quite hear you."

She gives a weak grin. "I *can* do it?"

Leaning forward until our noses are inches apart, I say through my teeth, "I. Can't. *Hear.* You."

Darby throws back her head and yells at the top of her lungs, "I CAN DO IT! Everyone! Get into marching formation!"

Students grab instruments, tuning up, jumping in place, moving toward the doors. Darby sticks to my side, holding her baton like it's a sword.

She suddenly seems like a totally different person, not the Darby who hung out in the back of the classroom every day, staying quiet and avoiding everyone. Now she shouts orders and even the seniors listen to her, everyone falling into neat lines and readying their instruments.

I find myself standing just in front of Jai, and with a deep breath, I turn around to face him.

"I was wrong," I say, before he can avoid my gaze. "I was stupid, and mean, and *wrong.* You're not a coward, Jai, but you *are* a good friend, a better one than I deserved."

He looks down at his violin, his thumb rubbing the E string. "You were right, actually. I *am* too scared to tell my dad how I feel. And I pushed you the way he's always pushed me, and I hate when he does that. I should have known better."

"Well, maybe I needed pushing. I was just so scared of messing up, I couldn't even try."

"Your magic *is* only as strong as your belief, Amelia *Grace* Jones."

I blink. "You—you guessed it. You actually guessed it!"

He laughs. "Nah, I just peeked at your student file when Mr. P. left it on his desk during detention one day."

"Kapoor!" snaps Darby. "Would you shut up already? It's time to kick some ghost butt!"

Jai whoops and waves his violin over his head. "Hey everyone! What're we gonna kick?"

"Ghost butt!" we scream.

"What are we gonna kick?"

"Ghost butt!"

"Blocking spell!" calls Darby. "Beethoven's Fifth, first movement! On my count, one and two and—"

We fall into two lines and strike up the powerful spell. Golden light explodes from our instruments and spreads overhead, then down to the ground, forming a glittering shell around us all. We parade through the front doors of Harmony Hall, almost the entire seventh-grade class and a few older kids, our spell ringing out. Even the cellists and bassists walk with the rest of us, their huge instruments strapped to them in marching harnesses. The drummer from Rebel Clef pushes Victoria's wheelchair, while she adds powerful guitar riffs to the spell. We're not the most organized marching orchestra in the history of Musicraft, but we just might be the *loudest*.

I spot my mom nearby, and she raises her hands together to give me a little victory cheer. I nod back, keeping my flute pressed to my chin. Above me, the rain hits our shield and slides down, so we seem to walk in a moving dome of water. All around, the other students play with all their might, the Chordos taking the melody and everyone else filling in the harmonies and counter-melodies. It helps that we've been practicing this particular spell in Orchestra for the last two months. I wonder if anyone could have guessed it might one day save us all.

For the first time, I really do feel like I belong with them. I play as loudly as anyone, my fingers moving with a grace and surety I didn't know I had.

But it's quickly clear that this is not going to be easy.

The tornado twists and writhes, ghosts swirling from its depths and diving at us. The storm is worse than ever, with thunder cracking and rolling while lightning streaks from east to west. Behind Harmony Hall the echo trees whip around like they've been caught up in a frenzy spell.

The ghosts who swoop our way bounce off the ward and flee, screeching in rage. It's like walking under a giant, transparent turtle shell veined with gold. Where the ghosts hit, shimmering dust rains down on our heads, but the ward holds strong. And my mother floats beside me, a few steps away, separated by the glowing barrier but sticking as close as she can.

"It's working!" Jai shouts, scraping furiously at his violin. "Don't stop!"

Darby walks backwards down the hill, flicking the baton, eyes focused and jaw tight.

When we reach the water's edge, she stands on the dock and faces us. Behind her the tornado writhes, churning up the lake's flooded waters. She looks tiny with that thing looming behind her. This close, I can see the edges of the rip fluttering like cloth. The depths are black and shadowy.

But worse, as I lower my flute to catch my breath, I can see the tear inside the tornado is getting wider. The spell I began months ago is bigger and stronger than I could have ever imagined. More and more ghosts are finding their way out, shrieking with delight as they see the world of the living open to them at last. I remember what my mom said about these ones being the worst of the worst, and what they'll do to stay in this world they don't belong in.

We *have* to make this work.

I have to make this work.

Or Mystwick and the Maestros and all these students will pay the price. This isn't about me anymore. It's not about proving myself or earning my place here. If I fail now, there won't even *be* a *here*.

Darby has us finish the blocking spell, and the students fall silent. The ward remains in place, but soon it will fade away and leave us all exposed to the ghosts and rain, so I don't have long. Everyone else looks as scared as I am, but nobody breaks. They await Darby's instructions.

"Ready?" Darby asks me.

"Ready." I raise my flute, inhaling deeply.

"Okay, Amelia," she says. "What's the spell?"

I stand beside her and start to play the tune I invented months ago. At first I'd worried I wouldn't be able to remember it, but it comes to me as freshly as if I were still lying in my treehouse. I played then with the fear that I'd never even *see* this school.

Now I play with the hope of saving it.

The melody is simple and sad, filled with longing. I know now that it's my love for my mother spun into sound, all my heartache and wishfulness and regret pouring from me, into my flute, turning to magic. Each note feels like a piece of me, raw and real, unwinding from my heart; it's like letting everyone look straight into my soul.

I feel more exposed than I ever have before.

And I also feel more powerful than I ever have before.

I run through the melody twice, and then Darby turns to the

other students and signals for them to get ready. They stand with instruments poised, as around us the ghosts gather and thicken, as if preparing for a full, organized assault. Their hollow eyes gape at us. They know our ward is weakening, and they're waiting for the moment to strike.

Jai is first to jump in, picking up the melody with his violin. Rosa and her saxophone join next, and then Claudia, and George and Victoria and Rabiah, and the rest of Rebel Clef. As the students begin to play, one by one joining in with my flute, our sound slowly drowns out the ghosts.

Then *everyone* is playing, following the melody or adding their own harmonies. And Darby Conducts it all, her baton flicking to keep tempo, her free hand reaching out to call for more from certain players. I don't know how she does it, keeping track of each instrument and its musician, weaving us all together, making my simple spell into something grand and intricate and beautiful.

These kids really are the best in the world. Who else could hear a melody two times and then turn it into a symphony with no practice at all? Not that every note is perfect. I hear a few that make me wince. But the nice thing about playing in an orchestra is that there's always someone to cover for you.

The ghosts seem taken aback. They aren't sure what we're doing, and some start to pull away worriedly. Before, the Maestros weren't able to join together in force against them, and so they became easy targets. But all together, our student orchestra is too strong for them.

My spell becomes *our* spell, and our united sound is more powerful than anything I could ever play on my own.

But I am still its Composer, and I must decide how this spell will end.

Go, I think, but it is only one ghost I think of. *I'm letting you go.*

And even though it feels like I'm telling my own heart to crawl out of my chest, I focus everything in me on the words and on the music. And I know, at last, what it means to Compose. I take the reins of my wayward magic and pull it back under control, this spell of my own making: a spell to summon the spirit of a lost soul, and then release them to their rest.

Go.

Rainbow-colored threads coil upward from my flute to join with the magic flowing from everyone else — yellow and green and blue and purple all twist together, glittering and brighter than any shades I've ever seen. A great stream of it swirls to the tornado, like thread feeding a spool. The dark clouds and water begin to glow as our magic weaves through it all. Black spells aren't black at all, just like Mom said, but every color at once, more beautiful than I could have imagined.

Finally, the tear starts to close, threads of magic knitting the seam together.

The ghosts start wailing as the tornado begins sucking them inward. All around us, silvery forms flow through the air and disappear into the shadow inside the funnel. They vanish into the tear and back into whatever afterlife awaits. But what about my mom?

I turn and see her watching me.

Since the rest of the students are going strong with my melody now, I am able to lower my flute for a few moments. I stop closer to Mom so I can hear her over the music.

"Your spell is strong, my love," she says, her voice slightly warped by the ward between us. "It's working. But that means I have to go."

I raise a hand, pressing it to the barrier, aching because I can't touch her. "Maybe there's a way," I whisper. "If you just hold on to me—"

"The tear can't close until I'm on the other side," she replies. "But don't worry about me. A part of me will stay here with you, as it always has. You must stay strong. Maintain your focus, Amelia, or the spell will backfire. Be strong, my love. Don't worry. Don't be afraid."

"But I still have so many questions. Especially about . . . I didn't think I cared, but I think maybe I do. My dad—"

"Amelia!" Darby is calling my name. I glance back to see her waving her baton at me, needing me to rejoin the others. But I can't. I have to ask Mom—

But when I turn back, she is gone, and only her last whisper hangs in my memory.

"Don't be afraid."

I look around, then spot her, growing smaller and thinner as she soars back to the rift. She presses her hands to her lips, then extends them toward me, a final kiss, as she joins the river of ghosts streaming back to the crack between life and death.

She grows fainter and fainter.

And then she is gone.

Again.

And it feels like my heart has been ripped from my chest.

"Amelia!" Darby is growing frantic.

Trembling, I turn around and raise my flute. I feel like I'm going to crumble apart. But I have to finish this.

So with all my might, I focus on my music, though it's kind of hard to see because of the tears in my eyes.

I can feel the melody reaching its conclusion. But I don't rush it. I think that's why I always messed up before, when I tried to Compose consciously. I was trying too hard to control the music flowing out of me, when instead, I needed to *listen*.

The tornado is getting smaller and smaller. The roar of the wind is dying. Overhead, clouds are starting to thin and scatter. The rain stops at last.

One by one, the other students drop away, lowering their instruments at Darby's command, until the only sound left is my flute's silver tones. Magic curls from it, scarlet and violet and golden, every color there is, to drift through the air and then fade.

I play through a slow measure, then another, and finally, I hold the last note until my lungs feel empty.

Then, lowering my instrument, I watch as the tornado dissolves and the water it had drawn out of the lake begins to rain around us.

For a full minute that rain falls, until at last, the sky clears.

The lake is still and silent.

Stars dazzle overhead.

Not a wisp of wind remains to ruffle the grass.

And behind me, everyone breaks into a loud cheer.

A few rush to help the bewildered Maestros off the ground, and Rosa and Claudia help Victoria, whose wheels are stuck in the mud. The others surround Darby and me and lift us up. Phoebe and the drummer from Rebel Clef have me on their shoulders, parading me around like some kind of hero. Darby catches my eye, and we exchange a look that — call me crazy — is almost friendly.

Our celebration doesn't last long, though.

The Maestros pick up their dropped instruments — most of which are no doubt ruined. But at least they're *alive*. The students fall quiet as they approach, and the seniors set me down.

Everyone parts for Mrs. Le Roux, who manages to look serene as ever despite her windblown hair and soaking clothes. She walks through the crowd of students until she reaches me.

"Amelia Jones." She gives me an odd look, like she can't figure me out. "We need to talk."

CHAPTER TWENTY-NINE

Overture and Out

I**T'S BARELY DAWN,** everything washed in thin gray light.

The joints of my flute slide together with soft clicks, the smooth barrel so familiar to me it's like an extension of my arm. I press the keys a few times, loosening my fingers, and take a deep breath. Crouched in the grass, I get dew drops all over my jeans and think it's lucky I wore my beat-up old boots, because I'd be slipping all over the wet ground if I were still in those horrible, pinching, tight uniform shoes. Those are deep under my bed again, right where they belong.

Standing up, I look at Mrs. Le Roux.

She gives me a single nod, not looking the least bit bothered by my ugly old boots.

The other four Maestros stand in a row beside her, and for a minute, I get a terrible wave of déjà vu. It's all so similar to two nights ago, and my first test with its disastrous result.

After the storm, Mrs. Le Roux had taken me not to her

office, but to her own private rooms in Harmony Hall. There, in a cozy chair by a crackling fire, with Wynk curled on my lap, I'd told her everything: about my Composing, my initial fear that Other Amelia was haunting me, and how the ghost had turned out to be my mom. The headmaestro had listened, asked a few soft questions, then fallen silent for a long while. I had no idea what would happen next. Would I be expelled? Punished? Barred from Musicraft altogether?

Instead, she'd surprised me with another option entirely: the chance to redo my test.

Jai was mad when he found out. "They're testing you *again?* After you just saved the whole school? They should be handing you the key to Harmony Hall!"

I pointed out that it was *me* who put the school in danger in the first place. And I *did* play a black spell, which is kind of illegal.

"Who cares?" He waved a hand. "They can't send you home, Amelia. They know you're a Composer now."

Looking down at my echo tree with the Maestros standing around me, I pause and consider. Do I try Composing a spell, and risk ruining this if I mess up? I know I'll never get another chance.

Mrs. Le Roux still doesn't tell me what she expects. She just waits for me to play. It's another riddle. Another shot in the dark.

Or is it?

I stare hard at the tree, my spirit rebelling. I'm tired of playing games with them, of trying to guess what they want, *who* they want. I couldn't be the other Amelia for them, and I couldn't be the perfect Mystwick student.

I can only be myself.

So that's who I decide to play for. Not for Mrs. Le Roux or Mr. Pinwhistle or Miss Noorani.

For Amelia Jones.

Me.

I Compose a short green spell, with a quick tempo and a major key. Instead of watching my fingers to be sure I hit the right notes, instead of watching the tree to be sure the spell is working, I close my eyes and trust the music inside.

When the spell is over, I lower my flute before opening my eyes. I wait a moment, knowing the risk I took was huge, and likely will cost me my dream of Mystwick forever.

But this time, if I fail, I'll know I truly gave it my all.

When I open my eyes, I see my echo tree leaning crookedly in front of me, bent at that awkward angle, imperfect once more. It's out of place, it's weird, and it's *real*. Not a copy of any other tree in the whole forest—just completely itself.

I smile at the tree.

Then finally look up at Mrs. Le Roux.

She's smiling too.

"Amelia Jones," she says, "welcome to Mystwick."

I catch Miss Noorani before she follows the others into Harmony Hall. We're standing on the front steps, overlooking the glimmering lake. Beams of sunlight stream through the trees and glint on the water's gentle waves. Hard to imagine that less than two days ago, that lake was a swirling funnel open to the land of the dead. Right now, it looks as peaceful as a painting.

"Is this real?" I ask her.

She laughs. "Go back to the Echo Wood later today and look at all those trees. Look *closely*." She raises her finger, as if letting me in on a great secret. "They may look perfect, but once you get close, you'll see each one has its flaws. Its crooked branches, its awkward knots, its lumpy bits. We never wanted a perfect musician in you, Amelia. We wanted an *authentic* one. Someone unafraid to be herself, even if that meant risking everything. Because that's what Musicraft is really about — finding your own voice, and being brave enough to use it."

Embarrassed, I look down at my shoes. "I guess it took me a while to figure that out."

"Amelia," she continues, "you're a Composer. That's no small thing, and we're lucky to have you here. We'll begin searching for a Maestro to instruct you. Unfortunately, none of us here have the gift, but don't worry. We'll make sure you learn how to use this skill, so nothing like this ever happens again."

"Thanks," I mutter, but it's an inadequate word for what I feel. My own Maestro to train me in Composing? It's more than I could have dreamed.

But there's still something I have to say to Miss Noorani.

I try to find the right words.

"That first test, before the storm happened . . . I know it was you who voted for me against the others. I wanted to say thank you."

Her eyebrows arch up, and she looks surprised. "Oh, Amelia. As much as I hate to admit it, I wasn't the one who voted for you."

"What?"

She smiles, patting my hand and then pointing down toward the lake, where a lone figure stands on the dock. "He was."

I blink hard, sure she's pulling my leg. "Mr. *Pinwhistle?*"

"I know he's a grouch, but really, he's one of the best teachers here at Mystwick. Mr. Pinwhistle is one of those special people who sees not how good you *are,* but how good you *could* be. And then he pushes and prods and aggravates you until you reach the potential he sees in you."

"I thought he hated my guts!"

"Yes, I imagine he's been a bit of a beast," she chuckles. "But now you know it's not because he hated you."

He *believed* in me.

When everyone else had written me off, there was Mr. P., fighting to keep me at Mystwick.

I don't think I'd have been more surprised if she'd told me it was a humfrog who'd voted on my behalf.

Miss Noorani pats my shoulder. "But Amelia . . ."

"Yes?"

She sweeps her hand, gesturing at the mess around us. The storm has left debris all over the grounds. Leaves, sticks, plants torn up by the roots, broken glass and trash blown out of bins, all scattered around the lake. "You're not *totally* off the hook."

All things considered, getting stuck with groundskeeping duties is a pretty light sentence, even if I'm not allowed to use magic to do it.

After breakfast, I head out with work gloves and a wheelbarrow to start on the mess. Looking around, I sigh, realizing it's going to take days to get the grounds back to normal. But it's a small price to pay for staying at Mystwick.

I start by the girls' dorm, picking up sticks and cracking them in half before tossing them into the wheelbarrow. Soon I get lost in the work, and it's much nicer than transposing homework.

"It'd go faster if you didn't crack the sticks before throwing them away," a voice points out.

I spin around. "Jai!"

He's standing with his own set of gloves and wheelbarrow. He grins. "Did you think I'd let you have all the fun? I mean, grounds work? Hello! It's the *best*. Gives me a chance to show off these." He flexes his skinny arms.

I laugh. "Yeah, keep that up and you'll pop those balloons you call muscles."

Then I see six more students walking up with wheelbarrows, gloves, and rakes. All are seventh-grade Aeros, including George and Claudia and Collin.

Seeing me stare, they just shrug.

"The storm knocked out the internet," George says. "No computer lab until it's fixed, and classes are postponed until the afternoon. What else are we going to do? Study?"

We all laugh like he told the world's biggest joke.

The sun rises higher. It's the warmest day we've had all month. I toss my jacket aside and work in my I'LL BE BACH T-shirt.

Good thing chicken poop washes out. It's my favorite shirt.

There's a fallen branch jammed in a pear tree at the corner of the gym, and I struggle to pull it loose. Instead, it breaks in half and I topple backwards, landing hard on my butt.

"Need help?" someone asks.

I slowly turn around, sure I can't be hearing right.

Darby rolls her eyes and steps around me. With her height,

she easily dislodges the branch and tosses it in the wheelbarrow. "Honestly, does it suck being so short all the time?"

With a grin, I take the hand she holds out, letting her pull me to my feet. "Does it suck being so tall that everyone thinks you're in tenth grade?"

"Actually, it's kind of awesome."

We stand awkwardly for a moment, then Darby blurts out, "I'm sorry. I shouldn't have treated you the way I did, or blamed you for things way out of your control."

I shake my head. "You don't have to apologize. Really. We've both had a rough time lately."

She pulls off a glove and holds out her hand. "I guess we're even, then."

I grab her hand and shake it. "Even."

She coughs and puts her hands in her pocket, looking suddenly shy. "So. Phoebe told me if we still want to change rooms, we can do it over winter break."

"Oh." I look down, wincing. "So . . ."

"So . . . I figured, it's just a lot of work to change rooms and I'm pretty sure I'm the only person who can sleep through your snoring, so —"

"I don't snore!" But I start to giggle. "Okay. Out of the goodness of my heart, I'll let you be my roommate in the spring, Hamako Bradshaw. But only because I'm lazy and don't want to move."

"Right. And only because *I'm* too selfless to inflict you on any other poor girl."

"You really are a saint."

"Yeah, well, all I can say is they better put a statue of me down by the lake. I *did* kind of save the whole school."

"*You* did?"

"You said it yourself. You couldn't have done it without me."

Impulsively, I step forward and hug her.

After a moment's surprise, Darby hugs me back.

"Oh, and Miss March asked me to pass on a message," she says. "When you're done cleaning up, she needs you to clear out your mailbox. Apparently it's overflowing."

"My what?" I look at her blankly.

Darby gives me an odd look. "Your mailbox. Where you get your mail. In the back of Harmony Hall. You didn't know about it?"

"Nobody told me I had a mailbox!" I bet it was announced the very first day, when all the new students had arrived—but I was up in the headmaestro's office, finding out I was never supposed to be at Mystwick in the first place. "I don't even have a key for one."

"Do you have your whistle-key?"

"Well, yeah," I reply, taking it from my pocket. "But—"

"Give it here, dummy." Darby grabs my key and twists it, and to my shock, the holes realign to form a new sequence of notes.

She hands it back to me, and I twist it back and forth, my mouth hanging open.

"You mean you haven't checked it even once?" she says. "You've probably got forty million letters in —"

But I'm already running away, ignoring the branches and leaves I'm supposed to be cleaning up. I run as fast as I can to Harmony Hall, where I finally stop to ask a senior where the mailboxes are. She looks at me like I asked where the sky is, and points to a hallway. Racing down it, realizing I've definitely never been back here before, I can feel my heart pounding.

Skidding to a halt in a room lined with little mailboxes, just like in the post office back home, my eyes fix on one with my name on it in gleaming gold letters. I twist my whistle-key so that the second set of notes is ready, then play them in quick succession — F–F#–B.

The mailbox bursts open at once, and a torrent of letters falls out. I stumble back and stare at the envelopes piling up on the floor. It takes a while. The last one, bigger than the rest, lands with a little thunk.

They're from Gran.

They're *all* from Gran.

She must have written almost every single day since I've been gone. And all this time I thought she was ignoring me on purpose!

Sorting through the pile, I find the envelope with the earliest date on it and rip it open. The letter inside is full of the kinds of things I'd expect—Gran asking if I remembered my shampoo, if I liked my roommate, if the food had enough fresh veggies in it—but the last line catches my eye: *PS There's no use in emailing me, as I have forgotten my password.*

My stomach sinks.

All this time I was emailing Gran, and all this time she was writing to me—and neither of us knew it. She must think *I* was ignoring *her!*

"Amelia?"

I turn around and see Miss March staring at my pile of letters in astonishment.

"Is it okay—" I stop and have to swallow, because I realize I'm on the verge of bursting into tears. "Can I have the morning off from cleaning? I swear I'll get it all done after—"

"It's fine," she says gently. "Let me get you a bag for all this."

Minutes later, I walk out of the mailroom hauling my bag of envelopes. It'll take hours to read all of Gran's letters, and then I know I have to do what I've been putting off for weeks—I have to call her and tell her the truth. The *whole* truth.

One envelope I keep in my hand; it was sent just last week, and it's the one that was heavier than all the rest. There's some kind of little box inside it.

I rip it open as I walk back through Harmony Hall. In the lobby, a few older students are lounging on the sofas and rugs, glued to a news story on the TV about some castaways being rescued from a tropical island.

"Wait a minute," says one of the kids. "I know those people. Isn't that—"

"Move, guppy!" calls out another, just as I walk by. "You're blocking the screen!"

"Sorry," I mutter, scurrying off as I unfold the letter.

> My Dear Amelia,
>
> I suppose you're still upset with me for lying all these years about your mother, and I want you to know I understand, and that I will always love you, even when you don't wish to speak with me.

I pause to wipe my eyes. No, Gran! That's not it at all! I have to explain everything to her. Wait till she hears I met my mother! That I got to *hug* her!

Gran's letter continues:

> This was your mother's. I suppose it will do more good in your hands than it's done sitting in my jewelry box. She would have wanted you to have it. I expect in a few years you

will have one of your own, but until then, perhaps this one will encourage you to always
follow your heart even when a stubborn old
goat like me is too afraid to let you go.

Love,
Your Gran

With a little gasp, I turn over the envelope and a little jewelry box slides out into my palm. Inside it is a glittering gold music note.

My mother's Maestro pin.

Heart pounding, I go back to my dorm room and spend the next three hours reading Gran's letters, my heart pinching every time she asks me why I haven't written back or called. The rest is mostly updates on our neighbors' vegetable gardens, and Mrs. O'Grady's chickens, and how Gran's book club is feuding again over what to read next—in other words, all the normal, boring, wonderful stuff I've missed most about home.

When I'm done with the letters, I carefully pin my mother's golden music note on the bulletin board over my desk. One day, not long from now, I *will* earn the right to wear it myself. If I work hard, and practice often, and always stay true to myself, then I can become anything. Even a Maestro.

But for now, I grab my flute case and head for the door.

As of today, I'm an official, no-strings-attached, honest-to-Bach student at the Mystwick School of Musicraft.

I've got class to attend.

Acknowledgments

As the third rule of Musicraft states: *The more who join into the spell, the greater will its power swell.* Mystwick would never have been possible without the influence, insight, passion, and time poured into it by so many people, each lending their own unique harmonies to this story.

The first to ever meet Amelia was my little sister, Madelaine, the original frog wrangler and chicken charmer, whose enthusiasm (and fan art!) was just the encouragement I needed to believe in this story. Thank you, Maddy, for believing in Amelia first, and lending her your red curls and freckles.

Several early readers were instrumental in this story's development. Megan Shepherd, thank you for all your insights into the tuning of Amelia's voice. Jessica Brody, you are always one of the first people I go to with a new story, and your wisdom, encouragement, and staunch faith are a steady beat that never fails. Ventia McConnell Webber, flutist, music teacher, conductor, reader, and friend—where in Bach's name would this story be without you? I am forever in your debt for the advice and musical expertise you so graciously shared. A Maestro position at Mystwick is waiting just for you!

My agent, Lucy Carson, thank you for that flash of inspiration when you saw just what this story could become long before I ever could have, for the incredible lengths to which you have gone for Mystwick and for me, and of course, for lending Amelia her name. All my love.

Heather Alexander, editor, inimitable Conductor of this orchestra of words and sounds, thank you for taking this story on with such tenacity and vision, and for keeping its many moving parts in sync. Thanks to everyone at Audible Originals and brilliant narrator Suzy Jackson for bringing this story to life in a whole new way for listeners everywhere.

Nicole Sclama, the other half of this peerless editorial duet, thank you for being Amelia's champion on the page and pouring such care and love into this book. Thanks to Opal Roengchai for her design work; Helen Seachrist, Christopher Granniss, Mary Hurley, Megan Gendell, and Erika West for their deft editing skills; and Alia Almeida and Anna Ravenelle for promoting this book. Everyone at HMH Kids who had a hand in this project, you have my deepest thanks.

A sonata of gratitude to Federica Frenna, whose illustrations perfectly captured these characters and brought Mystwick to life. I am so happy that you're a part of this story! Nat Osborn, you gave Amelia her most important voice—her music—and I am deeply grateful to you for the beautiful, poignant compositions you created for her.

Always and forever, my family, for giving me the time, encouragement, and support to do this work, for believing all these years, for enduring those hours of awful violin, piano, and recorder playing I did in third grade . . . ok, ok, and on through high school, too. I may not be Mystwick material, but my parents taught me to love music. Thank you, Mama, for all the Loreena McKennitt, and Daddy, for the Andrew Lloyd Webber and Elton John.

Ben, always. I love you.